OUR TOWN

a Novel

KEVIN JACK MCENROE

COUNTERPOINT | BERKELEY, CALIFORNIA

Library of Congress Cataloging-in-Publication Data
McEnroe, Kevin Jack.
Our Town : A Novel / Kevin Jack McEnroe.
pages cm
ISBN 978-1-61902-528-8 (hardback)
1. Motion picture actors and actresses--Fiction. 2. Hollywood (Los Angeles,
Calif.)--Fiction. I. Title.
PS3613.C426O86 2015
813'.6--dc23
2014044890

Cover design by Charles, Brock Faceout Studios
Interior design by Elyse Strongin, Neuwirth & Associates, Inc.

COUNTERPOINT
2560 Ninth Street, Suite 318
Berkeley, CA 94710
www.counterpointpress.com

Printed in the United States of America

Distributed by Publishers Group West

10 9 8 7 6 5 4 3 2 1

CONTENTS

ACT 3: 1982-1990

ACT 1

1939-1965

SERENITY SIDE DOWN

Dorothy White—whose given name was Joanna-Rae Cook—was born in October, 1939, in Americus, Georgia. She was born on a Wednesday, in the hospital, and she was the elder of two daughters. When she was nearly five, her father, her mother, her sister, and she went out to dinner in Eufala, a nearby town. Just a short drive. Only a few exits. Her father, Henry, an atomic scientist, wanted to go out to eat. Her mother, Etta—so beautiful, just like her daughter would turn out to be—was happy to stay in. She enjoyed cooking. She found the process meditative, and the ritual made her whole. Henry, though, wanted to go out. He liked cheap drinks. He liked a bargain. And so he decided on Rover's Tavern. Monday beers are two-for-one.

They had a nice meal—Dorothy had baked chicken, onion-fried potatoes, and greens. Swiss chard, I think. And Henry drank Schlitz, mostly. After eating, he switched to rye, neat. They weren't two-for-one, though, so he only had three. Everything was going swell—they were all, the whole family, smiles and happy. Happy and smiles. Just enjoying each other's company. Just happy to be full. On the way home, though, they were in an accident. On a dark road—a back way—Henry turned a corner and was blinded by another car's brights. Dorothy's mother and younger sister died immediately, while Hank passed that night in the hospital from internal injuries. Dorothy, somehow, was safe. She was broken about it, at first, but she'd be okay. She'd eventually be okay.

For a time, Dorothy was raised by her Nana, until her Nana became mentally and physically incapable of doing so. She was then adopted by a rich local family. Eugene Goodman was a doctor, and his wife, Iris, was barren, and they loved Dorothy dearly. They always, no matter their busy schedules, made sure to keep her close. It was here that she changed her name from Joanna-Rae to Dorothy. Because she felt different here. Happier, somehow. And she thought it'd be nice, and fitting, to recognize that change. Starting over would be a theme in her life. She always felt she could be better than she was.

As a teenager, Dorothy married Willis White, but they divorced soon thereafter. He didn't nearly deserve her. Wasn't nearly enough of a man. But she kept his surname—Dorothy White was just straight pretty—and, after that, moved home and enrolled at the local college. While attending, she entered and won a beauty contest—Miss Americus. Coincidentally, a Hollywood agent, Ricky, or something like Ricky, was visiting an acting client who was shooting a movie somewhere nearby. At night, and days they weren't shooting, Ricky became quite lonely and thought he might like to go out and have a few drinks. Maybe scout some new talent. Something young, hopefully. Fingers crossed. Yet untainted by the world. He attended the Miss Americus trophy presentation because he happened to be at the bar where it was being held. When he saw Dorothy, with her wreath and blue ribbon—*Number 1!*—he thought he'd maybe, for the first time in his life, fallen in love. And when he approached her afterward, pushing through the crowd of people that surrounded her, congratulating her, and he said hello, and congratulations, too, and she responded—"Thank ya kindly!"—he knew.

Dorothy then said good-bye to college, and Eugene and Iris— she kissed them on their foreheads after she'd hugged them both, hard—and moved to Los Angeles with Ricky. When she got to LA, though, Dorothy soon realized she could do better. Ricky was pretty small-time. His suits were never pressed. He couldn't reserve the right restaurants. She didn't even have a reel! He'd crowned himself enough of a photographer to shoot her headshots. And the picture he decided was best to send to the studios portrayed her wearing a red ten-gallon hat, sitting on a hay barrel, and chewing on a rigid piece of straw. This didn't quite get her foot in the door, so to speak, nor did it garner her the respect she felt she deserved. But finally—finally!—her career began when a producer for Universal spotted her at a cocktail party she'd snuck into—she knew one of the caterers from back at school in Americus. Even though Dorothy ended up just a B-movie actress, who only briefly experienced any true success, her beauty and her vanilla voice and her appetite for proper living earned her, almost, infamy. But she also wanted to be a good woman. A good wife, and a good mother. And a good grandmother, too. A good friend. But she always got in her own way. She never quite figured how to get out of her own way.

AVOCADO GREEN

Later on, between takes, in the corner of a television pilot's shooting set, behind a key grip with muttonchops who balanced a boom mic between his brown, wooden clogs, stood a perfectly handsome young actor attempting to remove his tan, collarless Barracuda jacket. His zipper was stuck, and he was pulling so hard that his thumb and pointer finger were growing more and more purple-red with each attempt. He kept trying, but he just couldn't get it unstuck. The set was a modest living room, made to represent the sort of living room you might see in a small midwestern town in the mid- to late 1940s. Its furniture was dressed almost entirely in pastel. A Navajo rug lay flat beneath an avocado-green-painted drop-leaf oak-wood table, mid- to late 1940s and behind that sat a plush, salmon-colored, L-shaped, partially pulled-out sofa bed. The walls were lined with light red stripes, and from those stripes grew yellow roses, painted very well—very accurately—almost as though you could smell them. Leaning against one of these walls, just beside a full-stocked, off-white, rolling wet bar, with matching white stemware and three ivory decanters, stood Dorothy White, smoking a Bravo lettuce cigarette—tobacco was prohibited on set, and the director, an asthmatic, had directed, even off camera, that such be the case—with her legs crossed one in front of the other and a quite curious expression on her face. It seemed as if she smelled something, but not something pretty, like the flowers. Something gone rotten. Something overripe. She was as perfectly beautiful as the young actor fighting himself on the other side of the room—both tens, grading on a scale from one to ten—and she stared at him. She watched him struggle. She noticed his pain. She saw a man she thought she could help. He had a structurally sound face—symmetrical—with kind eyes, a very masculine jawline, and a clean crew cut, barbered longer on top than at the sides, high and tight. Dorothy took a step, pulled once more from her Bravo, and, now, decided she could help. She was sure of it. So she pressed her cigarette into a decorative ashtray and made her way across the set—swaying past the key grip and the TV pilot's director, a few gathered producers, and a food cart with corn chips and salsa and carrots with a sour cream dip. And a few extras, and spotlights, and the director's and the producer's cloth-backed chairs—until, finally, she arrived at the actor's feet. She stood before him in a black shoulderless dress and an updo and placed her hands thoughtfully on her hips. A teacup. Short, not stout. Not yet stout. She had thin but muscular arms, a long, angular neck, and a waist that had yet to provide her any worry, but he didn't notice. He still looked down, consumed entirely by his full-stuck zipper. After about thirty seconds, she tapped him on the shoulder, and he jumped backward, frightened, but without letting go of his coat. He thought he'd got it loosened. He wasn't gonna let all that hard work go to waste.

"You mind if I try?" Dorothy asked as she stepped forward one long step, quietly but convincingly, as though she already knew him. Like she'd seen his type before. Like she knew what it would take to train him, like the dog she had when she was little. She'd put him in his place, if necessary, but still let him feel tough, like a man. She reached down with her long fingers—only one ring, an opal set in silver on her pinky— and pushed his hands gently to the side. She angled the gold latch down and twisted, and then pulled apart the jacket halves like an avocado, cut in half—the zipper half the pit half. And then young Dale was free.

"Thank you," he looked up and said. He was nervous. He didn't know what to do with his hands, so he put them in his tan jacket pockets and felt the tartan, flannel fabric on his palms. Then they started sweating, so he rubbed them against the soft lining before he pulled them back out.

"It's no problem, darlin'," Dorothy replied. "I saw you strugglin' over here and I felt like I could maybe do some good."

Dale breathed audibly. Loudly, with relief. "Well you certainly did that," Dale said and then smiled, and Dorothy saw how perfect his teeth were. And then she noticed his eyes—orange blue, a sunrise ocean—and fell straight into his dimples. And then she saw how shy he was. And how surprised he was that someone noticed he needed help. Dorothy saw all that and she smiled, too. She stepped one baby step closer and then put up her little right hand, palm down, parallel to the floor, so that he had to kiss it.

"I'm Dorothy," she said, and then she smiled bigger. Her teeth were perfect, too. "Dorothy White."

Dale put out his right hand and grabbed hers and reached to pull it toward his mouth, but he paused halfway near his chin as he wasn't sure what to do with his left, so he pushed it into his back pocket as if he were going to remove his wallet, but he didn't like that fit, so instead he came back empty-handed, then pushed it flat against his leg.

"Dale," he said quietly. "Dale Kelly," and he finally pulled her hand the rest of the way to his lips and kissed its smooth back. A little too close to her knuckles, she thought. A mistake, but a cute one. She figured she'd let it slide.

"It's nice to meet you, Dale Kelly. I guess we're playing opposite each other. At least that's what I can gather from our pages," she replied, pointing toward her pink leather purse with her pink-painted fingernail. Her pink purse housed her cigarettes—Lucky Strikes, she didn't switch to menthols until later—and her compact and a roadmap and her script, which pointed out from the top. "See, I'm new to all this, you know, and—"

"You have a really beautiful voice," Dale interrupted, much braver than before. Forgetting he was nervous. He'd stopped thinking about his hands. He'd stopped thinking altogether. Instincts took over. Speaking only as he felt. "Really amazing. Your speaking voice. I've never heard anything like it, really."

Dorothy stopped, too, suddenly short on breath. Now she was nervous. Struck by his newfound courage, she had no idea what to say. So she just smiled and hid behind her teeth. And she was usually quite the talker.

"Thank you, I guess," she replied, bashful. Newly bashful.

"No, no, I mean it," he said and put his right hand on her forearm and then pulled his left from his pants pocket and grabbed her pinky finger, the one with the ring. "It's like velvet, or something. Like the way velvet would sound. Or, I don't know. I guess that doesn't do it justice," he said and he waited. "I'll think of something better." But he never did.

"Well thank ya, again," she replied. "You know, where I'm from," suddenly aware of what he'd noticed in her cadence, and so willing to exploit it, "*every*body just talks like *this*." She held the *k* in "like" and the *s* in "this"—impersonating her more deeply southern kin, entirely aware of herself—and she knew it was over. She had him straight lassoed. The cat's in the bag.

And then she was the most beautiful girl Dale had ever seen. And him her. And she was right. It was over. Again, straight lassoed. Hooked. Both of them had each other hog-tied, but to each other, so it was sweet. He pulled his arm from her shoulder but continued to hold her pinky. Didn't want to give that up.

"Where was it you're from, anyway?" he asked.

"Georgia. Americus, Georgia. You prolly never even heard of it."

"No. No, I *prolly* never even heard of it," he parroted.

"You should go. It's real pretty. If you ever wanna get away from all this, I mean," pointing toward the hollow furniture.

"I'd love that." He paused. "You wanna take me?" impersonating her twang.

She cocked her head and smirked. "Yeah, I think I'd like that." She looked down at her tootsies but then back up. "I'll certainly try my best."

No one spoke for a time. Neither was much for cordiality. Dale eventually let go of Dorothy's hand, but they still looked in each other's eyes. Then, big and loud, they heard their names—both their names—being called from a megaphone, and they looked up to where they heard the noise.

"Dale Kelly. Dale Kelly. And Dorothy White. We're gonna need you on set for the high school dance scene. The high school dance scene, everybody. So let's be ready. Let's make this first one count!"

This was Dorothy's first acting job. And it was Dale's, in fact, as well. He'd done some theater in high school—but certainly nothing that ever paid. And she got hired for her looks and charisma and, most importantly, her accent. The role required a specific regional dialect, and her meter fit just right. And so the first time they acted they did so together. And they were both nervous. But more excited, still, because they were both new to acting and had gotten into it because they were pretty, essentially just leashed up and led around and told what to do. Which can be disconcerting, not knowing what the future holds. But now they each knew somebody else—somebody else like them—so now things might be easier. So they ran to their marks, and they hit their cues, and they acted, for the first time, together. Teamwork, you know? And they were believable—the swooning cheerleader and the varsity wrestler had real spark. They were young, not yet overdoing it. Not yet overapplying *the method*. Not yet overcompensating for their developing jowls. They didn't know how to act, yet. They were only being themselves. They just liked to be around each other, and their viewership, watching at home, believed that truth. And the confidence they built from that scene allowed them to be successful in their other scenes, with other actors. And they saw, in each other, a future. Just themselves. Themselves together. Just together. And then they were happy. Happy as baked clams.

* * *

Dorothy and Dale only had four more scenes opposite each other during the filming of the pilot for *Crossing Robertson*—neither of their characters was primary—but they all went quite well. On their last day of shooting, Dale finally asked Dorothy to drinks. After work, they went to a local bar that never checked for ID. Dale had three Budweisers and Dorothy drank Sazeracs. She knew her alcohol. Daddy'd taught her how. After that they went back to Dorothy's rented studio apartment. Dale still lived with roommates, and Dorothy preferred they be alone. They talked all night—and it was perfect—and didn't kiss until six in the morning, and an hour later they had sex in the sunlight from the window. And they were tired when they woke up at noon, but when they walked to breakfast they thought it was okay. When they got to breakfast they knew it was worth it.

AFTER THEY ATE, then went back to Dorothy's studio apartment, Dale had to return to work. It was past three, and they needed him in makeup.

"I don't think they need to make you up at all," Dorothy said and grinned as she rolled over—rolled up in her bed sheets like a sloppily rolled cigarette—as she watched Dale pull on his chinos. Dale winked and then, before he continued dressing, walked back to the bed and kissed her as best as he could, his ring finger hooked under her chin, to slightly lift her. But he was late, so he pushed off and pulled his shoes on and didn't tie them, and Dorothy watched as her door slammed shut behind him with his shirttail still untucked and his pants not even buttoned.

Dorothy wasn't needed on set that day, so she bought a *Daily Variety* and went and sat at a diner and read it—back to front—with a cup of coffee. Although her sensibility was quite continental, and catching up on her reading was usually something she quite enjoyed, she found the magazine, today, rather hard to take in. Her mind was elsewhere. She knew she'd fallen. Might not be able to get up. So she went home and sat and waited and Dale called after he was done shooting that night and came over, and then Dorothy had to leave early the next morning, and she left him there. They didn't have any more scenes to shoot with each other, but for the next month they saw each other every day. Dorothy temporarily suspended her audition schedule to ensure she'd have free time for him. And soon Dale vowed to find them a place where they could be together—just them!—and once he got his first real paycheck, that's what he did. He kept that promise.

* * *

Before Dale and Dorothy had found their first apartment, Dale had bought a ring. It was a modest ring—he hadn't made his money, yet—but a ring nonetheless. And it was pretty, for what it was. It was accommodating.

He'd ask for her hand, he'd decided, the day they found the place of their dreams. They'd seen a few apartments, but for Dorothy they weren't enough. And although Dale could've been fine anywhere—all he wanted was her—he supported how picky she was. It was endearing, in the beginning. So he held on to the ring, at every showing they saw, and he waited for the right time to ask her. He was under the impression that the only way an engagement could be seen as official, in the eyes of the law, would be if he asked Dorothy for her hand with a witness present. Even though this was, in fact, only true for the wedding ceremony, Dale was young, still, and had, until this point, traded on his looks to get by, forsaking the benefits of things like school. Or reading—that's for chumps and squares—relying instead on his looks and physicality to remove himself from trouble. But he was ready now, no matter what anybody told him. He'd found himself a woman, and he thought that made him a man.

* * *

"What do you think, baby?" Dale asked.

Dorothy stood in the living room and heard Dale's question. But before responding she left and walked to the kitchen, testing the room's balance and flatness. The way it felt against her feet. She took small, measured steps. Noiseless. She was always light on her feet. She opened the wooden pantry—painted fire-truck red, with shined gold handles—and smelled for dust. She ran her little fingers along the bottom panel then put them to her nose. Not much. Newly finished. All well and good. Then she went to the bedroom. Large, colonial windows. Clear panes, white shutters. Good light. Good closets, too. There were two of them, in fact, in the bedroom. His and hers, and also one for jackets in the foyer, with equal amounts of shelving. No squabbling over space. Although she knew she'd bleed into his eventually. She was a bit of a clotheshorse. Then she went to the bathroom. Firm cabinetry. Solid. Black and white tiled floors. And a toilet with a pull flush. How quaint. The kind she had when she was young. And a bathtub big enough for two. And then the mirror. A square mirror. A large, full mirror. Not bright enough to see your pores, but okay. Still pretty. The fluorescent from the ceiling would be fine for now. She could fix that later. She'd been gripping her hands—tightly—into fists at her sides but then she stopped and relaxed, and she looked into the mirror and tightened her black bandana around the bun atop her head. She unbuttoned her blouse's top button. Too much. Act like a lady. She buttoned it back up. Then she squeezed her hands together in a ball before her and smiled, as big and natural as she could.

"You install some vanity lights in there and this place is perfect," she said as she walked back into the living room—past the female real estate agent—and toward Dale. She neared him and ran to him and jumped into his big arms.

But Dale pushed her away, and Dorothy fell back surprised. He put his hands to his temple and waited a while. Nobody spoke. Not even the real estate agent.

But then—but then—he pulled his fingers from his face and opened his eyes—sunset eyes—and got down on one knee and pulled the ring from his pocket. He snapped open the box and asked her, as sincerely as he could.

"Well, I guess it's now, if this is where we're livin'. Would you want to marry somebody like me, honeypunch?"

Dorothy blinked and squeezed into herself, but then she put her hand to her head and fell to the floor in a heap—real dramatic-like—her white dress spilling up and exposing her undergarments. Dale ran to her, and even the realtor took two steps, but without letting go of her clipboard. He spooned her up and carried her and dropped her onto the staging couch in the room's corner—just strong enough to hold her. It was cheap but she was light. And she opened her eyes—her blonde eyes, even more perfect than his—and she said to him, with sweet breath, "You didn't have to bother with all that, baby. You know I'm always yours. Yours and only yours, baby. Yours and only yours."

And Dorothy and Dale were beautiful and young and engaged, and they always held each other tight. All the time. Even tighter when they were tight—when they were drinking—but they always liked to be together. As much as they could be together they were. And so the real estate agent began to scribble, fairly sure she'd made a sale.

* * *

As they left their condominium—515 North Crescent Heights Boulevard, Apartment D, West Hollywood, CA 90048—Dorothy noticed a strange set of tropical trees and shrubbery in the corner of the courtyard. Just two small palms, with a thick, green bush connecting them. She stopped and cocked her head. She stood there a moment, looking into the greenery, while Dale turned and stared at her. Then she pointed.

"Look, baby," she said.

"What is it?" He walked up and stood beside her and he looked, too.

"There's something in there."

Dale didn't see it at first, but then he locked eyes with a large, green iguana, whose yellow irises around his black pupils were all that stood out in the thatch.

"See, baby," Dorothy said, as she pulled Dale's arm over her shoulder and tucked her head into his chest. "He's green like the trees so you can't see 'im. That's his thing. That's his ticket."

Within one month they were all moved in, and happy, and within four they were married. Their wedding was beautiful, and white, and took place at a local church nearby. A progressive one. They only invited a few people, and Dale didn't even wear shoes. The world was changing. People were less inclined to judge. Dorothy had never experienced anything quite like this and, as it turned out, she would never—ever—be happier. For Dale it was harder to tell.

RIGHT AS RAIN

Two weeks later, Dorothy and Dale drove up Highway 1. They left their new apartment in Hollywood, which Dorothy was just starting to feel was her own—she'd just put up her pictures—and they drove north, to Big Sur, for their honeymoon. They took Santa Monica to the Pacific Coast Highway until, eventually, they got on Highway 1. Highway 1 runs along most of California's Pacific coastline and is, supposedly, one of the most beautiful drives in America. They could see mountains for miles, and driving by the water made driving not so bad. But sometimes the road got too twisty and they both became nauseous. But they looked out the windows anyway, and they saw the craggy rocks stick up from the green water. Sun-glowy and wet. Carsick but beautiful. And then it got later, and the water turned blue. They stopped, before the sun went down, at a designated stopping grounds, to take pictures before it got too late.

"How do I look, baby?" Dorothy asked Dale. She held an unlit cigarette in one hand and rested the other against her waist. She wore a yellow sundress with red polka dots. She tipped a little to the side. A teapot. Yellow more right for summer, but Dorothy wore it anyway despite the late December cold. It was her honeymoon, she thought. It's whatever temperature I want it to be.

"How do I look, baby?" Dorothy asked again. "Do I look pretty?"

Dale was adjusting the Polaroid, still sitting in the driver's seat. He couldn't quite figure it out. Wasn't big on technology. Fucking technology.

"Hold on a second. I'm trying to get this stupid thing to work."

"Well, would you at least tell me if I look pretty? Am I posing the right way? How's my pose?"

"Yes, honey. Of course. You're the most beautiful girl on the whole planet," Dale said but didn't look up from the camera.

"Oh, please. You didn't even see," Dorothy said to herself. She turned around and looked out on the ocean.

"It's really amazing here," she said, louder now. "Forget the camera, baby. Just come look with me?" She waited with her hand out. "Jesus, would you just come look with me, please?"

"Give me another minute," he said. "Oh, for fuck's sake," and he tossed the camera to the right side of the bench seat in their peach-colored El Camino.

The sky was pink but lined with green. The ocean was green but lined with pink, reflecting the sky. Dorothy stepped near the cliff's edge and looked down. The waves broke anxiously against the shore. The rocks were stacked like sugar cubes beside a saucer. The air smelled like the best sorts of seafood. Fresh seafood. Lobster tail, maybe. With melted butter. Or a perfect oyster. East coast—small, not too briny—with cocktail sauce, mignonette, horseradish, and a forehead kiss of lemon. Dorothy appreciated oysters properly dressed, if that wasn't clear already.

Dale pulled his cap over his ears and then put his hands in the pockets of his wax cotton jacket. This jacket wasn't lined.

"It's getting sort of cold, honey. Should we try and get there before it's dark? I don't wanna get lost."

"You don't like it here?" Dorothy spun around, and her too-blonde—ghost blonde—now damp hair fell and hung loose and stringy before her eyes.

"I do. I really do. It's beautiful," Dale said. "I think I'm just hungry, is all. A little cranky. Yeah, I'ma go wait back in the car." And then

Dale walked back and closed the door and sat and held the steering wheel too tight. Dorothy looked up. The hills above them rolled down and were green like spearmint. There were telephone poles along both sides of the road—some tilty—and they were all connected by long, black wires that hung down, precarious. There were dark trees and there were light trees. There were full trees and empty trees. But everything was full green. Steep-sided and sharp-crested ridges separated v-shaped green valleys. Streams fell off flat canyons and fell onto hard boulders. At the tops of the hills were houses. Some looked like rich houses, and others looked poor, but all was covered in chaparral. That brought them together. They liked to be together. They liked to be close. Somewhere, between the two, was a cow farm. If you looked hard you could see them—the cows—sucking on grass and chewing, spitting out the parts they didn't like between round bites. Dorothy thought so, anyway. She imagined. There were endemic firs, rugged slopes, and rocky outcrops. Here and there, one at the top, and another at the bottom—one near, another faraway—there were rare madrones and spire-like sycamores. And everything was lush, green. And everything was bright, perfect.

Dale honked the car horn and Dorothy woke up startled and turned around. She walked back to the passenger side of the car with her head down. She got in and slammed the door behind her. Dale turned the keys and looked at his new wife before he geared to drive. They were young, and they were beautiful. She looked back out on the water. She liked it out by the water. It was cold but she wasn't cold.

COCKTAILS AND VACANCY

They couldn't afford to stay in Big Sur—yet, anyway—so they stayed just outside in Carmel. Dale's cousin was a travel agent, and he'd suggested it. He said it was nice. Or nice enough, at least.

They drove through a long stretch of redwoods and abandoned VW buses and made a few wrong turns before they finally arrived that night. Just before nine, they pulled into their motel, the Carmel Inn/ Lodge. They found a parking spot and unloaded their bags and walked toward the reception area. The first room they walked into was dark and empty, but they saw a red sign that read *Lobby*, in bright neon script. Like a bar sign. *DRINKS*. They followed an exit arrow through an empty doorway, and then it was bright. Before them, a family from Spain—six kids, three parents—Europeans, you know? They're pretty out there—spoke curtly to the clerk behind the desk.

"But we wanted *tres* rooms," they said, thickly foreign but clearly English capable.

"But you only booked two, sir, and unfortunately we're otherwise at capacity." The man behind the counter was small and meek, and maybe even from Carmel. It's hard to trust people from resort communities. Locals are liars. Xenophobia pervades. But he was tough, seemingly, and he handled being spoken to rudely. Like he was used to it. Maybe even above it. He stood his ground, and he took it, and he smiled.

Fake. Big and toothy. Overly nice, to the point of condescension. Like a waitress at the end of her shift. Or a stewardess on a red-eye.

"Well, just give us a cot then. Put it in his room. I'm tall. I need to stretch my legs out."

"Sure, sir. Here're your keys," he said, coy, forcing his mouth to smile.

They fleeced out the door and went to their two rooms. Dorothy approached the desk, tilted her head, and smiled back.

"Hi," she said.

"Hi, there. What can I do for y'all?" He looked down for a while, filing papers. Then he looked up. He noticed Dorothy's eyes were pretty—real pretty—and his head fell and matched her tilt. "Yes, ma'am?"

Dale stood in the corner. He read a map and attempted to piece together their trip's itinerary. Tonight they'd just barely have time for dinner. Tomorrow they were booked full through. He liked to keep moving. The stewardess gave them their keys. And he served them free hot tea. They were cold. And cookies. But they didn't want the cookies.

Oh, it's 9:30 P.M. now. And the year's 1960.

* * *

They spent the next few days in Carmel. They went out to eat, and they appreciated the dogs, the ice cream flavors—"peach?"—and the elderly. Dale, though, missed LA more than he would've preferred. He began to grow restless. One day, they hiked through the woods, all the way up the cliffs, and then soaked in the mineral hot springs, and another they went to the beach. The beach was wider than those in Los Angeles, and whiter. And thinner, and softer. The sand was covered in dogs like ants on an anthill, and as you stepped it felt good through your toes.

"Maybe we should get a dog," Dorothy said to Dale as they walked along the dunes. Dorothy often thought of where she was in her life— her place in her timeline—to rationalize her decision-making process. Now—here—she feels her role on the show—their show—is being minimized, but she feels this is justified. Because she wants to focus on her relationship, anyway. She's happy to be with Dale. She's happy to be married. She wants to be a wife. That's her out. And with that out she feels, justifiably, that her career is not just secondary, but more so incidental. A lateral move. And so she'd focus on her future—her future in her happiness—and she'd prioritize as such.

"I don't know, hun. We're both pretty busy with the show and the rest of it. And I don't want some little rat to ruin everything."

"I know, but I think I'd like it. And I think you'd like it. You'd be a good papa. And I think I'd be good with something little. And I've always wanted a dog. Always, you know? Maybe it'd be good practice." She looked up at him and made herself small and fluttered her lashes, knowing she was already pregnant but prepping him before she broke the news.

"Well then maybe we should have a kid. You're not getting any younger."

Dale enjoyed reminding Dorothy that he was younger than she was, even though it was only by one year. Dale's twenty, so Dorothy's twenty-one, it seems.

"That, too, I guess. Yeah. But a dog, too, I think. A dog and a baby ain't really the same thing, ya know? A baby's prolly a little more precious."

"All right, well maybe we'll get a dog then." Dale pushed a blond curl back from his face and pulled up the collar of his red tennis jacket. It hadn't gotten any warmer. Clouds covered the sun, and the sky was gessoed gray. Dorothy ran ahead and a few beagles chased her. She was light but heavy-footed. She left deep imprints in the sand.

* * *

Their last day in Carmel they drove the half hour to Big Sur National Park. They would have a hike—Dale was an athlete, at least in terms of build—and then they'd have New Year's Eve dinner. Dale had found a place that he knew Dorothy would like. Tonight would be for her, he thought to himself. He'd be okay, but she could be hysterical, so tonight he'd take good care.

After they were finished in the woods—they went awhile not talking—they stopped at a gift shop where Dorothy could buy souvenirs to take with them back home. Dale waited in the car. She walked past the canned peas and bags of pretzels of the Post Mercantile Shoppe before she reached the gift section. She found a mug with a picture of Bixby Bridge—lit up bright orange from the headlights from cars—a signature rabbit's foot—dyed green, like the foliage—an ashtray shaped like a ten-gallon hat, and two T-shirts—one with a print of a chartreuse convertible, graying rotten beneath a cliff, and another that read *Big Sur*, emblazoned in the same design as the Budweiser logo, *King of Parks*.

THEY PULLED INTO the Three River Ranch and drove past a loud pink *BAR* sign. They'd begun their evening at a hotel restaurant in San Simeon, but Dale didn't like the waiter or the clam chowder—a cheap prix-fixe menu was all they offered—and neither did Dorothy, so they paid the check early and left to find somewhere better. Before they got in the car, Dale made some calls—he insisted on using the bar's phone—and discovered that an old friend owned a piano bar nearby. An actor. Another actor. And so a gravel driveway cracked and spat up beneath their tires as they pulled into the parking lot. They saw two girls sitting on a hanging, swinging, brushed-wood bench. They both had short hair. One wore a white blouse and a brooch shaped like a beetle, and the other wore a gray pantsuit. One held books, while the other held the other. They were both smoking and, between pulls, they kissed.

"I like this better than the other place," Dorothy said as she turned back to Dale while he looked around for parking.

"I like it better, too," Dale replied, his eyes focused on the lot.

"I'm happy you decided we should go. I don't think I could've."

"I know, baby. You leave the tough stuff to me."

"Even though I wanted to."

"I know."

"I like when you take control, baby. I like when you're a man."

And then he finally looked at her.

"I know, baby. I've got you," he said, and he put his hand on her knee as his eyes traveled back to find parking.

THEY WALKED INTO the foyer and Dale walked up to the podium and spoke with the hostess.

"Hi."

"Hi there."

"My name's Dale Kelly. Table for two?" Hoping for recognition, the kind he'd sometimes begun to receive. But thus far it was just from young girls. Young girls were his demo. Girls, however, unfortunately, who were just too young, even by his standards.

"I'm sorry, sir," she said, stepping sideways and turning her head and looking out onto the floor, "but I think it'll be about forty-five minutes to an hour before a two-top opens up. If you have a drink at the bar and wait, I'll come get you the second something becomes available. K?" Wink.

He frowned, looked at her in the eyes—red eyes—and squinted.

"I know Ron, you know?" he posed. "He's an old friend of mine."

She sighed.

"Sir, everyone that comes in here knows Ron. He tries to stay relevant. And we don't really advertise much. Anyway, it's New Year's Eve, sir, you know? It's busy."

Dale looked the hostess up and down and then walked back to Dorothy. He might have gotten more upset if so much of the girl's bosom wasn't abreast.

They found a seat by the piano. Dale let Dorothy sit. The stool was three-legged and periwinkle-painted metal and its cushion was covered in cracked white leather. The piano, too, was white. Off white, actually, or ivory. But the bar's ceiling was dark wood. Maybe cedar—aged and slatted—like an old farmhouse. Candles lit in highballs covered the tables and the marble bar top and were lined an inch apart on the floor along the wall. A colonnade tore the room down the middle—separating the bar from the floor—and a fire burned in a masonry stone hearth. The walls were covered in tarnished mirrors and the various menus—Dinner, Dessert, Drinks—were scripted on them in white paint stick. The guests looked to be between sixty and senile. Dorothy liked to think of her and Dale as old already. She thought they'd always be together.

"Can I get you a drink?" Dale asked. He'd just come back from the bathroom.

"Yeah, honey," Dorothy answered southern, like she did when she was having fun. "I'll take a white wine."

Dale had a whiskey. Cutty Sark, one cube. Then another. He had a few.

AROUND MIDNIGHT THEY finished their dinner—two steaks and cheesecake. Dale paid the check and then they went back to the piano bar, where Dorothy preferred to be. The music gave her energy. When an elderly couple got up, the newlyweds took their two seats. The piano player stopped singing and sopped up her brow with her shirtsleeve. Now, in what seemed to be tradition, people wrote their names on pieces of handed-out slips of paper, then put the slips in a top hat that a waiter walked around the room. Then the ginger-red-haired piano player got to choose a name from its innards. If you were chosen, you got to sing. And everyone wants to sing. Everyone likes attention.

Her hand in the hat already, she pulled one out with glee. She uncrumpled it and read, "Bruce!" she shouted. "It's Bruce's turn to sing!"

Bruce had buck teeth and hair parted from the middle and a white suit, and he sang Sinatra. Then Enid, wearing a jacket with shoulder pads and gold jewelry—her earrings matched her bangles and were plated, too, it seemed—performed the Four Tops. When she was done, Bernard, in tweed and a beard, took off his porkpie hat, pressed his hair back, and did "Sea of Love," without ever looking away from his slender wife's angel orange eyes.

"They really love each other," Dorothy whispered at Dale as she clasped her hands and craned her arms from his shoulder.

"Yeah, I guess so."

"I really love you, too."

"I love you more, baby."

Dale reached up and broke Dorothy's grasp and held her right index finger with his right hand.

"I love you more, baby," he said again and looked into her eyes and kissed her. Right then he meant it, he thought. The tawny port was helping, too.

A cocktail waitress in a black mini approached them from behind with a tray of half-full champagne flutes. They took two. A waiter then came from behind her, and he had black and white plastic bowler hats—inscripted *Happy New Year!*—feather boas, and kazoos. Dorothy took white, and Dale took black, naturally. He put a boa around his wife's neck and felt the grain of the feathers on his fingertips. It was soft, and he thought back to the dog Dorothy had said she wanted. He, again, wasn't sure it was a good idea.

Everyone cheered and kissed after midnight. Dale and Dorothy sipped on what was left of their drinks. A black man with clean white teeth in a baby-blue tuxedo took their picture with an Instamatic and then gave it to them. Dale let go of Dorothy's hand and shook out the Polaroid. Then the piano player took back the mic. "Does anyone want to sing one last song?" she shouted, her head shaking, her red hair bouncing and alive.

No one responded for a moment. Then a cowboy stood up from one of the dinner tables, his checked shirt tucked into his jeans and belted in a silver buckle, hat down low over his eyes. Everyone seemed to know him. Everyone applauded. Local celebrity. Around here, a star. He emerged from the crowd at the front of the room, took the microphone, and then whispered in the piano player's ear.

"I'm gonna do something we all know." He closed his eyes. "Something yellow, for old time's sake. So let's all sing," he said, his voice gruff and tired. And then, sardonic, "Let's all sing. Johnny Angel, everyone! How I love him!"

And they all sang together. In harmony, together.

And I pray that someday he'll love me
And together we will see how lovely heaven will be . . .

* * *

They were drunk when they got back to their room. Dale opened the door, and Dorothy walked in and fell toward the bed. She lay on her back. She'd had the most fun. She was just so happy.

"I loved it there," she said.

"Yeah, baby. Me too."

Dale'd brought another bottle of champagne back with them to the room. He'd stopped at a gas station. It was cheap, but he wasn't finished.

"I'm gonna go get some ice," he said.

"Okay," she replied. "Wait, what do you need ice for?"

"I like it," he responded. "Hot champagne's disgusting." And the door slammed closed as he left.

When he returned, Dorothy had undressed to her underwear, and she was laid back with her hands behind her head and her legs crossed at the knee. He handed her a plastic cup and poured champagne to its brim. Then he poured some for himself. He put an ice cube in each glass and hers overflowed. He'd already started sipping. He sat down on the bed. She swung around behind him and straddled his back. She began to unbutton his shirt. But, with her glass in her hand, filled all the way up, she spilled some. Champagne soiled his pants—new pants—and he felt it in his boxers. He got angry, and he pushed her off. When he did so, she fell back, and, in attempting to catch herself, her plastic cup flew from her hand. It struck Dale in the side of his head and now the bed was soiled, too. And Dale got angrier.

He took his shirt off and walked to the bathroom with brut in his hair. As he stood before the mirror angry, he decided he had to pee. Hanging his wet shirt around his neck like a scarf, he unzipped and went and then felt better. But he was still mad. As he went to flush, he stumbled back and, trying to catch his balance—trying to right himself—he knocked the car keys, which he'd placed on the sink when they'd arrived home, into the toilet. He tried to catch them, but they were already in the bowl. The water stayed yellow. It didn't go down. Dale stared for a while at the calm water. Then he went back to bed with crunchy hair. Went back to bed with crunchy hair more angry.

THE NEXT MORNING, before noon checkout, Dale called a local plumber—Allen's Plumbing. It was nine thirty. The plumber promised he'd be there by ten. In the interim they tidied the room, and packed, and got ready to go back to Hollywood. Dale stuffed his clothes in his duffle. Dorothy folded and pressed and placed hers in her overnight bag. She wore a long-sleeve turtleneck to cover her bruises.

There was a knock at the door. Dorothy turned off the TV. Dale went and got it. He unlocked the chain lock, then turned the door-knob and pulled it open. Before him, with a grin, stood a tall, white-haired, white-bearded plumber in blue overalls over a white T-shirt, tight on his biceps. Handsome, which Dale hadn't expected. Straight silver fox. He raised up his leathery paw. And Dale shook his hand hard, trying to impress him.

"How are ya, big guy? I understand you lost your car keys in the toilet?"

"That's right."

"Well, then. Let's see here what we got."

Dale ushered in the plumber and he strode forward into the room.

"How are ya, ma'am?" he spoke at Dorothy.

"I'm okay," Dorothy looked up and replied but then went back to folding. "I mean, as good as I can be, I guess." A pause, with her head on her chest. "Under the circumstances."

The plumber sniffed.

"Thanks for comin', though," she said and looked up again and smiled.

"No problem, ma'am. Everything's gonna be all right. You called the right guy," he said, and he smiled, too. "I promise."

He made his way to the bathroom and pulled open the door.

"Oh boy," the plumber crowed. "You've got one of these old guys, huh?"

"Yeah, I don't know," Dale said as he walked up behind him. "We've only been here a few. But I guess it's not the best I've seen, no."

"Well that's an understatement," he laughed, then sighed. "But I'll figure something out." He got down on his knees and dropped his tool bag beside him. "Always do, big guy. Always do."

AT ELEVEN THIRTY, Dale walked back over to the closed bathroom door to check on the plumber. They only had thirty minutes 'til checkout. Do was getting restless. And, now, again, becoming scared.

He pushed open the door and its unoiled hinges squealed.

"How we doing in here?"

"Well, it's funny that you're comin' in now," the plumber replied, seemingly exhausted, but with a piss-wet set of keys dangling from his thumb and forefinger as he stood up from his knees. "'Cause I just got 'em."

Dale put his hands on his thighs and dropped his head. From behind him his wife started clapping. They were so happy. They might be okay.

"But I'll tell ya," said the plumber. "These fuckers weren't easy. I used my closet auger for a while but then the damn oar got stuck. So then I had to take the damn thing off at the hinges. But, of course, some asshole decided to cement it down to the ground. So I've been chippin' away at the thing the last half hour, until finally I could pull the bitch up. But then," he dangled the keys before Dale, and they jangled. And Dale smiled. "But then I got 'em. I got the fuckers. Man against mechanism, I guess. And you know what?" More dangling and jangling. "We fuckin' won."

It was fifty-seven dollars. Dale gave him one hundred in twenties. He saved them. They had won.

The plumber gathered his things, victorious.

"Every day's a new adventure," he said, and winked, before he left them.

THEY DROVE BACK home to Hollywood in the rain. Dale drove, and Dorothy slept most of the way. Dale had given her something for sleeping, and a headache, while he took something to stay awake. He'd drive the whole way. She wasn't much of a driver. And, anyway, he needed some time to himself.

DALE GOT HUNGRY, later, driving. While Dorothy slept more—curled in on herself like a puppy—he saw a sign that read *MADONNA INN* as he continued down the 1, which he'd heard of, he thought. Maybe he'd read about it in the trades. Maybe it was just one of those places. Those places they put in brochures about California. *California: Find Yourself Here!* A real, true landmark. The only place to be. Dale took the right exit, at Madonna Road—exit 201. But it wasn't on the right. And it wasn't on the left. They pulled into a desolate shopping area—a sign read *In-N-Out Burger, Obispo Community College—Go Pelicans!*, and *Lou's Handsome Thrift*—but it wasn't there either. Walls looked fake, like they were only an exterior. Light and empty. Overly described and under-important. Like cardboard. A set.

Dale rolled down the window to ask two men directions, but, on second glance, decided otherwise. They didn't look right. Hollow like the walls. He turned back around.

As he left the complex, he realized it must be on the other side of the highway. He got back on then and got back off on the right side.

A rectangular piece of whitewood was erected in the middle of the parking lot. At the top was an oval painting, surrounded by round white light bulbs like those on a vanity mirror, of a carriage being drawn by two horses in front of a cloudy white sky—a cowboy at the front steered the reins. Underneath was a lit-up square pink sign. The words *MADONNA INN* were electrified neon in turquoise. He pulled past and found a spot. The lot was near empty. He poked two fingers into Dorothy's ribs and she woke up; she was sore there so she woke up.

"Hey," she squeaked.

"You hungry, baby?" he asked.

"I'm tired," she answered, rubbing her side and scratching her eyelids. "Really tired. But yeah, I guess so."

They got out and walked toward the hammered-copper stairs. They didn't hold hands.

"What'd you give me?" Dorothy asked.

"What do you mean? Nothing. Same as always."

"I just really slept and now I'm groggy."

"Good, baby. You were tired. And you'll wake up with some coffee. I mean, if you want to, that is."

They walked up the crimson carpet down the center of the coppered stairs—her to the right of the handrail, him to the left—and, as they pushed through a large, wooden saloon door with a heart cut out and filled in with pink stained glass in the center, a hostess greeted them. "Howdy!"

"Oh, hi," Dale said, surprised. The woman stood close and shouted, her podium too near. Her stand was too close to the doorway.

"What can I do for y'all?" She wore a pink pilgrim dress with a muffled pink apron, a pink headband, and pigtails tied in pink bows. She was freckly. Pale-pink skin, tawny red hair, and an affected accent. Dale couldn't tell whether that was part of the job description or something "cute" she'd picked up along her way.

"Table for two, I guess."

"You got it, darlin's," and she grabbed two oversized wood menus. "Follow me."

She led them to their table. Dale made sure to stand one step behind her. Do was by his side.

"This place is weird, right?"

"Yeah, very," Do replied.

"Very, very," Dale repeated and looked around.

"Should we just go with it? I'm suddenly starving."

"Yeah. I mean, I guess we have to. I'm real hungry, too."

They walked past a pink bar with pink and gold bar stools and a foamy-pink ledge. They walked over a pink-and-red carpet with pink roses blooming and splats of blue hyacinths growing from the pink rose stems. Pink stucco pillars led the way—faux Greek classical—but fashioned to look as though they were really carved from one piece of pink stone. All from the same rock, like they used to be. They arrived at a red booth with a navy chandelier. Gold trim. Pink bulbs. And above them a portrait of frontiersmen. And a square wood table, which housed, on its center, six different types of mayonnaise. One of which was pink, with a label that read *Thousand Island*. And went on to say *Our Very Own*.

"Y'all have a nice lunch now, would ya please?"

"Yeah, thanks. You got it."

The hostess patted Do on the back, then winked at Dale, then spun as she walked away—knowing that her pink-pleated bell skirt would inflate and show the tips of her pink, ruffled panties.

DALE HAD A BLT and Do had Caesar salad with grilled chicken. Dale didn't request "no mayo" because he assumed you added the condiments yourself. But his rye bread was already soaked through. The bottles on the table were for if you wanted extra. It seemed most people wanted extra. Dale's sandwich came with steak fries and coleslaw, extra-thick-white. Do's Caesar was wilted and mayo-drenched with croutons. But their fat server was very attentive in refilling the happy couple's coffee cups throughout. Dorothy liked unsweetened and skim. Dale liked half-and-half and white sugar. He liked to be able to drink a lot. He liked to feel it in his fillings. Made him feel alive.

* * *

Dale and Dorothy took two years off acting when their first child was born. They'd saved some money, Dorothy more than Dale. *Crossing Robertson* hadn't hit its stride, yet, but Dorothy continued to get side work. Some TV. A few B movies. Something with Elvis. Something else with Nevada Smith. Dale continued wading downriver—his role on the show slowly, but exponentially, grew—while Dorothy fought upstream. Against the current she swam hard at first, but fairly soon relaxed her muscles, and eventually she made her way to the shore. Dale, though, was beautiful but maybe not angry enough. Not yet, anyway. He needed some time to figure it out. So when they were going to have a baby—between seasons—he took a break. It was getting harder—he'd become unsure—and being a daddy seemed like a good excuse. It seemed, to him, quite masculine. So he smoked all day and grew a beard for the first—and only—time in his life. He liked his few months off, and he was happy, then. They were happy, then. She was twenty-four and he was twenty-three. He wished to be a good daddy. And, although that never quite came true, he tried. At least until he stopped trying. A lot of the time he got in his own way. But again they were happy still, for the most part. They loved each other. They only ever wanted to be close.

AFTER THIS BREAK, though, their careers took perpendicular paths. Dale's face was discovered, and Dorothy's quickly forgotten. *Crossing Robertson* finally struck a chord with audiences in its third season, its first without Dorothy—given her relative fringe status, and the fact that she never tested well with the flyover states, they felt she'd become expendable—and propelled Dale to relative TV stardom. Not so much for Do, but she was a mama, so that didn't matter. She considered their finances shared—this wouldn't become a problem 'til later. Critics said it was something in Dale's dimples and his candor. His passion and his eyes. And, with all that new attention, he couldn't really muster the spirit to be home anymore. It just didn't seem that important. And all the smoking and drinking didn't help. And then later all the coke.

But let's not get ahead of ourselves. As I said earlier, when Dorothy was pregnant, they were happy. Dorothy only ever just wanted a family. A family's all it took to make her whole.

"I love you, babyskins," he said, high—red-eyed—in a holey, having-had-it-since-high-school, threadbare, loose, white, sleeveless track tank.

"I love you more, babyskees," she replied with a smile. Such a genuine smile.

She'd let her dyed blonde hair go dark—sandy, and natural—during the pregnancy. She'd read that the chemicals weren't good for the baby. When she was pregnant nobody forced her to do anything. She could eat whatever she wanted. And she was doted on. Whatever she needed, she got. She loved that. She loved it all. She was an actress, but she didn't need acting anymore. She didn't need anyone to tell her that she was the prettiest. She got brave. She loved Dale, and she believed in him, and that was enough for her. What woman needs anything more than a man who loves you? You find a man with a big wallet—or at least a wallet with big potential. And she believed he'd make it to the top. Straight to the top. Even with the beard, he was the handsomest man she'd ever seen. And she didn't need to be more than a good mama. They'd rented a place in Malibu on the beach and spent much of the time in the cabana, where Dale kept red-labeled bottles of Budweiser—*Budweiser Lager Beer*—on ice in a plastic bucket. Sometimes he'd blend up frozen margaritas. She didn't drink much during those nine months. For the first time in her life, she cared. She watched Dale fiddle with his bathing suit drawstring underneath his guitar and then go back to playing. He couldn't really play, but he tried. His beard made him look like a foreigner, but she didn't mind foreigners. Not if they looked like Dale, anyway. He got up and went to the bathroom. She could see him unzip his pants through the window. Everyone in Malibu has a bathroom outside. A bathroom outside, she found, in her experience, to be a problem for the poor and a luxury for the rich. Low-high. She liked low-high. But she preferred the latter.

Dorothy grabbed her big stomach in one hand and her horn-rimmed, green wayfarers in the other and got up and walked toward and then slid open the cabana door. She stepped down the two wooden steps and across the flat-brick path through their yard and past their peach tree. Green-tiled, with Mexican shingles falling from the roof, and gray stone siding. Having a family—just being a wife—was growing on Dorothy. She couldn't imagine much better. Couldn't imagine much better at all.

She was hungry and in the mood for tortilla chips and spice. Everything nice. She'd read that salsa was good for the baby. Kept her humors clear. Kept the baby on its toes. As she stepped over the hot red bricks they burned her feet. The Jacuzzi was on; it didn't need to be, but it didn't matter. Worry about the heating bill? Please. Dale left for the beach to jump in the ocean—which he liked after a sauna—but now he was coming back. He wore a towel over his trunks and carried a half a beer in his hand and his sunglasses on his head. His body hadn't started aging, yet. He felt strong. He put his sunglasses back on and then watched her open the door as he dried himself.

The cool air from the icebox stuck to her and she lifted her stomach and rested it on the fruit shelf. She wasn't hungry anymore. She thought she heard the garden door open, and she grabbed a half-gallon jug of wine from the sauce rack.

"You good, baby? You need anything? I'm having some chips. I'm hungry."

Dorothy thought she heard Dale coming, but as she looked over the icebox door no one was there. Then suddenly, below her knees, their new dog Butchie stretched straight up on his hind legs and reached for her like he was attempting to catch a bouquet.

"Oh, my little," she said, and she scooped up Butchie and his ears went back like a rabbit's. She pet back the wiry gray fur from his bangs and he smiled. And she smiled. They were happy. Then he tucked into her chest and balled up. He was happy to be with his mama. When Dorothy bought him, a month before, the store clerk told her they looked just alike. Like twins, almost. She kissed him, and she liked his breath, and she thought it'd be good for the baby to have a friend. And she could raise them together, and love them together, and she was sold. And Butchie was sold. He'd just come now from pissing on their rented teal sofa bed, but when Dorothy found out she didn't care. She let him get away with everything. And, anyway, they could afford it. She just loved his face. She gripped Butchie from under his pink stomach and poured some wine into a water glass with her other hand. She was pregnant, and she had a dog, a tan, wine, freckles, real hair, and a beach house. And that all seemed like more than enough.

DOROTHY AND DALE spent much of that summer—and the rest of the next eighteen months—in each other's arms. With the new baby, and the dog, and each other, she'd made a family of her own. And she'd always, more than anything, just wanted a family. Only wanted a family. And even when Dale got angry, or jealous, or resentful, and then more angry still, Dorothy tried to be there for him. A man needs his woman's support, no matter. That's just the rules. When she was a little girl in Americus, she remembered her father driving a car, with her mama in the passenger seat and her sister and her in the back. Mama opened the windshield, when you could still open windshields, and let in some fresh air. It was hot, that day. But when they opened the windshield, even from the backseat she felt the breeze.

* * *

Now, a year later, Dorothy and Dale still get on, for the most part. Again, for the most part. Their baby, Clover, had just started walking, and Dorothy was pregnant again. Almost Irish twins. Dale was still working his way up, and soon he'd be bigger and better than ever. He began to go back to the gym. He thought if he got big and strong it would help his career. He remembered the confidence he used to have when he boxed as a teenager, and it helped. It made him strong and kept him scary. The girls always liked that. And he liked the way he felt after sweating. A good sweat and a liter of water? Brand-new man.

MASTER BRUCE!

Dale bought Dorothy jewelry sometimes because he knew it would help their sex. This time he bought her a Native American—Iroquois—arrowhead on a long silver chain from a gypsy jeweler—well, gypsy-looking, anyway—at the mall—Dorothy liked things with "character"—and, as he pulled it off a mannequin's hairless foam head, he thought of what he'd tell his wife as he hung it from her neck. He'd say, he thought, "It's for your protection, baby," and he'd brush her hair from her face and hold her head by her ears. "An Indian carved it outta rock to keep 'emselves safe. And now you'll be safe, too, baby. When I'm not here, 'cause I can't always be here, you'll be safe, too." And he squeezed it in his fist as he walked it to the cashier. He attempted to talk her down—gypsies love a haggle—but eventually a hundred was decided. All twenties, no change. Most likely stolen—again, gypsies, you know?—she didn't bother with sales tax. And when he gave it to his wife she said she loved it once he performed the lines that he'd rehearsed. Lines that he'd run with himself in his rearview while he drove it back home. And she loved it so much that she'd wear it that night to dinner. They'd planned a fancy dinner. She said she wanted to look pretty tonight. She said she wanted to look pretty for him. And this'll go swell with my purple dress. I just know it. The one with the ruffles. Lined down the fringe.

THEY ARRIVED AT the restaurant and left their Jaguar—Dale's Jaguar, hunter green with a pale, sand interior—with the valet. Sorry, Dale left it with the valet. Talk about self-importance. Narcissism. Grandiosity. Sheesh. They left the car and walked inside and looked around. Dale signed an autograph for an overweight young woman. Believe it or not, moments like this actually hurt his confidence—his insides spoke to him, fanned him, only if, and when, his fans were actually pretty. Dorothy had become known as "budding star Dale Kelly's side dish"—sorry girls, he's married—but she was comfortable in this role. She liked being in the background. The set. The decoration. She liked being the scaffolding that held up Dale Kelly and made him whole. And he liked it, too. For her, that is. He smiled for the camera, and as bulbs cracked and flashed in his eyes he felt alive. This was, in reality, what made his foundation strong. This was his scaffolding. And he'd chase it, and build it, as tall and high as he could, until his days were ultimately numbered, until his book was finally read.

DOROTHY WASN'T HAPPY when she received her food. She was hungry. They made friends with the maître d' once Dale slipped him a twenty for the table by the fireplace. Do loved a fireplace. So warm. The maître d' was an actor, too. He recognized them. Both of them, which wasn't usual. Dale from TV, he told them. Dorothy because she sometimes came around when Dale was busy shooting. As they finished their appetizers—a cheese plate and charcuterie, with pickled vegetables, olives in a walnut vinaigrette, and garlic shrimp in a sizzling skillet—the maître d' came back and carried two small envelopes—folded in half and both reading *Preferred Customer*—in his ringed fingers. He removed the plate before Dale and replaced it with one of the envelopes.

"Spread this on a roll," he said. Then he took Dorothy's food, as well, and placed her letter in her little fingers. "And enjoy this with your pasta. It'll pair well with the Bolognese." And he clasped his hands together. "Enjoy," he said and curtsied, long-necked like a swan. "We appreciate your business so."

So Dale ate his pot butter on a rosemary seed roll and Dorothy swallowed her mushrooms with a forkful of spaghetti. Dorothy's mushrooms were bitter as she chewed them but she felt their effects fast and smiled the rest of the night through. Dale's butter, though, was hard to get down—earthy. Gamey—and he didn't feel it hardly at all. He couldn't feel anything, he thought. Just fat from eating bread. And butter. He'd spend the rest of the dinner trying to swish the taste from his mouth. That made it hard to enjoy his steak. And Dorothy's big grinning didn't help much either.

DOROTHY DIDN'T USUALLY enjoy dancing. She thought of herself too outside of herself, and then she imagined she looked stupid, usually. That's what Dale figured, anyway. That's why she never danced. It must be. But once they arrived home—oh, they lived in Topanga now, briefly, Dale complaining that Dorothy was getting too much sun and looking leathery. Dale also moved when he began to feel unsettled, overwhelmed. This is called a geographic. A series of starting over by which, you hope, the freshness of your new reality will displace your shame and your past and the fear of your present and your reluctance to look into the future. Dorothy, though, hadn't yet noticed this pattern, distracted by the shininess of all her new things. And, anyway, right now, she could only think of dancing. That's all she wanted to do. She slid open their glass sliding door and pushed past the screen and started spinning on the patio. The patio floor—gray-slate tiles, still hot from the daytime sun on the bottoms of her feet. She'd already taken her shoes off. She danced with the standing parasols, their umbrella heads still opened from afternoon sunning, now providing temporary reprieve from the moon's unwavering eye. She spun from one pole to another—swinging from the grounded white aluminum like Tarzan to a vine—before she twisted off the patio and into the yard—short grass, slightly unkempt, a lemon tree, planted by previous owners, and a few corner cactuses. But pretty, still. Right now, anyway.

Dorothy certainly made it look pretty. She opened her eyes momentarily, so as not to fall—she'd stepped on something sliding under her, and her eyes were open enough to see a salamander glide away, hidden almost immediately by a few brown shards of grass. She held her lids open long enough to whisper, "Bruce. Master Bruce," while he was still in her presence, but then she went back to pirouetting. She put her hands up and her hands down and spun, more and more. Quicker each rotation. She grabbed her skirt and pulled on it. "Dance with me, baby," she yelled at Dale with her eyes closed as she bounced her head from shoulder to shoulder. "Come on, baby. Please?" She kept her eyes closed. "I love you more than the earth, the moon, the sun, and the stars," she opened them now, but not to look out, just to flutter her lashes.

"No. I can't," Dale answered. He'd followed her out and sat on a lawn chair. "You look too happy. I'll just screw it up."

She kept spinning. A top. "Suit yourself," she whispered with her eyes closed, and she kept on dancing more. She danced like it was just her instincts. Like she was happy—actually happy—and she didn't care that people saw. Even if it was just Dale. Even with him she usually seemed self-conscious. But not now. I guess that's what mushrooms are, Dale thought. It just makes you who you wanna be. Not like pot butter. That just made me feel fat. And then hungry. So then I ate more. So then more fat.

"I CAN'T FIND my necklace," Dorothy said as she shook Dale awake. He usually woke before her. But not today. He was up late forcing himself to throw up.

"What do you mean? It fell off?" he answered, pulling sleep from the corner of his eye.

"I guess." She grabbed at her neck, but nothing. "I don't know."

"All right, well." Dale strained forward then pulled the covers off and got up. He pulled jeans on without underwear. But it was hot so no shirt. "Let's look in the bed. Start there."

It wasn't in the bed.

"Do you think it fell off last night?" Dale asked from his knees, checking under the frame.

"Maybe," she sniffled. "Yeah, maybe." She tapped at her neck as though she still might find it dangling against her rib cage. She pulled at her blouse between her breasts. It was a long chain, the kind you could take off without unclasping. It must have just fallen off.

Dale walked to the glass deck door and unlocked it and pulled it open. A car drove through the canyon down the street.

"How you feeling today?" Dale smiled a smug smile.

"What do you mean?"

"I don't know," he slid open the screen. "Aren't mushrooms supposed to give you a bad hangover?"

"Oh, please. I hardly took any."

"Really?" Surprised. "It didn't seem that way. The way you were acting, I mean."

Dale looked under the folding deck table—a turned-up ashtray. A flip-flop. A deck of cards—then under the hammock.

"What is that supposed to mean?"

"I don't know," he said and stepped onto the grass, cool on his feet, not from the air but from the sprinklers. He didn't answer awhile. And then, "You just seemed, like, really happy. Really happy to just be you."

She was on her knees, crawling, searching in the grass for where it could've bounced off. She got up fast when she saw a snake hole. She breathed.

"I think I was just really happy. Actually, you know?" And she thought about what she'd just said. "Yeah. I loved my necklace. And dinner. I was just having fun," she looked at him in a way she hadn't in a while. Concerned. "Weren't you?"

"Yeah. I was," Dale replied, then looked back to the ground. "I just liked your dancing. I just really liked your dancing."

DALE DIDN'T REALIZE he'd never be able to forgive her. At the time, he pinned his anger on her losing the necklace, and it was this lack of care—this callous disregard for his feelings—that allowed his rage to be justified. From this point forth, he looked back at this as the beginning of the end. How could she care about him—how could she care about anything—if she could lose something so important? What kind of priorities does she have? What in the world is wrong with her? How could she? Just how could she? From this point on, he began to look at her with a certain level of disdain, in that he began to ask what if? *This grass is always greener*, he'd propose, often aloud, attempting to feel better. He didn't want to feel this way—he wanted to be happy. Happy where he was—but he couldn't help but wonder if he'd settled. If too early he'd settled. He loved her—or he tried to—but once this thinking—this termite—began to gnaw at the wood of his brain— began to feed on his foundation—he was unable to beat it. He was a winner—he wanted to win—but perhaps this match was already over. Perhaps what they'd been through, as large or small as it seems, to us, was simply too much to bear. Because, how could she? Just how could she? And so it is from here, henceforth, that it isn't fun any- more. And he began to choke on his own resentment. Resentment is like swallowing poison and expecting someone else to die. And Dale's particular poison is aged Scotch, and it seems to have gone down the wrong pipe. And now he chokes, and he chokes, until he's finally forced to spit.

PAPICHULO

But now it's 1965. The kids are young but getting older. Things are rather prickly. Things are rather thorny. As their son and daughter grow, Dale and Dorothy began to enjoy themselves differently. I mean, if at all, really. Dale seemed rather perpetually annoyed. Dorothy tried as hard as she could to please him, but Dale begrudged her nonetheless. He felt as though she was taking his youth away. Like she was stealing from him. How could she? And almost every opinion she expressed he viewed as disrespectful. And so the space between them grew and grew. You could measure it with a yardstick. Eventually a first down. And they'd moved again. As Dale's career began truly to bloom—movie offers and the like—he wanted to be closer to the studios. So they moved to Encino: 17801 Santa Rita Street, Encino, California 91316. Just off Ventura. Sometimes, though, when Dale looked at Dorothy, and he saw her shine, he wanted to be with her again, even though that feeling was fleeting. When he saw her glimmer, though, he sometimes attempted romance. He wouldn't usually bring her places. In his eyes, she'd already begun to decompose, like a corpse would—moments away from rigor mortis. But today she looked shiny. They'd be dead, but then alive again. Alive again all over. But that didn't usually last long. Until he fucked another hostess, say. But tonight they'd attend a movie premiere. And then the after-party, too.

* * *

Dorothy got ready by the mirror in the master bedroom. The house in Encino—meant to provide a dichotomy to the lush nature of the lot—was modern. Simplicity—bare—and materials meeting at ninety-degree angles abounded. It was colder than before. It was different. Dorothy didn't want to move. She preferred antique. Something with character. But Dale liked this. It cost more. She'd at least promised herself she'd always, no matter what, have a vanity mirror. A vanity mirror was essential to her as a woman. Essential to womankind.

She applied makeup in front of the bright-white round bulbs, patting a squarish yellow sponge across her forehead, from temple to temple 'til she reached her hairline. Foundation first. Coolly tinted, powder based. Only one thin layer. Otherwise she might break out. Then concealer. And mascara. Dark mascara. The more the better. Persian eyes. With a smoky finish. Like Cleopatra. Liz Taylor. She'd make a statement tonight. This was her chance. Maybe her last one. She'd have to be beautiful. She needed to pop, like the light in a chiaroscuro. So bronzer. And a tight pink lip line, just above the upper lip, which she'd recently gotten fattened. Her lower was full enough. As she finished, she stopped and rested her sponge and compact on the counter to the right of the sink. She looked her reflection up and down in the artificial light. She still had a towel on her head, cream-colored and wrapped up like vanilla soft-serve ice cream. A towel on her head and a towel on her body, nails done, toes done, and a face on—finally a face on. She opened a small drawer with a white handle and found her pillbox—an overused cigar tin that read *Red Cloud—high grade, handmade*—and featured an Indian, smoking, in traditional Confederate garb as he sat on a mare on a beach by the dunes.

When Dorothy first moved to Los Angeles, she was told she was too heavy to compete with the other girls. Thin is in. That's what they told her. Always is, always will be, they said. You can always be thinner. So they sent her to doctors who gave her things to lose weight, and when those things kept her up at night, they gave her other things to put her to bed. Then things for if she was anxious, and others for after a long day. Things for going out, and others for staying in. Things for if she felt like crying. Things for if she became frightened, and others for if she felt lost. Things, and more things. Every type of thing. They were all different colors, but, outside of baby blues—which were only for sleeping!—it didn't matter much. They all helped. She picked up a varied and wide-ranged assortment. She closed her eyes and swallowed the handful without water. She didn't need water anymore. Then she opened her eyes. Now soon she'd be pretty.

Dale changed in the other room. Today—these days—he wore his sideburns longer and his hair longer and his shirts more open, with a gold cross medallion against his hairy, manly chest. It hung askew, above his heart. The stone in the jewel's center was rock crystal—his moonstone—surrounded by a white-gold crucifixion. He leaned forward at the edge of the bed and pulled on his brown suede moccasins with a shoehorn, his necklace now dangling between his chin and ribs. His green dinner jacket lay folded in half beside him and beneath that were a white-dusted razor and straw and mirror. He'd just finished what he had left over from yesterday. He didn't yet need more. Not for an hour or so, anyway. Once his shoes were on, he stood up, rolled up the white sleeves of his shirt three folds, and walked to the bedside table where a rocks glass was filled halfway with Scotch whiskey. His ice had melted. His drink was watered down. Dorothy entered, still swathed in towels, and the light from the bathroom behind her provided a rather lovely silhouette.

"How long's it gonna be 'til you're ready?" Dale asked, swishing the contents of his glass back and forth before him.

"Fast, 'cause I already did my makeup," she replied looking for her hairbrush. "Can't you tell?" she said as she smiled and turned toward him, looking up at the ceiling and clasping her hands and blinking and fluttering, like a bug.

"Yeah. Yeah, yeah. You look great. You know you look great. But you have to get ready. You gotta be ready soon. I don't wanna be late." He paused. "Seriously, Do. I don't wanna be late again." He sat back down on the bed and looked down at his shoes' ornate brown tassels.

Dorothy stood in front of her bureau and stared at her drawers. She stared awhile longer before, newly energized, she reached into her purse beside the bed and took out a Lucky Brand cigarette from a crumbling soft pack. She didn't, yet, smoke menthol 100s. Next they'd be Mistys. And then eventually Virginia Slims.

"What are you doing now?" Dale asked at Dorothy.

"I'm thinking of an outfit."

"How long is that going to take?"

"I don't know."

"What do you mean you don't know?"

"I don't know, okay? Once I figure something out I'll give you a fucking update." Black eyes. No pupils. "And anyway you badgering me is only making me take longer."

Dale put his fingers to his closed eyelids. "Oh my God," he said, dropping his head and shaking it and sucking on the inside of his cheeks.

"Oh yeah?"

Dorothy got angry and hot and her voice showed it. Good hot, though. Her skin was crawling with euphoria. She seemed to have gotten today's pharmacological cocktail just right. So right. But she didn't know how or why. Too bad. It wasn't always this easy. She spoke again. This time louder.

"Don't fuckin' bug me right now, okay?" Her eyes were wide, even blacker. Parrot-like, she squawked, "I'm getting ready. I'm figuring out my fuckin' outfit. And you asking me these dumb questions is only getting in my fuckin' way."

Dale looked up at her and then back down at his drink. His glass was empty. "I need another drink then," he said, and he got up and left for the kitchen. His dinner jacket remained on the bed, still atop the mirror. Fuck an hour, he wanted another bag. He'd have to stop at his guy's house before the party. He thought he'd stay out late tonight. Have some fun. Enjoy his youth. I'll sleep all day tomorrow, he thought. Sleep's for pussies, anyway. I'll sleep when I've got nothing to do.

"GOODNIGHT, MY DARLINGS," Dorothy whispered to Clover and Dylan. She'd gotten a nanny—Roberta—to watch the kids for the evening. Dale's success to this point—he'd already made a few films and just recently booked his first lead!—had allowed for certain conveniences that they were once unable to afford. Roberta rocked in a white-framed rocking chair in the corner. She'd kicked off her shoes. She read a cookbook—Tex-Mex, *True Tooth: San Antonio*—and flipped the pages slow.

"Where you goin'?" Clover asked. She was blonde, just like Mama. Pretty eyes and all smiles, too. She shared a room with her brother Dylan, who still slept in a crib with a spinning mobile. Clover slept on a springy twin.

"We're going out, baby."

"Why?"

"Because sometimes parents need to go out. Sometimes your daddy and I need some time together. Alone, that is," Dorothy said and brushed the bangs from out of her daughter's eyes. "We haven't been seeing too much of each other recently," she said, which was true. "Plus, baby, you're in bed already, anyway."

"But," the little girl said and paused, "I love you." Clover blinked and blinked. Her eyelids, dewy with sleep, stuck together. But she found the strength to pull them open one last time.

"I love you more, baby," Dorothy said and kissed her daughter on the forehead. "More than you know." Then she squeezed her daughter. Almost too tight.

Dale, now, was silhouetted in the doorframe. He stood before a standing lamp.

"We gotta leave."

"Okay." But Dorothy didn't let go of her daughter.

"Now."

"Okay, okay. Jesus H. Christ." She let go of Clover and pet her head.

Then she walked to sleeping Dylan and pet his face. Then she found sleeping Butchie, underneath the crib, and pulled on his beard. He purred asleep. She stood up and headed for the door.

"Get Clo back to sleep, okay, Roberta?" Dorothy said.

"Yes, ma'am. Real soon, ma'am."

"We love you guys," Dale said, fast. "Don't wake us in the morning," he said and closed the door behind them.

Dorothy went to the bathroom another time before the road. When she returned, Dale held the front door open. She walked through and he put on his dinner jacket. Before the door closed, though—

"You're not wearing any cufflinks?"

Dale stopped and looked down at his loose sleeves and sighed, and then went back upstairs. When he returned, two shined shark's molars encased in platinum reflected off the paleness of his wrists.

"Finally," Dorothy said, and smiled. Dale, however, did not.

DOROTHY ARRIVED AT the party before her husband. After the movie, which was a bore, Dale dropped her off at the Hollywood Hotel and then drove home to pick up a different shirt. The one he'd worn itched him, he said—"You over-starched it, again"—and he said he couldn't wear it another minute. "Not another minute!" But that most likely was just an excuse to be alone.

Dorothy walked to the bar. The hotel's décor was earthy but still oddly matte. Green leaves sprouted from potted plants at the corners of the room, and an Indian man wore a tan suit with white bucks with gum soles beside a painting of a red sun rising while a ship, below, sank. The room was filled to the brim with people, but the Indian stood alone. He leaned against the painting and it tilted slightly. He listened to a girl with a strawberry-blonde bob play the guitar. Girls who play guitar don't have nice fingers. Dorothy never understood those girls at all. Not even a little. The guitarist played "Für Elise" and sat beside a dartboard. In the room's center burned a gas fire from a black chrome fireplace—a fire that you could turn on and off with a switch that sat on the damper—and along the leather couches were royal-blue and apple-red feather pillows. Dorothy arrived at the bar. There was a line of people. She waited her turn for a drink. Fatigue had struck her and, as she licked her dry lips and tasted the stink of incense and patchouli, she reached into her purse for her cherry Chap Stick. She applied her cherry Chap Stick, and then licked her lips, and she was better. She put it back.

"I'll have a white wine, I think," she said as she reached the front of the line.

The bartender wore a tuxedo and had a moon face with his hair parted neatly to the side. He corkscrewed a bottle and poured full a plastic highball and handed it to her.

Dorothy walked around the party, switching her plastic glass of wine from one hand to the other, from time to time making her way back to the bar. It was crowded, but she'd begun to enjoy herself. She knew some of the guests from when she used to go to her own premieres, years prior. They remembered her, and they missed her. Many asked why she'd stopped. She wanted to be a good mother, she replied. Really, though, there wasn't room for two successes in her household. Too much personality. One person had to float while the other floundered. One sailed, one sank. Highs and lows. Peaks and valleys. It didn't matter which one, she thought. It used to be her, but now this had to be. In this world—on this side of the country—there are some people who carry the piano, and some people who play the piano. But Dorothy wanted both. But, again, Dorothy had begun to enjoy herself. Enjoy the party. She was chatting, and being cordial, and then she started laughing—even laughing!—and nobody judged her. She was free, for the time being. It had been a while. Nobody told her what to do. And as the hours passed, people's ties began to loosen.

Then, from above, Dorothy saw Dale enter. She was upstairs and could see the front door from her vantage point between the shoulders of two men. She was speaking with two executives who had some ideas about her career, and from below they were all you could see. They said they could help her get back to where she was and even further. That *she* should be in the movies! That *she* should have a name! Her own name! That she should be on top, like she was supposed to. And she was talented. And she was prettier than she ever was. She liked to hear that. My goodness, she loved it. As Dale walked in, though, the party was at its most full, so he couldn't see Dorothy's ear-to-ear. She began to see her name in lights—MARQUEED—and she smiled, and the suits then further beamed. He'd changed into a red shirt, and, paired with his green evening jacket, he looked like a Christmas card. Dorothy wore white. She was over statement pieces. I mean, in terms of what she wore. Dale looked around the front of the room, but he didn't see her. Then he walked to the back. He looked up, for a moment, toward the second floor, but he couldn't see her past the men in suits. Dorothy saw him, though, and pushed between their arms. "Dale!" She hung out over the railing. "Dale!" she called. But the music was loud, and he didn't hear. "Dale," she called again, but again he didn't notice. People were dancing near the entrance, and a woman swung around and elbowed him between his shoulder blades. She apologized, but he got angry, because she hurt him, so he left. He slammed the door behind him once he'd walked through. So Dorothy shoved her way along the wall, down the stairs—making herself small—across the makeshift dance floor—and then finally outside. She followed. She saw him walking toward the parking lot. He was nearing their car. In his eyes his car.

"Dale!" she yelled. "Dale," she yelled again.

He turned around. He finally saw her. But he kept his mouth closed shut.

"Come back, baby. I was just upstairs." She reached him and reached for his forearm but he pushed her off. "I'm having the best time, baby. Why are you leaving? You just got here. I was only just upstairs."

Dale stared at her, again. This time longer than before. He grabbed the sides of her head. He pressed his hands around her ears and then held tightly on to her hair.

"I missed you, baby. It's so good to see your face," Dorothy said and closed her eyes and opened her mouth and waited for Dale to kiss her. Kiss her to say hello.

But he just looked at her. Then he head-butted her as hard as he could. Her head whipped back as her nose started bleeding and she tried to put her hands to her face but he blocked them. He still held her head by the ears. He took a clump of her hair and wiped at the blood pouring from her nostrils. He watched it pool up at the edge of her lip, and dye her split ends hot red. And then he let go. He left and went back to the party.

Dorothy fell to the ground in a ball. She cried and cried. Her face was ruined, and her hair was ruined. Her tears mixed with her blood as she wiped her face with the back of her hand and soon it was covered in a mucousy, salty pink. The valet, who had looked away when Dale was with Dorothy, walked over to her. A long, black Johnny Chen moustache framed his face—like mouse hair—and his nametag read *Chulo*. He reached down to help Dorothy up.

"Are you okay?" he asked.

She breathed through her mouth, not through her nose.

"I guess I'll be okay," she said. She'd stopped crying. But still she bled.

He pulled her up and steadied her. He rubbed her back and she leaned into his arms.

"Do you want me to get security?" asked Chulo.

"No," she replied, and sighed and pushed off Chulo. Her nose still ran bloody. She breathed through her mouth. "I just need to clean up."

She made her way to the inside bathroom with her head down. She borrowed Chulo's grease rag to cover her face. She'd draped it over her forehead and got through without being noticed. With a piece of tissue pushed up her nostril to clot the bleeding, she attempted to make up her face. The swelling would be hard to hide. After she finished with a layer of foundation—only just foundation—she heard a knock at the door.

"I'm in here," she shouted. She was angry, and had already taken something for the pain. But now she was really hurting.

"I know, ma'am. This is Eddy, from security." He stopped, then continued. "I have someone with me. Someone who says he knows you. Your husband, actually, he claims. Is it fine if he comes in?"

"No, it isn't, actually. Tell him I'm busy and I don't wanna see him or talk."

"What did you say, ma'am? I'm sorry."

"That I don't wanna see him or talk!"

She could hear them speaking from behind the door but couldn't make out what they were saying; the music was too loud.

"He says he wants to apologize," Eddy shouted over the noise. "He says he's sorry."

Dorothy sighed again, this time through her nose. Her brick-red tissue clot fell out into the sink and the blood ink ran along the porcelain. Blood continued falling from her nose and past her lips and she tasted it. Mixed with makeup, she didn't mind. She balled up another tissue square and patted her face and then put it up her nostril. She looked at herself. She looked ugly. She hated herself, again. She'd forgotten about the executives.

"Fine," she replied. She turned the lock counterclockwise—lefty loosey—and Eddy opened the door and peeked in. He was handsome. Tough handsome.

"You all right?" he asked. Real sweet.

"Yeah. It's fine. Thank you."

"No problem, ma'am. I'm gonna let him in, okay?"

She nodded.

Dale entered, his once slickly parted hair now hanging down before his eyes, covering the bump—his unicorn—he'd procured on his forehead. His shirt was more open than before. He sucked in through his nostrils and felt more energetic. Alive again. These days he only breathed through his nose.

"Let me look at you," he said, quietly, and he grabbed her face again. He turned it from side to side in his palms. He was checking if he'd done enough damage. Then he held it straight and looked back at her, flat in the eyes. He let go with his right hand and he slapped her. Then he slapped her face again.

"Don't ever embarrass me like that again," he said, coolly, calmly. "I told these people we were coming here together. Coming together. As man and wife. And then I can't find you. And I ask someone. And they say you're upstairs, talking to two guys. *Two* guys. Do you consider that acceptable behavior? As a married woman you think that that's okay?"

Dorothy rested her face against Dale's hand. She could feel her cheeks getting hotter. She thought she must look red. Redder than before, even. Tomato faced.

"Do you hear me?" Dale asked, and then let her go.

Dorothy turned toward the sink, away from him. She squeezed the porcelain in her hands until a fake nail cracked off and landed against the blood-clot tissue.

"Let's hope so," Dale affirmed. And then he opened the door and left. He left the door open behind him.

Dorothy looked up at herself in the mirror. She grabbed a new tissue and blew out the old tissue and threw them both in the toilet and watched them tie-dye the water as she flushed.

SHE TOOK A cab home. Dale took the car. She was nervous as she entered the house and walked upstairs to the bedroom. The lights were still on. She crept through the door and saw Dale on the bed. He lay in his underwear and dinner socks with the TV remote in one hand and the rocks glass—the same rocks glass as before—in the other. An ice pack rested on his head. He looked up at her.

"I kind of hurt myself, if you can believe it," he said, chuckling. Then he looked back toward the TV.

* * *

Months later—actually probably less—Dale woke up in the middle of the night. He wasn't sure why. He hadn't heard anything—instinct, I guess—but he was suddenly filled with energy. And, perhaps even more so, fear. He reached over to Dorothy's side of the bed and felt for her, but no one slept beside him. He breathed in deeply. He pulled off the covers and stood up. He noticed the bathroom door was closed, but low light was streaming through the half-inch space beneath the doorframe. He walked to it, quietly, with measured steps. He opened it. The shower curtain was pulled, but two pedicured feet stuck out the far end. There was a hand-painted antique lamp—an East Coast winter scene, children sledding in the park—which just yesterday was on the bedside table, plugged in, and lit, sitting on the toilet bowl. It sat perched on the lid. In the tub, one leg and foot was crossed over the other. Dale stepped two steps and opened the curtain. Dorothy lay sleeping. Peacefully sleeping, in an empty tub, with an avocado-green face peel, dry and cracking, still on her face. Her hair was pulled back in a bun on her head. Her hands were clenched just below her breasts, one of which showed through her bathrobe. Her breaths were soft and mechanical. Her heart rate was slow. Content. She breathed now only through her nose. In and out only through her nose.

Dale stared—disdainful—awhile, scratching the stubble on his neck and breathing, also, solely through his nose. His doing so, though, was because he was angry. His doing so, though, was because he wanted to control his breath. He realized his doing so, though, was because he'd lost control, and he wanted control, and he would do whatever it would take to regain it. He stopped breathing and opened his mouth and spoke.

"Dorothy?" She didn't move. "Dorothy?" Louder. He grabbed her ankle and shook her leg.

She opened her eyes and turned toward him and smiled, before closing them and pulling her leg away and getting comfortable and attempting to regain her rest.

"Hi, honey," she replied, eyes still quiet, as though he'd caught her catnapping before an oh-so-important soiree.

"What are you doing in here? Why the hell are you in the bathtub?"

"What do you mean?" She nuzzled. Butchie was on her and he nuzzled, too. "I'm sleeping."

"I can see that you're sleeping. Why are you sleeping in here?"

"I wasn't cozy in bed."

"What does that mean?"

"You kept hogging all the covers."

She curled back into herself and looked quite comfortable. Dale left and went back to bed. The next day, Dale went out for a pack of cigarettes. And Dorothy was rather suddenly, in her eyes, all alone.

ACT 2

1970-1981

I ATE THE FROG FIRST

Dorothy met Seth about a year ago when she decided she wanted a pool. She'd gotten a good settlement from the divorce—it was decided that she'd take the kids; he could have a weekend a month, if he wanted—and they'd sell the houses and split the money. And with that money she bought herself a ranch in Reseda, with a few acres of barren, dry land—she'd, of course, find that out later, trusting her young, handsome real estate agent when he described the lot as "plush, revitalized, and a gardener's delight! With some work, you can truly express your vision! With some work, this place will truly be yours!" And she thought his face was just so honest. Just look at him, she thought. He couldn't tell a lie. But, in light of all that, Dorothy was getting by, attempting to enjoy her newfangled independence. Not yet forced to work, and with some money in the bank, she thought a pool might be good for the children. Might keep them out of her hair. When the pool men came for their consultation, though—Tranquility Pools, a father/son pool team she'd found in the yellow pages—she decided it unwise to spend so much money, given that she wasn't such a fan of the water herself. Water's no good for hair. Frays your ends. So she said sorry for the trouble to the father, and sent him on his way, but slipped her number, penned on the inside of a deli matchbook, into the back pocket of the son's black dungarees. She knew he was young, but she thought she was young, too, still. Even though her hair had started thinning, and she'd therefore started wearing wigs—she loved wigs!—she was still young, right? Thirty-one was still young. She was still pretty. So Seth called her back later that week, and since then they'd pretty much gone steady.

* * *

Dylan aligned and prepared his kill shot, far removed from his target. He hid behind a green-brown shrub. He kneeled in the dirt with his right hand on a splintered skateboard, and he rolled it backward, then forward. Forward, then backward. Backward then forward, again. Eight years old, he wore a ratty T-shirt and holey briefs. The top of a sport water bottle, with its long plastic straw, sheathed—a knight—between the underwear's elastic and his freckled right leg. He counted upward in his head. He started at one and only planned to three, but got there and didn't fire—too soon—so he continued counting. When he reached fifty-three he wondered if she'd ever start riding. "How long does it take to oil your hands?" he thought to himself, remembering the sight of his sister yesterday wearing their mother's long, white prom dress gloves—lace and satin—lying asleep in a bikini on a round patch of dead grass in the sun. Tanning, baking. Coloring her pale. But today he was at the back of the driveway, and Clover was preparing herself at the front, and he felt the hot, tarry, sandpaper-tough top of the board as he glided it back and forth on uneven wheels beside him. He reached ninety-three, and then he put his head down, about to give up. But then—how exciting!—Clover mounted her turquoise bike and put her shiny hands on the pink tasseled handles. Dylan grinned. "Onehundredthree, onehundredfour, onehundredfive!" he whispered, angrily, and he pushed it off with all his might. And he watched, quietly, as the board flew forward in front of him. Straight as an arrow. Sharp like a sword. Hard enough to knurl up the bike's wheelbase beneath her. Strong enough to really do some hurt. And, just as she'd begun to pick up speed, the board reached her and jammed up under her front wheel. The rubber tires screamed and the board cracked in the spokes as she flew forward over the handlebars and onto the hot cement. But she was strong and resilient—it was in her little genes—so she held on tight to the rubber handles, even when her instincts told her otherwise. She landed on her shins, instantly bleeding. Her spine was curved like a crescent moon over the frame's front wheel. Her mouth hung open—limp and dogged. Her arms were raised. She still held on, though, but just barely. Just to the tassels. Dylan walked back to the house chesty. Like he'd won. For, when she was upside down in the air, he saw her feet touch the sky, momentarily, and beautifully, eclipsing the sun. And her hands still glowed bright white—her own personal stigmata—shining, glistening from the morning dew.

CLOVER EVENTUALLY MADE it back to the house. By that time Dylan was sitting on his bed Indian-style reading pornographic magazines. The spine rested between his knees. Dorothy sat at the kitchen table halfway through a cigarette, nooning quietly on the phone.

"No, I can't bring the car in to get serviced later 'cause I can't get there without the car. So you have to come get me. I need you to come get me," she said with a tone change. She said with a smile. "I could go for some servicin', anyway, myself." She stopped talking and nodded instead. "Okay. Bye, Sethy. Come soon."

It made Dorothy giddy speaking in a manner that she deemed youthful—a bit crass—with her young boyfriend Seth. Made her feel vital. She was still alive. And the phone, itself, felt good. Cool, pressed hard to her ear, when her little ranch house was always hot. She put the handset back on the receiver, then hung the receiver on the wall.

"What happened to your legs, baby?" she asked, just noticing Clover. "You're all scraped up."

Clover stared down at her feet and held her hands—palms up—before her. She didn't want to show Mama. She felt ugly. She didn't reply. She put her head down and walked toward her and then Clover crawled up Mama's legs to her lap.

"Are you okay, darlin'? Angel? This doesn't look so good," she said and rubbed her back.

"I fell, on my bike. I don't know. Dylan made me fall." Head drop. "His skateboard comin' at me and it jammed under me and I fell over the bars." She wanted to cry but she didn't like to cry. "It all hurts. I just wanted to stay out there and ride my bike and tan my hands. But it started to hurt more," she sighed. "And then it started to hurt a lot more, so I came in."

"I'm gonna get you some ice." Dorothy plucked Clover from her lap. She laid her down on the table and rested her dirt-blonde head—brighter in the summer than the winter—on a stack of paper plates. Then she went to the freezer to get some frozen peas. She turned and looked back at Clo. Then she turned back to the freezer. "What do you mean you just wanted to tan your hands?" she questioned.

"They're all white."

"Well, I know that. But so's the rest of you."

"Yeah, but when you put the oil on me yesterday, I fell asleep and forgot to take off your gloves."

She showed her mama her hands. They were like ghost's hands.

"Oh, my sweet. I've got ya. I'll take good care of ya. Let me put this on your knee. Hey, you know what? Are you listenin', baby? You know what?"

"What?"

Dorothy placed Clover's little hand on the peas to steady them and let go and pulled her chin up with her long-nailed fingers and looked her in the eyes.

"Maybe later we can use some of my self-tanner to cure those see-through hands of yours. I don't know why you wanted to wear those old gloves anyway. Now look at 'em. White like ivory."

"Really, Mama? You can fix 'em?" Clover asked, misty.

"Really, my sweet. Really," Dorothy said, and Clo hugged her mama. "I've got you, baby. I've got you."

When Dorothy stumbled to get the peas, she also grabbed a bottle of bourbon from the liquor cabinet and uncorked the top. A sour mash.

A blend. When she came back, she hid it behind her ass in her right hand and with the other pet Clover's freckled-out face. When Clover closed her eyes and grabbed Mama's hand with all her might in her little fingers—Clover was excited, she finally felt safe—Dorothy took a swig and it burnt her throat and it made her even hotter. Ah. Her cheeks reddening, she poured the rest on Clover's scratches, understanding that this was best for her in the long run, and without much belief in the present. So Clover yelled, and kicked Dorothy in the gut, and then ran to the bathroom and slammed the door behind her. Dorothy—stunned—looked around, her daisy-print sundress stuck to her sweating belly. She hadn't eaten yet that day. Recently she hadn't really been eating. She felt the whiskey more than she had expected. Suddenly slightly nauseous, she walked to the bathroom and knocked on the door.

"Had to do it, baby," Dorothy shouted. "Like a Band-Aid, baby. Needed to make sure you didn't get infections."

No answer.

"Baby?" Dorothy knocked. "Baby, what'd you do with my cigarettes, baby? Where'd you put 'em, baby? Where are they?"

Dorothy was itchy. There was a long silence, and then the toilet flushed.

"Baby?"

"Yeah?"

"What's happening in there, baby? What's wrong?"

Sometimes, some mornings, when she felt like acting "better," she'd write herself lists on napkins, or envelopes, about the ways she'd try and change. How tomorrow would be different. About how much more she'd do. About the kind of woman she could be. Work out tomorrow. Call Pony. Get better. Do more. These same mornings, Dorothy often asked Clover to hide her cigarettes. "And when I ask, baby," she'd say, "don't give 'em to me still." This morning was one of those mornings. She usually remembered, though, to buy more from the Sunoco on Saticoy Street and hide them in her truck's glove box— or near the boiler, or in a box of tampons underneath the sink—before she really needed one. She made sure not to tell Clo about those. That way she could smoke and Clo would think she wasn't and Clo wouldn't judge her. But Clo always knew even if she didn't let Mama know she knew. Today, however, she'd been too busy. Actually, it was just too hot. And the truck was broken. Something about the rear compressor. She couldn't go drivin' herself to the store when the truck wasn't functioning. And she didn't know a damn thing about how to fix it. Isn't that what she keeps the boy around for?

"Nothing's wrong, Mama. I'll be out in a second, okay?" Exasperated.

"Do you have 'em?"

"What's that?"

"My cigarettes?"

"No." She paused. "They're gone."

"What do you mean they're gone?"

And silence.

"Where are they?" Dorothy lifted her voice now.

"They're gone, Mama. I flushed them."

Clover opened the door and came back out. She walked past Dorothy and out the door as Dorothy shook her head with her hands to her eyes.

"Goddamn bitch," Dorothy said, and then she went back to the kitchen.

The screen door pushed open—filled with holes, like Dyl's undies, it didn't do much to keep the bugs out—and Seth entered the front room wearing a yellow hard hat. He'd got off work the hour before. He'd left early. Couldn't take it anymore. Had enough. His pants hung low, and his black-and-blue, short-sleeved, checked, silver-snap, button-down shirt was stained with oil. He usually parked his truck—which he'd borrowed from his father, he had two—underneath the fir tree in the yard. The ranch was eighteen acres. The ranch had a long, low roofline. Stucco. Paneled brick and brown wood siding. A rambler, single-story, with vaulted ceilings and exposed beams, large, overhanging eaves, and a hip roof. The ranch had two yards—front and back. Both were covered in grubs—long, white, wood-eating larvae, which made for a suspect back porch. The fir tree was in the backyard. Seth walked to the fridge for a Coors—*The Banquet Beer*. A tall boy. He was Dorothy's boy. He worked with his hands, and thus they were rough, and coarse, appropriately. He'd recently dropped out of school. He was fifteen. Well, almost sixteen. Fifteen and three-quarters. From his back pocket hung a red bandana, once soaked with sweat but now salty-dry from a few days straight of long work.

"Where you been, baby?" Dorothy asked.

"Workin'."

"I thought today was your day off?"

"Yeah. No, I had to work, but I got off early. There was a lot of pools today. They're all mucked up from the drought, and Dad made me do the last two by myself so I said forget it and left when I got finished." He cracked his cold one. "There were still some leaves in the last one."

Dorothy ran toward him and then jumped up on his back as he leaned down looking into the fridge. They were about the same size so Seth could only hold her like that a moment before his knees buckled beneath him. Dylan was in the bathroom staring into the mirror. Clover sat on her half of the bed staring at her still-pale fingers. Sad. Dorothy could see Clover through the doorframe from Seth's back. The kids' room was off the kitchen. She hadn't helped her daughter, yet, but Dorothy didn't care much anymore. She'd do it later if Clover asked. But she had to prioritize. Right now she was busy. Happy in Seth's hairless arms.

Seth held Dorothy as long as he could, but when his hands slipped off the small of her back he spun around and gripped her to him—with his forearms—and pushed her up on the kitchen counter as the icebox door swung closed. This took all his strength. He leaned between her. The cracked porcelain counter was cold on her hamstrings. She was sitting on the ledge. Like she didn't care. She hooked her feet around Seth's back. She was drunk, by three, and happy. He stared at her. She stared back.

"I have to go to the bathroom," he said.

"Can I come?" she asked.

"No. No. Not this time," he replied. "I really have to go. Stay here. Make us some drinks. I'm tired, and I really have to piss."

"All right, sweetheart. Okay, baby. I get it."

"But be ready for when I'm back."

"You know it, baby. I've got you. I'd never leave you in the lurch, baby. I've got you forever."

He walked back to the fridge, found his beer, sucked on it, then brought it with him to the bathroom. After he flushed, he walked back into the kitchen and finished his beer and threw it at the silver trashcan in the corner. Missed. He forgot something in the truck so he walked straight out to the yard. Dorothy moved gingerly as she jumped off the counter, her bare feet enjoying the cool, mosaicked, slate kitchen tile. She went to the fridge and took out an orange, then went to the cupboard for molasses. Then she went to the bar cart for bitters and bourbon. Old Fashioneds were her favorite cocktail. Her grandfather—Blackie—used to let her sip his when she was Seth's age. He was called Blackie because he played football in college and he was fast. An athlete. He used to say, when she was little, "In Georgia, you put molasses in everything. That's just our way. That, and peanuts." But maybe he just liked molasses and spun that out for houseguests to get away with everything he made being so sweet. Dorothy took two rocks glasses off the drying rack and placed them in front of her, in line with her left and right leg. Left for her, right for him. That's how she'd remember. She cut the orange in half on the countertop. She let the juices drip all over. Then she cut the halves in half. She took the two handsomest quarters and put them to the side, then took the remaining two and squeezed them into the tumblers and dropped in the rinds. She removed the bottle's yellow twist-off top and then added two dashes of Angostura Bitters—always mix bitters with plea-sure—to each glass. She swirled in a teaspoon of molasses to both. This was her favorite part. She liked the way the oranges looked all dark. Half-covered in black. Inky. No longer beautiful. Marred. She went to the freezer and got an ice tray and put two fat cubes in each glass. She splashed around the glasses and saw she'd spilt some. She knelt down and licked the juice from the counter. The coarse grout between the tiles was tough on her tongue. Like a cat's tongue on your face. Grainy. Perfectly grainy. Then she took the pretty two orange quarters and stuck them, like half-moons—on the left side of the right glass, and the right side of the left—so that they were touching. Together. She liked them to be together. *Life is only a paper moon, sailing over a cardboard sea. But it wouldn't be make-believe if you believe in me. If you believe in me. If you believe in me.* She hummed and swayed. She reached for the open bourbon bottle. She filled his glass halfway. She filled hers full. He was young so she had to monitor. Then he walked up behind her and took off her wig and reached into her housedress and undid her bra. She tried to squirm away, but he held her to him with strong arms.

"What are you doing, Sethy? Hey."

"Come on, Mama. I missed you today."

"Oh, Sethy. I missed you too. But the kids are here. The kids are somewhere."

She gave in and leaned back into him.

"Oh, Mama. Come on."

"Oh God, fine." She grabbed his hand and pulled him closer and backed further into his groin. "I don't know where they are. I don't see 'em anywhere. Just go close the door to their room, babyboy."

He did and then came back. She'd already put her wig back on. She stood on her tiptoes and kissed him. She pulled on his greasy hair. It was thin like her real hair. She pulled him closer and kissed him harder.

"Babyboy, I just licked the counter. Kiss me, babyboy. Kiss me and you'll kiss the 'lasses."

HISTRIONIC PERSONALITY DISORDER

Single Dale enjoyed being single Dale. He enjoyed the freedom that came with sleeping with a variety of women—always lookers. Always. Please. He was a star. He, too, enjoyed being able to do drugs when he wanted, as much as he wanted. He enjoyed being able to do drugs without anyone knowing he was doing drugs, even though most of the time everyone knew he was doing drugs because, where he often was, everyone else was also doing drugs, and thus assumed everyone around them was doing drugs as well. But he didn't like the camaraderie that came with standing around a glass table—at least not yet, anyway—and instead preferred doing lines with Scotch before he left the house and then, out, doing key bumps in the bathroom, alone. When people asked him why he had to go to the bathroom so often—jokingly, even though they sincerely wondered—he'd say he drank a lot of water during the day. He'd say he'd been exercising. He'd say his doctor told him to do so. Eight full glasses, he'd say. "Good for the body and the mind. It is. That's how I stay clean," he'd say. "That's how I stay clean." He liked the idea that people thought that this personality—this "energetic yet spiritual" personality—was how he always was. Was how he was born. He'd always had a certain pep to his step. He was always this together. It was easy to stay out this late. He enjoyed the world, and he loved his friends, and just wanted to be around them longer. He just loved their company, and he didn't want it to end. Having to do drugs to feel alive was weak, he said, even though he was doing drugs and just pretending not to. When he awoke at girls' houses with nosebleeds after long nights, often, he'd say it was the changing weather. Or that the climate in, say, Marina del Rey was so dry this time of year. You know? "You know what I mean, baby?" he'd say. I'm just getting over a cold. And I really do feel better, but for some reason I just keep getting these damn nosebleeds. So I have to keep blowing it, and blowing it. I've had to use so many tissues, honestly, it's just nuts. Let me go clean up, though, baby. But be ready by the time I get back, 'cause I'm gonna get right back up on ya. And then he'd go to the bathroom and sit on the toilet with his head tilted back and a hand towel in his nostril until the blood finally stopped.

He also enjoyed the nights he stayed in. The few nights he stayed in. Or, in the morning—to be able to watch sports on television, something Dorothy always gave him flack about.

"Can't we watch something we both like?" she'd say. "Or can't we just be together? Snuggle? Maybe just talk?"

Jesus Christ, that was annoying. Because Dale loved sports, in particular boxing—having been, as a youth, a Golden Gloves boxer himself. He's thirty, now, but eventually his favorite fighter will be Gerry Cooney, referred to, during his time, as Gentleman Gerry or "the great white hope." Cooney's style was unorthodox. Cooney was known for not throwing punches at the head, aiming instead for his opponents' chests, ribs, or stomachs. But this made him, at times, vulnerable. Anyway, he liked being able to watch him whenever he was on. For every fight. He was from the same hometown as Dale—Huntington boys—and Dale would come to feel, with him, a certain kinship. They both had their troubles, but they both continued fighting. Continued fighting on.

Single Dale, though, also had his moments of doubt, and friability—in other words, the ability for a solid substance to be reduced to smaller pieces with little effort. The opposite of friable is indurated. Dale certainly hardly felt indurated. These moments, moments when the appearance of solidity began to crumble beneath his toes, came when Dale had to spend too much time in his new home alone. When he'd come home from a girl's house in the middle of the night, say. Or during the day when he didn't have to be working. The middle of the night when he'd done too much cocaine also comes to mind. When he couldn't sleep and so he'd go to the wet bar in his bedroom's corner and pour himself a Scotch, and then another, but then he still couldn't sleep so he'd lie in bed and listen to birds chirp-chirping outside his window as the sun came up—he could tell even through his navy blackout curtains—until he finally put a robe on and made his way downstairs to the kitchen and opened the freezer, removed the vodka, and poured himself a highball full—no ice, forget the ice—and drank it all in three medium-sized sips before sleeping from noon to nighttime.

* * *

The phone rang. It wasn't day anymore. Dorothy woke up on the floor of the bathroom. It stopped ringing. Her head ached. It was ringing again. She let it ring as she got up and pushed open the sink mirror to get to the medicine cabinet. There were four pill bottles on the top shelf, but three of them weren't what she wanted—they were only for bedtime. She removed the farthest to the right. Still ringing. She took six without water. She put the bottle in the back pocket of her jeans. She closed the cabinet door. Then she walked to the kitchen window and looked out. Seth's car was gone. She reached and got the phone. It felt good on her ear. Cool. She'd forgotten she'd switched into jeans. She was awake again.

"Yeah?"

"Jo? Jo? Hey, it's me. It's Pony."

"Ponytail" Jones was her last manager. Since the divorce, she thought she'd try and get her career back. She'd fired him, though, the month before. And that wasn't the first time. She often fired him. He once even discharged her. But she hadn't begun to look for new representation, yet. She hoped that'd be the last of him. But now.

"Don't call me Jo. My name's Dorothy, Pony. I don't know how many times I've gotta tell ya."

"Fine. Jo, then, Dorothy. I'm sorry you're still Jo to me."

"That's because you changed it for me, Pony. It was your dumb idea."

Ponytail insisted on having her billed as Joanna Cook—her given name—in an attempt to distance her from her reputation. To show that she'd tried to change. It never much worked, though. And, anyway, she found it too revealing.

"Fair enough. I just thought it had a nice ring to it. How you been, gorgeous? How's things?"

"I don't know. You know. The same, I guess."

"Nothing new at all?"

"No. Not really."

"Well, we need to get you working again, then, beautiful. You're the best. Always my favorite and always the best. My first. I found ya. I found ya before nobody else. I let you shine. The way you're supposed to shine," he exclaimed proudly.

"No you didn't. It was over before I found you," she sniffed. "Boy are you dumb."

"Well, I tried to get it back for ya."

"Yeah, but it was already over."

"Come on, gorgeous. I just—"

She interrupted.

"I just don't wanna right now, Pony. You know that I don't wanna. In fact, I don't want to ever, I don't think, and you know that. I've told you that a million times." She closed her eyes and pressed the phone between her ear and her shoulder and pushed back up her wig. "I'm not interested in anything you have to say."

"Yeah, but I'm not gonna stop askin' 'til you say yes. I need ya." He waited.

"Oh brother," she replied.

"Even if you never do. Anyway, I've got somethin' for you. Somethin' real came in. *A Christmas Carol*. A lead. The ghost of Christmas future. It's dinner theater."

"What? Dinner theater. Are you crazy? Jesus, Pony, quit janglin' so hard. It's unbecoming. In fact it's just pathetic."

"I know what it sounds like, Jo, but it's good. It's a good production. And they'll make you look beautiful, again. They're known for that. They'll bring you back. They'll bring out your gold and silver."

"Oh, enough, Pony."

"I'm just working, Jo. I'm always just working for you."

"No."

"Listen, Joanna."

"Dorothy."

"Well listen then, Dorothy," he paused. "It's five thousand dollars. And you don't have to audition."

"It's what?"

"Five thousand dollars."

"Five thousand dollars," she repeated, eyes open, now wide. This was a lot in 1970, you know? Wide wide.

"Yeah. No audition, too."

"How no audition?"

"I don't know. Some sort of nostalgia production, I think."

"Oh."

"Well?" loudly.

"I don't know," she waited. "I guess I'll get back to you."

"Oh, Jesus," he sighed. "Fine. Are you okay, Jo?"

"Yeah, I'm okay, Pony. I promise."

"All right, beautiful. Okay. Just know that I'm gonna keep tryin'. As long as you keep gettin' offers I'll continue to try."

"Good-bye, Pony."

"Good-bye, beautiful. We'll talk soon, yeah? You're gonna get back to me?"

"Yeah, yeah," she said. "I promise."

She hung up. She put the phone back on the wall and walked toward the kids' room. She stood in the doorway for a moment before going in. Clover kept the lights off. Clover didn't like the heat. Clover had, the past few hours, been drawing pictures of cats with a red pen in her right hand while holding a Maglite in her left. She just outlined them. Didn't fill them in. Drew their silhouettes. She'd always wanted a cat, but never asked for one, because Mama was allergic. And when Butchie got sick, Mama was just so sad. And then Butchie got better, but Mama got worse. And she knew that if she got one, and it wanted to leave, Mama wouldn't let it, and so it would be trapped. Trapped on a ranch with dumb Seth—who Mama insisted she call "Daddy"—and a brother who watched her in the shower.

Dorothy got up and walked to the light switch and flicked it and then walked back to Clover and placed a hand on her shoulder. Clover squinted and stopped drawing. Then she looked up at Mama shy.

"There's something wrong with your head," Clover said, her eyes half-closed.

"What? What do you mean, baby? What do you mean?"

"Your head. Your hair's all sideways."

Dorothy got up and went to the mirror. She looked at herself. The mirror was supposed to be slimming. It wasn't. Not for her. Not today. She was fat today. Her wig clung to her head like a flower of broccoli. Or a cauliflowered ear. She'd probably slept on it the wrong way. Or she didn't pin it tight enough. It was hard to be sure. And she looked squat. She hated her real hair. Her thin hair. *Her* hair. As she got older her wigs grew larger. The uglier she felt, the more she covered. More makeup. Bigger, faker teeth. Chiclety. Skin more taut. Fewer wrinkles. No more furrowing her brow. The wigs, too, had grown exponentially recently. And they'd continue to. Essentially for forever. She never quite got her confidence back. One thing always led to another. Her perfume got stronger, too.

"Mama? Mama, are we gonna go to town and get our nails done? Last Wednesday you said we were gonna go Sunday."

"Ugh, is that today? Is today Sunday?"

Dorothy wiggled her head sideways looking into the mirror as she spoke. Then she pounded on her left ear like she had water in her right.

"Yeah, Mama," Clover looked back down with her head shaking. "Today's Sunday."

Clover started drawing again. The cats were suddenly filled in. And they all grew very long whiskers.

"Come on, baby. Don't act bluey."

"I'm not, Mama."

"It's just too late now."

"I know, Mama."

"We'll go tomorrow."

"Okay, Mama."

"I promise."

"Whatever you say, Mama."

"Please, talk to me, beautiful girl. Look at me." She turned back to her daughter—hair fixed—and sat back down. "Don't be mad at me. Do you want me to fix you something for dinner? I think we have eggs. In this heat I could probably fry 'em on the counter. You want two eggs? Maybe two fried eggs? Maybe three? You look hungry. You've been eating all that horseshit recently. All that sugary cereal. That jar of rotten olives. I should fix you something. Yeah, I should fix you something. How about some chicken? I can go to the store and buy a chicken. Oh, but the car's beat. So eggs. I know we have eggs. Unless. That'll do, huh, baby? That'll do."

She pet her daughter's hair down flat to the back of her neck. She then stopped supplicating, suddenly, when, without warning, a foul smell entered the room. It hit them both hard, freezing them frozen. Like amateur boxers getting hit—really hit, like a hook not a jab—for the first time. They'd had their bell rung. Dylan walked by them to the bathroom and closed the door without a word. The bathroom off the kitchen didn't have a sink—just a toilet—and Dylan needed a sink. And no one was allowed to use Mama's. Unless you wanna get your ass spanked. Do and Clo finally looked simultaneously toward the door. Starting at the doorknob, a crack crawled up—sprawling like a tree branch—to the door top. Slammed too many times. They wondered what he'd gotten into. It smelled like ethanol, but he never showered. Dorothy had given up on asking him for that. And antiseptic. Gamey, too, and familiar, like the after-hours at a bus depot.

"Dylan," Dorothy yelled. "What are you doing in there?"

"Nothing," he replied through the closed door. Dorothy and Clover heard him turn the faucet on.

"Oh, really?"

"Yeah," he yelled back. "Really."

Dylan's voice was like that of a lifelong smoker who'd never been through puberty. When he didn't get his way he screamed. For attention. He sometimes liked attention. Once, at an airport security check-in— Dorothy sometimes flew to Manhattan for sale season; she used to bring the kids—he lay down on his back and pounded the ground with his fists and the balls of his feet. He pounded and pounded until his pinkies started bleeding. A flight attendant brought them peroxide, but once he got cleaned up they'd missed the plane. In the car, on their way to the airport, Dorothy'd lost the plume for the sugar-sack hat of his toy knight. That plume meant the world to him. His knight was nothing without it. So he cried until Dorothy missed her flight. To punish her. Dorothy went back to Manhattan the next year. She spent two weeks that trip to make up for the one she'd lost. Dylan wasn't invited. He stayed at Dale's. But Dale didn't really like him, either.

"Baby, what are you doin' in there? What's happening in there? And what in the world is that smell?" Dorothy walked to the door and knocked and asked, angry.

There was no reply. Dylan turned off the faucet. Dorothy knocked again, this time more violently. Even angrier, still.

"Dylan, baby? Dyl? Let me see what you got in there. Let me see what you're doin'."

She knocked again and the mirror rattled. Her nose burned and her arms itched. Perhaps a side effect from her lengthy, and plentiful, use of pain medication. Like her cottonmouth. Or she was just itchy. And the house was just hot.

"Dyl?"

"Yes, Mom?"

"I need you to come out now." She put her ear to the door and tried to hear him. But she couldn't hear him. "I need to see what's wrong with you, baby. I need to see what you're doing. So come on, baby. Come on."

Dylan opened the door. He had another straw from a water bottle sheathed in his blue-lined tighty whities and wore once-white holey socks. He spent most of his time, when he could, in the sun. It made him warmer. His face was, thus, so covered in freckles that it was hard to see between them. Especially this late in the summer. When he tried to run past his mother—he faked right then spun left—and almost made it!—she grabbed him by his neck and he stumbled back and fell on his tail bone. Bruised. She stood over him, but he refused to meet his mother's eyes. He lay there with his juice-belly stomach heaving up and down like a fireplace bellows. He'd drunk too fast. Distended. He was always thirsty. Again, it was always so hot. Dorothy stepped on his chest in her house shoes and he wiggled like a turned-up centipede. But then she understood. He smelled like champagne and musk and rainwater. Like he hadn't showered in a while but wanted to fool somebody into thinking otherwise. He smelled like perfume and disobedience. He smelled like her.

"Dylan, did you take my perfume? Did you take your mother's perfume? The one I got from Bergdorf's?"

He didn't look at her or reply. He shook some more, then stopped. He moved his hair out of his face, then sneezed in his hand and rubbed it on the rug.

"Dylan? Dylan? Do you hear me? Do you? Jesus, you better not have. You know I can only get that in New York. When I go away— not when *you* go away! I can't get that here, goddamn it. Answer me now, Dylan. And don't answer me snarky. Dylan!" she yelled. "For fuck's sake, Dylan, answer me now."

And he finally looked at her and met her eyes. His nose, gray-crusted from years of untreated sunburn, pointed up. And his ears, as though he controlled them, stuck out as though he might lift off from the ground and fly. His eyes were fixed on her hair. It was teetering, again. And half her scalp and head cap showed. He thought it might fall on him. This made him nervous. He didn't like her wigs.

"I had to kill them, Mama. They were in my fort in the yard, and they were crawling on everything."

"No, Dylan," she moaned and pressed her thumbs on her eyes. "No, no, no."

"I had to, Mama," he said and leaned up now. "I was making sandcastles outside in the dirt and they were ruining everything. I swear they were. I was playing with my knights and they were crawling all over. The critters were hiding in the moat. The bugs. So I had to fill the mote up. Fill it up with poison so they'd die. I had to kill them, Mama. They were gonna ruin everything, Mama. I swear."

"You two are so fucking annoying!" she yelled. "Such spoiled brats. Ingrates!"

Dylan's eyes glazed over and he began to tear up. But he wasn't crying. His mother lit a cigarette and was blowing the smoke in his face as she held him under her foot. She'd found a pack. Earlier. In the fridge, beneath the cream cheese. She stood over him angry, spitting smoke in his face. But she perked up when she heard Seth pull up in the truck. She stepped off her son and went to the window and watched as he backed it in under the fir. He slammed the door and ducked under a branch as he walked toward the house. Dorothy left to meet him in the kitchen. But first.

"Wake up, Clover. I'm tired of you always complaining, too. You can't help me out with Dylan ever? He just does whatever he wants. Wake up. Wake up, and grow up. I can't take much more of you, either. Neither of you!"

Dorothy walked through the narrow, picture-lined hallway to her bedroom. She opened the door, stepped two steps to her bedside table, picked up the spring-loaded, dancing hula-girl figurine—dancing in her hand as she surfed through the air—and grabbed up a small copper key. She put the figurine down. She also noticed a rolled-up twenty, which likely meant she had a line left over. She picked up a newspaper—the arts section, the *Calabasas Beetle*—and there she was. She put out her cigarette in the ten-gallon hat ashtray—the one she got in Big Sur. At times she could be sentimental—then she rolled the twenty tighter and took the line—half up her right nostril, half her left—then she went back out the door and closed it behind her and locked it. She'd lock it from now on, forever. Her hand was oily from the doorknob—freshly greased—and she rubbed her palms together. As she walked to the kitchen, she outstretched her arms and spread out her fingers. They grazed the white walls to the left and right of her. And she painted the walls with the grease from her fingers like the flame decals on a muscle car. She got to the kitchen and stared into her toaster reflection and smiled and then reached up and squeezed her wig down. And she was okay. A hopeful disposition. But then Seth banged in through the door.

"Seth, I need your help, baby. Sethy, I need your help. I need you."

He walked by her and went to the fridge. He stood—staring—awhile, then looked at her over the icebox door with a large pretzel in his mouth. He must've come in with it. Maybe his daddy'd bought them for the crew. Seth called Dorothy "Mama" because it turned him on. His actual mother wore stockings and was gray and was a paralegal. He held an orange juice carton in one hand and dropped the cap on the floor. In the other was a stalk of celery. A seemingly odd combination of food.

"What?" He exchanged the pretzel in his mouth for the celery. He crunched the stalk.

"I need you to go get Dylan. I can't do it right now. I need you to go get him. He's done it to me this time, for cryin' out loud!" Her nose was runny so she wiped it with her thumb. "How am I supposed to live with kids like these? You tell me. And stay pretty for you, too. I'm tryin' to stay pretty for you!" She stomped her foot on the ground. "You get him. Maybe you can show him. Maybe that way he won't do it again. He's a brat. He's a brat. Just like his father. That fag."

"What'd he do, now?" he asked, still chewing.

"He used my perfume to kill some bugs in the yard or something. Perfume that I'd bought in New York that they don't sell here. Real one-of-a-kind stuff! Can you believe it? He went into my room and stole my things. *My* fucking things. He used my expensive perfume to kill fucking bugs. Bugs!"

"All right. I'll do it," Seth said, putting down his food and jokingly saluting her. "Whatever you say, boss," he laughed.

"It's not funny," she screamed. "Do it! Now! While he still stinks, so he remembers."

"In a sec." He picked up the OJ and took another swig.

"No. Now. It needs to be now."

"In a sec. I'll do it in a sec. Jesus. Let me eat a little."

"No, goddamn it." She ran up to him and pushed him in the chest.

"Jesus, Dorothy." He stumbled back and dropped the carton. "Fine. Fine. I'm going. You clean that shit up." Luckily for her all the juice was already drunk.

He took a bite off his pretzel then dropped it next to the juice carton on the floor so it rested against its paper side. He continued chewing as he walked to the kids' room.

"Don't forget to get a switch," Dorothy chirped.

"Oh. Right," he said, and turned around and went to pick a branch from the fir.

CALL ON ME. I'LL BE THERE ALWAYS.

Dale was also competitive. When the kids visited from their mother's, he'd often garnish them with presents, not because he thought them things they might enjoy—he didn't even know what the gifts were much of the time, gifting the buying responsibilities to his personal assistant—but he liked to win, and in this instance he wanted his children to prefer his house to hers. And they did eventually. They had fun when they were there—when he wanted to win, that is. And when he eventually did win, when they no longer wanted to go back to their mother's, most of that fun stopped. Because he was just being competitive. He only just wanted to win.

This competitive nature—his edge, most likely how he became successful—applied to other aspects of his life as well. His dealings with women, for example, since Dorothy, had become rather extreme in nature. More extreme than one-night stands. His ability to get off became contingent on his ability to have stolen a woman—a variety of different hers and shes—from someone else, and the closer he was to the situation, the more exciting he found it to be. In other words, he only liked fucking his good friends' girlfriends. Or wives. Especially wives. And so his friendships didn't last long. But when you're famous it's easy to make new friends. That's what they say, anyway.

He used to joke that, while he looked at himself in the mirror, before he left for the night, he had to go "find his pups a new mother." And then he'd wink at himself, and smile, real devilish, knowing that in fact quite the opposite was true.

Tonight, Dale was meeting with a friend. A new friend and that new friend's new girlfriend. A friend who didn't yet know better than to keep his new girlfriends away from Dale. A friend who still trusted him. They were to meet for dinner and then perhaps go dancing. Dancing was Dale's idea. He knew some people. People that worked at night. The night's more important than anything. But you already know that.

Dinner went fine. It was somewhere that didn't matter. Dinner didn't matter. Never did. Afterward, they'd go to Downstairs at the Upstairs, which was a tough door. They walked past the line at Downstairs, as it was called, and past the door guy—"Hey, Rob," Dale waved. "Kells!" Rob answered. "Just you three?" and he showed them around the ropes. Dale ducked—the door not seemingly befit for tall drinks—ducked and waited for the others to enter before he shepherded them along. The hallway was dark, brick—a catacomb—and candles were the only light. The walls inherited the music, which you could not only hear, but feel, as you made your way "downstairs." They arrived—the couple before Dale—to the light at the end of the tunnel. They looked down a naked flight of stairs to a beach of dancers—each body compressed to another, grains of connected, kinetic sand—and the couple smiled at each other and then they took their first step toward the sea. But Dale grabbed them by the shoulders and held them there still. "No, no, no," the imp smiled. "That's for everybody else. We keep going." And he cocked his head and winked, pressing his hand too hard against his male friend's shoulder, and pulling his female friend along. As they continued to walk, Dale, now leading, moved past the bathroom and, to its left, stepped toward a small door, painted black, with a black doorknob, so as to blend into the dark, black wall. If one didn't know better—wink—one might think this was a utility closet. Just simply a place for mops. But no, it seems, as Dale reached into his pocket with one hand and pointed up to a sign—block print letters etched into plastic, no different from a company nametag—with the other. *The Upstairs*, it read. Dale removed a small black key from his pocket. He turned the handle and pushed the door, and they heard music—different music than before. Better. His friends' eyes widened as Dale held the door open for them, and when they stood frozen, Dale quit waiting and pushed them through. A long bar edged along one side of the rectangular room, and a few booths lined the right wall. The scattered few that had made it all smoked—weed if they wanted. Whatever they wanted. A blonde in a backless white leather suit and luscious figure was tending bar. She nodded to Dale as she wiped down a flute with a dishrag.

"Hey, Daddy," she said to Dale.

"What's up, gorgeous?" he replied. He was fucking her. So was Warren Beatty.

"We good in the corner?" he asked.

"You know it's already reserved for you, beautiful," she pointed.

"Thanks, hun. You feelin' good tonight?"

"Yeah, I do, baby. You know I do."

"Okay, good. But if you need anything now or later you just let me know."

"Ten-four!" she saluted.

"Very funny," he shrugged, jokingly, but also enough to make her stand down. "Could you do me a favor and send us over some vodka pineapples? With lemons? Two lemons on mine? And make 'em strong and keep 'em coming? Thanks, honey. You're the best."

He left a twenty on the counter, which he never normally did, but tonight he wanted her to know she was an employee. He wanted her to know that she was working. He wanted her to know that he was busy. He wanted her to know the night was his.

They sat in the corner enjoying their drinks and then more of their drinks and then some tea sandwiches, which they'd ordered from the club next door. Dale loved tuna salad, and The Roxy's were the best.

Dale bobbed his head along to the music for a while, waiting, until his new friend—let's call him Bobby—eventually leaned in and asked

Dale if he had any drugs. Dale did have drugs, and he removed his cigarette pack from his leather jacket's pocket, where his drugs were, then removed his drugs and handed them to Bobby under the table. Discreet, even though that wasn't really necessary. It's the early '70s, you know, so Bobby's attempt at concealment was really rather precious. Anyway, Bobby promptly got up, walked to the bathroom, and helped himself to Dale's drugs. There was a line, so he waited. And when he finally got inside, he took his time, too, wiping down the toilet with tissues before drawing long lines with a credit card on its white porcelain hat. Then he rolled up a fifty—a fifty he was saving just for this—and then he put it to his nostril, and then he breathed. And then he switched nostrils, and then, again, he breathed. Then he poured two more, and he breathed again. This was Bobby's one night out this week. He'd better enjoy it, right?

Dale, back at the table, waited awhile before he made his move. He watched the dance floor—smaller in the private room, but still filling—and he watched the people dance. Bobby's girlfriend—let's call her Sam—looked at the dance floor, too. She wore a Kentucky Derby hat—black, but blooming with red flowers—over her long black hair, which hung down over her ears and then down over her shoulders. Over her pressed white button-down shirt, she'd strapped men's suspenders to her high-waisted jeans, and her bellbottoms flared out so wide that you couldn't even see her tan clogs. She sipped on a vodka pineapple—this one mostly pineapple, given that she'd already had three. She finally looked away from the dance floor and smiled at Dale, shy, still sipping on her drink through two red straws. Three red straws. She was shy, again—or playing shy—so then she looked down and then back out at the dance floor. Oh, and she was beautiful, too.

"Why haven't we ever talked?" Dale leaned in, finally, and asked.

"What do you mean?" she asked and blushed. Dale made her nervous. Because Dale was a movie star. And Sam wasn't used to movie stars. How excited she must've been.

"I mean, we've met a couple of times, when we've gone out with Bobby. But I feel like we've never talked."

"I don't know," she answered, still talking through her straws. "What do you want to talk about?"

"I don't know either," Dale answered as he slid toward her in the booth. "I guess I just wanted to talk, you know?" He took her drink from her hand and drank from it, evading all her straws. "Just get to know each other. For curiosity's sake."

WHEN BOBBY RETURNED from the bathroom, he found that Dale and Sam had already left. Later that night, after they fucked, Dale convinced Sam to leave Bobby—"You don't think he's sort of a loser?" he asked—and so Sam left Bobby to be with Dale. But after a few weeks Dale stopped calling Sam back because Sam wasn't with Bobby anymore and he found her boring. Question: what's interesting, or exciting, about a stupid, single girl? Answer: nothing. Nothing at all.

* * *

Later on, another day, Dorothy was still upset with Dylan. And when she was upset with one of them, she took it out on both her kids. But she couldn't discipline them these days. She was just too over-whelmed. Exasperated. So she asked Seth for another favor. And Seth liked Dorothy—she let him be, and the sex was good. She kept him happy. Kept him satisfied. So he said sure. Whatever you need, baby. I've got you. He brought the kids down to the lake by the edge of the property, and he told them to bring their pet rats. Clover would sometimes wander around the yard near the trees and the bushes, near the bounds of the property, and would find rats and bring them back home and would keep the rats she found in a wood-flapped shipping crate beside the porch. And she'd feed them and give them water. And she'd walk them, and pet them. She'd take care of them—make sure they were safe—and give them love. Always give them love. And they loved her back. And Dylan, too. They liked being taken care of. They weren't used to it. But now they followed her and Dylan down to the lake. They arrived, single-file—Seth then Clover then Dylan then rats—then Seth told Clover to put the rats in the box—he'd carried the shipping crate down to the water with him—and then made the children sit in the love swing in the gazebo. As the children swayed back and forth, Seth reached into the box and then took each rat, by the tail, and swung it into the water. And with each one he swung harder. The last one almost made it to the other side of the pond. And the children wailed from the gazebo. And soon the shipping crate was empty except for droppings.

"Now," he spoke succinctly at the kids. He'd teach them a lesson. Something his father had taught him. The way he learned how to be. "Rats don't drown immediately. They swim, like polliwogs, but they can't make it from the water onto the land. Their legs ain't long enough. So they will drown, eventually, but it'll take a while." He stopped and picked up a piece of long grass from the ground. He put it in his mouth, and he chewed it. Real old-fashioned-like. Maybe like something he'd seen in a film. Like a cowboy. John Wayne'y, almost. Randolph Scott. "And don't try and go get 'em. Don't even think about going out there and trying to get 'em," he said and cocked his head and fixed his corduroy jacket collar. It was half up from all the swinging. "Don't think you can save 'em," he laughed. "'Cause I'll just go and sink 'em again," he sniffed. And he sniffed again. "There isn't any way they're gonna get saved," he said, and he continued chewing on his long grass. Then he tilted his head back, peacocking. "So leave your mother alone," he said finally, and then he lit a cigarette, orgasmically, and he walked back up the hill to the house.

The kids went on crying awhile but eventually they stopped.

EVERYTHING IS PURPLE

The white paint on the door to the office of Paul Jaunt, Esquire, was peeling as Dorothy waited to get buzzed in. Her feet click-clacked and her legs were wobbly. Bowlegged. She had a hard time standing up straight. The white lettering printed on the glass door had faded. The *P* in Paul was missing, and the *J* slithered down like a garter snake. But you could still make out *Legal Practitioner*. That, it seemed, had been touched up. All he could afford, presumably. Pretty chintzy. Only what was needed was done. The buzzer sounded. She stumbled in. A receptionist looked up from behind a wood-paneled desk. She pointed a pursed smile at Dorothy through winged, purple reading glasses and bucked teeth with a gap. Snaggle teeth and a bob. A mustard-yellow pantsuit. Just awful, really. Disgusting.

"Hello, miss. How can I help you?"

"Hey there," she said, then righted herself and straightened. "I'm Dorothy. I have an appointment. With Paul."

She held the *l* in Paul as she shook her shoulders even straighter, attempting upright.

"It's you," the woman replied, suddenly interested. "I think we've only spoken on the phone before. I'm Sue," she said, waving her pen like a wand.

Dorothy nodded.

"Is he in?" Dorothy asked.

"Yup. Yup. You bet he is. He's waiting."

The door to his office door was big and light and flimsy. She fleeced in.

"Dorothy. It is very good to see you. It really is. It really is," the lawyer said as he stood up and buttoned the top button of his three-button jacket. Then he put his hand out, which Dorothy shook. Then he unbuttoned the top button of his three-button suit before sitting back down with dignity.

Paul Jaunt was Dorothy's divorce attorney. Like her latest agent, he wasn't the first. She went through them. They ripened, then over-ripened, then she tossed them. His gold watch, with a red watch face, looked past his white shirt's cuffs and cufflinks. Greased-over hair and tortoiseshell reading glasses. When he looked up from his papers, those were removed. Like a government agent, he might be, on the weekends, in a diner, reading the paper—maybe the Metro section—eating a club sandwich—extra mayo, yuck—wearing a plaid button-down tucked into dungarees. No belt, though. Sunglasses on as he ate. Saving his pickle for last, most likely. And his coleslaw probably, too.

"Mr. Jaunt. I . . ."

"Paul, Dorothy. Let's use the *tu* form in here, honey. *Usted*'s entirely unnecessary."

"Okay, Paul. I hope all's well, Paul. Anyway, I . . ."

"They're okay. Things, that is. I raised my golf average. Finally broke a hundred. Just kidding, I've been breaking the century mark about a year now. I did beat John the Weatherman, though. That was a good day."

She stared at his eyes. He put his glasses back on.

"Well, enough small talk, I guess. I know what you're here about, Dorothy. Don't worry, I know. I spoke to him."

"I knew that, already, Mr. Jaunt. You told me on the phone."

"Paul, Dorothy."

"I knew that already, Paul." She sat down with her knees closed tightly and her purse on her thighs. She wore a light, powder-pink blouse and linen pants—which breathed—but she was still sweating. She was nervous. And her wig made her hot. This one was heavy. At least heavier. But maybe it was just a side effect from her medication. Sweating, that is. Or maybe from not taking it. That makes you sweat, too.

"Well, what did he say?"

"He says he's angry with you, Dorothy. Well, I guess that goes without saying. That's the status quo. But he says he's angry and he just can't trust you. He heard about you leaving the kids alone with your boyfriend. How he hurt the pets. I mean, yikes, Do. I don't know about that. Seems crazy," he said and paused. "He's understandably irate."

"He doesn't know anything. Anything! He thinks he does, but he doesn't. He really fucking doesn't."

"Yeah, I mean, he knows some things. You know, your boyfriend's a kid, Dorothy. He knows about that. And you left your kids with him." He leaned in and looked down at her over his glasses, then spun in a circle in his leather desk chair. He did this when he was nervous. An over-obvious poker tell.

"Did Clover say something to him? It was fifteen minutes. Fucking Clover! Ugh." She put her head in her hands and shook it. Sympathetic like. Please, feel bad for me now, would ya? I'm the victim. Poor me, poor me, pour me a drink. "Oh, God, Paul. Oh, no. What do we have on him? What can we do? He's got me backed in a corner, Paul. He's got me in jesses and fetters," she said, phraseology she picked up recently while shooting an after-school special about falconry. "We've gotta come back and get at him!" She stomped her feet on the ground and lost her heeled balance, but then she caught herself and she was okay. "I can't lose those kids. Really! They're all I have anymore. You know that, right?"

"Well, Dorothy. He's been comin' on strong. And there's not a whole lot we can do. He's pretty steady. I mean, we could boil down a lot of these recent problems you've had to your excesses. If you think about it—if you really measure it—that really is the root of all these problems, you know? If we could only curtail some of your excesses, just even a little, I'm sure most of these issues would just simply float away."

"What the fuck is that supposed to mean?" She removed her hands from her face. She hadn't really been crying.

"Um, well, maybe you're drinking a little too much? Maybe taking things a little too lightly?"

Dorothy looked at him blankly. She put her head back in her hands and now tried to weep naturally. An inch-long pink acrylic nail from her pinky finger fell onto the floor. But she just left it.

"Jesus, Mary, and Joseph in the stable."

He spun around one more revolution in his leather desk chair.

"Dorothy . . ."

"Jesus, Mary, and Joseph in the stable he's gonna take 'em. He's gonna take my kids."

"There you go again."

"He's gonna take 'em."

"Always acting."

"Paul, they're my everything." Now her mascara really ran. She could act if she had to. She could be good. "And I need that child support, Paul. He's gonna take away both my babies and there's nothing I can do!"

"Well, actually, that might be the only good news in all this. If there's any good news. But yeah, well, I guess this could be considered that."

She cocked her head, curious. Her fingers were desert-colored from her makeup. Feeling suddenly ugly, though, she took out her compact and looked into its oval mirror face as she spoke.

"What do you mean?"

"Well, right now, as you know, you two share custody of both Clover and Dylan—full split custody, two weeks and two weeks—and that's how it's been since I took over your case. But Dale's never been so keen on that. That's not to say that he necessarily deserved full custody at the time, or anything like that, either. But he wanted it because, as you know, he'd like to control the situation. He likes control. He wants the ball in his court. He wants to do what he wants to do. So now he's interested in full custody, and if he wants it he'll probably get it. Because you've been acting out, as you know—again, your excesses—which he's decided must be some sort of cry for help. And since then he's been lobbying for it. But it seems, strangely enough, that he only wants Clover. He wants to continue as is with Dylan, but take full custody of Clover. He wants Clover to go and live with him in Malibu. A unique situation, to say the least. *I've* certainly never heard of anything like it."

"But why? Why does he only want her?"

"He's too busy for Dylan, he claims. Dylan's too much of a headache." He paused and looked down and then spun around another revolution. Then stopped. "He told his lawyer he thinks Dylan's too much like you."

Dylan caused trouble, sometimes, but if she gave him a *Playboy* he usually disappeared. He let her be her. He understood her. The part of her that loved Clover loved her more than anything. The love, she felt, she deserved. Clover, though, didn't want to love her unconditionally, the way she hoped. Clover held her accountable. Clover let her know when she thought she should be a mom. That sometimes it's important to just be a mom. Sometimes she'd ask her to iron her blouse or boil some water. Can you take my temperature, Mama? Teach me how to sew? But Dorothy wasn't good at those things. They made her feel old. She got by on charisma. Clover wanted Mom's hair in curlers, and for her to put on an old apron—would ya?—and slippers, but Dorothy thought that was old-fashioned. She didn't like slippers. She was a modern woman. She was progressive. Those clothes just don't fit.

"Okay. I guess that's okay," she replied breathy. "I don't need her anymore anyway. She's really been dragging." Dorothy was energized. "I don't need her. She's old enough. I taught her enough. And anyway she's really never needed me. She doesn't even like my cooking. And she thinks all my health drinks are weird."

"Well, you've still got joint custody of Dylan. And you can have supervised visits with Clover, if you'd like."

"Did I get a raw deal?"

"No. I mean, he let you keep your money."

"Exactly. That's exactly what I'm saying. I'm gonna still see her. I'd never let her all the way go."

And after she said it she realized she meant it. She'd never let her all the way go.

"Okay, Dorothy. I've gotta run. I've got a late lunch. I'll let him know that you're okay with the new terms, okay? I'll get this thing settled."

"He's still gonna pay my alimony? For keeping Dylan? The same as before? 'Cause Dylan's not easy, you know?"

"He said if you didn't argue and just went home, then the original financial arrangement could stand. If you don't want to fight him on Clover, then you're all set."

"Oh, he can have her. For now, anyway, he can have her. She'll come back once she realizes what kind of man he really is. What kind of man he becomes when it's dark out. What kind of man he is *all* the time. She'll come back when she realizes Irish people aren't meant for the beach. Trust me. She won't like it there at all."

She loved Clover, but she couldn't help herself. She couldn't help but be excited to regain some of her independence. So she gave up her only daughter, because she loved to do the wrong thing. The wrong thing made her feel vital, and she was addicted to that.

"Okay, Dorothy."

"Okay, Paul. When's he gonna come get her?"

"She's already there."

"How'd she get all the way there?"

"He picked her up from school, I believe. Caught her before she got on the bus. Surprised her."

"Oh. Okay," she breathed. "Okay. I don't get a chance to say good-bye?"

He shrugged. She stopped pat-patting her face for a moment and looked at him.

"Okay."

She finished blushing and got up and put her hand out. They shook, and she turned to leave. She opened her purse and looked for a lighter.

She swung open the office door, then waved and closed it behind her. But as she made her way toward the stairwell, she stopped and turned toward the receptionist.

"Tell Paul to remind Dale of my largesse. Tell Paul to tell him he's lucky I'm so easy. I'm so generous. I've always been so generous. Do you hear me?"

"Yes, ma'am."

"Am I speaking Chinese?"

"No, ma'am."

"What do you want me to do? Count to three like they do in the movies?"

"No, ma'am."

"What'd I say then?"

"Your largesse, ma'am. You want me to tell Paul to tell Mr. Kelly about your largesse."

"Yeah, exactly. Yeah," Dorothy said as she picked gum from off the bottom of her slate-gray heel. "Tell him. Tell him about my largesse, and make sure he hears it," she stomped her foot down. And then she stomped again. "My largesse, ya hear? Make sure he hears it."

She left. Outside there was a breeze. And the breeze made her think of a tornado. And she thought a tornado might be fun.

* * *

She'd recently run out of Seagram's, and she didn't feel well. Not well, and not happy. Nauseous, most of the time. She stood before the mirror. She noticed that the toilet-paper roll had run out, so she reached behind the toilet for another. In case she needed them for later. When there weren't any, she went to her room, got the tissues, and put them atop the toilet seat. Then she saw she had lipstick on her teeth and started wiping it off. Pieces of tissue stuck to her fangs. She tongued those off and spat them out. After a few moments, she pressed the mirror in front of her, and it bounced open. She took out the burnt-orange-flavored mouthwash. It was the generic kind, which she preferred. It was stronger. Then she gargled for thirty seconds. Then she spat. Then she gargled again. This time she swallowed.

* * *

Dylan wandered around the house alone in his underwear and freckles and dirty hair. The bottoms of his feet were black from being inside shoeless then going outside shoeless then coming back in. Clover was at school in Malibu. Malibu Middle. She went because she wanted to. Dylan didn't because he didn't. Dorothy didn't care. She was busy. At ten he was old enough to make his own decisions. He was fine. Dylan walked from room to room exploring. Every door was open. Except his mother's. During the day, that was locked. That was always locked. She was writing, or napping, or something, she used to say when he used to ask her. She was busy. So he stopped doing that. It's best to just leave her alone.

He walked to the bathroom. He closed the door. He looked at himself in the mirror. He wanted to shave. He'd already tried—hearing that shaving early would bring forth coarser hair—but nothing. Once he'd cut the fur from a toy panda and Elmer's glued it to his face, but that didn't fool anyone either. It was just really hard to get off. And Clover made fun of him when she saw it. And when he thought about it he always felt sad. He walked to the toilet and saw that it was pissed in and flushed it and watched the water wash down. He touched the water once it was clean and felt that it was cool on his forehead. He walked to the sink and turned on the hot water and then walked back to the toilet to see if that water heated, too. It didn't. It was still cool, and he used some to slick his hair back on his head.

He left for the garage. He opened the garage door and left it that way, just in case. He crept toward the El Camino. It had begun to rust at its burnt-orange hinges. He needed two hands, and all his strength, to pull the door open. He hopped in. He reached up toward the leather wheel. His hands barely grappled on. He pretended to drive, steering left and right. He turned the keys—already in the ignition—but the car sputtered, and sputtered, and refused to start. Wouldn't catch. He couldn't reach the pedal. Also, he didn't know that's what was necessary to start the car. He stopped trying. Damn. He scooted over to the passenger side of the bench seat. He locked and unlocked the door. Then he turned on the radio. Talk radio. So he turned off the radio. He opened the glove box. Inside were a few maps—Pasadena, Rancho Cucamonga, Modesto, San Jose—a pack of cinnamon gum—Big Red, *deliciously different since 1937!*—a pack of cigarettes—Camel heavies, quarter-full, about—and a dirtied, greasy plastic bag. He ate a stick of gum—but it was old so it shattered in his mouth—so he spat out the sticky shards in the ashtray. He pulled a cigarette from the pack and put it in his mouth. He pressed in the car's lighter but it popped back out. Required the car to have been started. Shit. He pulled out the plastic bag. He let it rest against his naked legs. He opened it. There were four syringes inside. He removed one, white-flecked and overused. He pulled out the plunger and then pushed it back in. A crusty flake fell and floated down to his kneecap. And he felt the stale air against his fingertip as it was expelled from the barrel through the needle tip. Then he pricked his finger with the dull point. It took a moment, and he pressed hard, before he saw any blood. But then his fingertip turned red, and a drip fell splat on his knee, and then another. And then another. He put his finger in his mouth to clean it. His blood was warm and thick. It tasted like boiled, salted asparagus. He gulped it down.

PART-TIME HEAD TURNER,
FULL-TIME JAW DROPPER

Dale was filming a movie in New York and they'd rented him a room at the Plaza for the entirety of the shoot. This was a studio picture. They had the money to treat him right. He'd brought Clover with him along to the city, even though she'd miss school, because he thought she might have fun. And that they might have fun. Just the two of them. Just the two of them alone.

Clover spent much of the time in Dale's trailer over the course of the trip, but one beautiful fall Sunday that Dale had off, they spent the day together, enjoying New York. They went to the Bronx Zoo—Clover's favorites were the gorillas, then toucans—and the National History Museum—there she was partial to life-size Native American dioramas, trading wampum with the pilgrims, buckled loafers fresh off the boat, and the cafeteria whale, looming over them, large and precarious, as they finished their tuna salad sandwiches. Again, Dale loved tuna salad sandwiches, and this trait was inherited by his daughter, too. They went to the top of the Empire State Building, where Clover paid a nickel—well, Dale paid a nickel, but Clover dropped it into the slot—to look out at New York through a shined silver tower optical and down at all the people from above. Like ants in an ant farm, or moles in a molehill. Or lemmings, following each other off a cliff, off into nothing. And then just dead. Or cockroaches, when you leave your dirty dishes too long and then you turn the lights on; Clover looked down on New York and felt above them. And not just physically. Above them like she felt about her rats. Of a different ilk. Just better than they were. More independent. Much more free.

After the Empire State Building they walked to the Chrysler Building, and from the Chrysler Building they took a yellow cab to FAO Schwarz. Within the toy store she found an oversized, overstuffed gorilla—even bigger than her, almost the size of the one in the zoo!—and she made Daddy buy it.

With the gorilla on his back, holding it by its stuffed forearms, Dale walked with his twelve-year-old from the corner of 59th and Central Park South to their hotel's entrance. They'd had a wonderful day together, and now they were both pooped. I'm exhausted. You wanna go get some rest, angel? Yeah, I do. Daddy, can we order room service tonight? Of course we can, baby. You better believe it. I'm gonna get a sundae. You want one, too. Yeah, I do, I think. Vanilla with caramel. And walnuts. And a cherry. Make that two.

However, approximately thirty yards from the lobby's steps—57th Street and Central Park South—Clover spotted an advantage over her gorilla-gripping father and yelled, "Race!" before sprinting toward the marble. Surprised, he mumbled, "You little shit," before sprinting himself, still gripping the tan hands of the gorilla. He chased her the half a block toward the hotel, and, while doing so, considered his options. He could let his daughter win, perhaps make her day even more perfect. He could, perhaps, with some guile, attempt to tie, and they could celebrate their day together. Or, or, he could really run and, even with the gorilla, he could win. He could win. Yeah, let's go with that one. That seems the most fitting. That seems the most true.

"I told you you'd never beat me," Dale spat out with his hands on his knees, panting. He'd let the gorilla fall to the cement floor.

"Fuck," Clover replied. "I thought I finally had you."

"Don't curse."

"Yeah, whatever."

"Seriously, Clover," he stood up straight. "Don't curse."

"Whatever," her head dropped. "Don't forget my gorilla." And Clover walked up the red-carpeted steps toward the lobby's gold revolving door.

DUTCH ANGLES

And then Dorothy was at a bar. Gray gravel gargled underneath a brown Dodge pickup's winter tires as it pulled into a parking spot beside her El Camino. Dorothy sat in a window seat sipping a drink on the rocks—"Bourbon, with just a splash of juice," she'd told the bartender. "What kind of juice?" he'd asked. "Any," she'd replied—and watched as Calbert stepped down from the cab of his truck. Everyone called Calbert "Shoelace," but she refused. She said it was too common. She said it was untoward. Calbert wore a Hawaiian shirt—royal blue, with a golf club print—and carpenter's pants. He had yellow-tinted lenses in his nearsighted aviator frames, and thinning hair. Wispy, but still long in back—he wasn't gonna look conservative. And he always—always!—had full pockets. That's because he dealt pharmaceuticals. Calbert was Dorothy's latest. She met him on the bus. He sometimes gave her presents. She sometimes pretended she cared.

Calbert slammed his truck's door and walked in through the linoleum-framed entrance. In his right hand he carried Georgia tulips.

"Miss Americus," he said, his voice thick with cigarettes. "A Georgia tulip for my Georgia tulip."

"Hi, baby," she said. And then, "Oh, you shouldn't have," because she was bashful. Because she liked to play shy.

"How long you been waitin'?"

"Like two cocktails' worth," she replied and drank up the rest of her drink. All that was left was ice. She crunched it. Then they both turned around in their stools. Calbert then stood.

"You want another?" Calbert asked as he wandered toward the bar.

"Yeah. I think I do. I think I'd love that," Dorothy said and smiled.

This was Dorothy's locale. Since Dale had taken Clover, she'd decided to move and live smaller in Venice. She'd been in her apartment a month now, but it was still not entirely furnished. She was still living out of boxes. The biggest things in the apartment were her new Rottweilers, Sarge and Tiara. She'd left Dylan at home to take care of the dogs. They used to be LAPD sniffin' dogs, but they protected her now. They licked Dylan's face when he got dirty and even let him pull their tails. Well, once Sarge snapped at him, but Dyl just thought it was funny. They got along with little Butchie, and they kept him safe. They kept them safe. And Dorothy loved them dearly. They made her feel secure.

But back to the bar. Stamped-down wood—flattened by brown shoes—and bright-lit beer signs. Neon clocks and dried-whiskey smell. Bourbon-flavored Lysol. Prints of four-leaf clovers and a pool table with leopard print. And a bartender in a white button-down shirt with ribbed, white undershirt and gold chains with his sleeves rolled up, showing off half of his bicep tattoos—an anchor, a flower, and a cross within a heart underneath the scripted word *Mama*. His back shirttail was tucked into his dungarees. But not his front shirttail.

Calbert walked up to the bar and leaned against it. Dorothy admired her beau. He pulled up one of his elbows and looked at it with a sour face. He'd placed it in a puddle of beer, and the worn-frayed edge of his Hawaiian shirt had sopped up some Belgian witte. Dorothy laughed. Then lit a cigarette.

"I'll have a—hmm—what do you have on tap?"

"Dark, light, foreign." A beat. "And Americ—"

"I'll have an imported," Calbert interrupted. Calbert drank imported. He thought he was fancy. Extra fancy. Cosmopolitan. That was rich. "And a shot of bourbon. And whatever it was she had. What she had, again. Rocks."

They sat and held hands and enjoyed their drinks. Dorothy let Calbert catch up. He drank a few beers quickly. They talked about their days. Do worked now when she had to. The money from the divorce was drying, but she still collected some alimony. She felt this was deserved—in fact, she felt shorted—but, at this point, that's a losing battle.

Today, she'd done a radio commercial for a new mop detergent. Commercials paid, and exposure had no longer become a priority. Well, at least that's what she told herself.

"Your robot again?" a handsome voice asked Dorothy as she ate dinner on the floor.

"Nope."

"What then?"

"My Mop 'n' Glo."

"Your Mop 'n' Glo?"

"My Mop 'n' Glo!"

Calbert asked Dorothy about the kids. She said they were okay. Dylan was eleven, now, and Clover was twelve. Pubescent. Do smoked another cigarette. And another after that. She asked Calbert about being a locksmith—his day job. And about how much money he made selling drugs. He said speed was the most profitable. He said that these days, with everyone always partying, that that was most in demand. That it was all about demand. But he preferred selling downers, like Quaaludes, because he preferred the customers. Better clientele. In other words, very mellow people—their demons tending to surface more in the recesses of their mind than in their presentation. A lot less tweaky. And a lot more teeth.

"You look pretty today," Calbert said as he finished the last part of his beer. It was flat. He'd taken too long with this one.

"Well I think you look handsome as all hell." She leaned in and kissed his receding forehead. "I think I'm gonna run to the ladies'."

"You got it, baby. You want another?"

"What do you think?" and she looked at him, and she smiled, and she winked.

* * *

She looked at herself in the tarnished mirror after she used the toilet. *You cunty bitch* was written in cursive at the bottom in marker. She pulled up her wig. Her hair was getting thinner. Poor nutrition, her doctor told her. You don't eat enough, he said. She thought she ate plenty. Too much, even. Her shakes were filled with nutrients! She adjusted her wig. She pulled it up to see if that worked better. Looked better. Didn't. She pulled it back down. She smiled and looked at her newly capped teeth. She thought about Calbert. She thought of him drinking another beer and how, perhaps, she'd settled. Again, she'd settled. She hadn't introduced him, yet, to the children. Or to Dyl, that is. She hadn't seen Clo in a while. She couldn't figure out the right time. The cheese seemed to be sliding off the cracker. But she liked Calbert okay. Calbert was someone. Calbert was nice to her and spoke sweetly. It was hard to be alone. As a woman, she needed a man. She needed someone. A woman needs someone. Someone was better than no one. That's for sure. And Dylan wasn't someone. Not yet, anyway. So Calbert was it. Calbert gave her what she needed, which these days was a comfortable shoulder to lean on. Pick up a bar tab. A nice dinner out. Flowers every now and again. Valium.

SIN BOLDLY

Dorothy arrived at the set of *Crack the Whip* having slept only two Scotch hours the night before. This followed a three-day-straight motel stay with amphetamines and two new suitors. She'd had to glug something, when she got home, just to relax a little—crawl out of her head. Scotch—Dewar's—was all that was left in the wet bar. Try to get some rest. She had a busy day tomorrow. While those few hours were much needed, they weren't nearly enough. She slept, but it wasn't restful. She'd passed out. In the morning, she rolled out of bed with one of the men—she brought one home, Lorenzo—and got dressed quickly and so did he. He dropped her off on set—"Thanks, baby. I'll call ya. Swear." She'd got a part as a saloon girl in a western. *Tramp # 2*, according to billing. "We meet here before, baby? In this here bar-room?"—her only lines. But she'd flub those. Didn't care for repetition. Or alliteration. And allegory. Or both. But she walked onto the set with a smile. Her wig hooked into pigtails. Youthfully. Joyfully. Head up high. Still high. Happy just working. A disposition just for work.

Because she was late, small talk was skipped. She was rushed to a tin trailer for makeup and hustled into an avocado-green chair. They dolled her up like porcelain—dark red lips, chocolate-covered cherries— and then she got stood up and spun around and dropped into white leggings and lace and white frilly frillies. They pulled on white gloves, and a white seashell necklace hung down her neck. She had white talc thrown into her blonde wig and even white nail polish. And then she was ready. She couldn't quite see straight, but that's what they said. They pushed her out into the sand and past the high-noon backdrop. And then up the baroque stairs and columns and through the swinging double doors. They propped her up on a white bar stool. They crossed her legs. "Like a lady," they said. "Yeah, okay," she answered. "I can do that." They handed her a Bravo—lettuce cigarettes, remember?

"I've got one, baby," she told the stagehand as she pet his face. She pulled a brushed gold cigarette case from deep within her undergarments and folded it open. She pulled one out—now nine left, having just refilled it—still not yet Virginia Slims, now she was into Viceroys—and leaned into the prop boy for a light.

Barely on the stool, but trying, she attempted to steady herself.

"Everyone's in place, yeah? These fuckin' extras. Okay, now. Freeze! And . . ." Pause. "Action!"

The cowboy sauntered in—pushing through both sides of the shuttered doors with both hands—and clomped toward the bar maiden. Spurs spinning, sepia serape sheathed. He stepped past her and put up two fingers for a drink—a double—which the barkeep placed before him, and then waited. And then waited. Dorothy just looked up with flutters. Boy, was he cute.

"Cut! What the hell is happening?"

The director walked over.

"What's going on here?"

"What do you mean?" Dorothy replied.

"That's your line there. After he orders the drink."

"Oh, really? That's where I go?"

He stared past her eyelashes, one inch thick.

"You didn't get your sides? You didn't have to audition?"

"No, no. They called me. I can do this shit with my eyes closed," as her eyes began to close.

"Um, okay. Well do it then," he walked away with his head shaking. "Let's try that again, everyone. From the top."

"That was rude," Dorothy said to the cowboy. But he just shrugged and then drank back the double shot of flat ginger ale that was made to look like rye.

* * *

Dorothy always counted, which I'm not sure I've yet mentioned. It wasn't entirely conscious—the numbers she got to disappeared almost as quickly as they arrived. It was, instead, a sort of mental bookmaking, where the quality—say, if something was even—meant something to her, in a sort of spiritual, and yet arbitrary, way. This allowed her to escape the thoughts of her day-to-day responsibilities, relying, instead, on the cosmos to decide her fate. A chance to be led allowed her a break from accountability. Like it wasn't her doing the choosing, and so she had another excuse. Everywhere she went, and everything she did, had a number. The steps she walked up and down. The pages she'd read and memorized. Or didn't. And didn't. The candy she ate as a girl—she used to have a sweet tooth. And then she had to go to the dentist. And she didn't like the dentist. But then she realized the dentist was an easy way to get pain medication. But that didn't come 'til later. Everything had to be symmetrical. Everything had to be round. Numbers were the only thing she could count on. If she was drinking, anyway. If she was drinking wine, she could have a glass, but that never happened. She could have two, though. She could have three, too, because three is half six, and six is the number of glasses in a bottle. At least that's what they told her. Depending on the pour. So there must always be six serving-size glasses in a bottle. So that number should be considered natural—a baseline—and so everything should work around that. She could have four, and she did, because four was, at least, even. She couldn't have five. Never five. She could have a sixth, and that one felt the best, but not in the morning. She was, already, so tired. To some, six was too many. So she'd wait until she was alone. Maybe until she was at a bar. At a bar, there wasn't somebody looking at you. Judging you. People are more concerned with themselves. And bartenders want you to drink, even though they had their limits. So she'd reach her limit, then she'd go. She just wanted everyone to be happy. And when she drank—the more she drank—the quieter she became, so nobody wanted to talk to her. But that was okay. She didn't think she had much to say, anyway.

She could have whiskey, too, but there had to be an underlying symmetry. One whiskey, one wine. One whiskey, two wines, because that's three, and three is half six. Also one is half two. So that works two ways. Two whiskeys, two wines was okay. Two whiskeys, four wines made a lot of sense, because two is half four, and two plus four is six. Three whiskeys, six wines. Half six equals three. And, sometimes, like when Dylan was elsewhere. When she could be by herself and nobody could judge her. Not even her big dogs and their black, judging eyes, who she crated in the other room when she decided that was necessary. RIP Butchie. When she stared too much and there was no other way. When she didn't have anything to be but herself. When she didn't have to be accountable—six whiskeys, six wines. Six whiskeys, six wines was twelve. Six whiskeys, six wines was twelve, and twelve was six times two. And six was the natural number so two times six was twice as perfect. But one more than that would be too much. One more than that might cream her spinach. But, no matter, Dorothy always kept track, even if she had to write on her hand with a Magic Marker. Even if she had to mark it, with a black marker, in stilted Roman numerals, Dorothy had always counted, and she forever would.

Drugs, though, were different. Harder. Drugs were different because there was no way to keep track. Except for pills, or bags, which she did try to keep symmetrical, but in a more generic way. Like speed early, slow down late. Or, more specifically, analgesics with a headache, anti-psychotics when she was nervous. Amphetamines when she was too tired. Sedatives when she was awake. But when she was partying, like she did with some of the guys, that's when it became harder. With cocaine she had a hard time not finishing whatever she had. She liked to see the bag torn open from the corner and licked clean-empty dry. And it wasn't because she loved it so much. I mean, she liked it for a while—the night of, anyway. Certainly not the morning after—not the birds—but eventually she wanted to do it all just to get rid of it. Just so she didn't have it tomorrow. So she didn't have to do it tomorrow. So she didn't have the choice. When she had some left over, and she had a martini or two—maybe something more brown, if the guy she liked was manlier—it always came up. In her head it always came up. Because she didn't want to just go home. And, far more importantly than that, she didn't want to want to. She just wanted to stay out later. Enjoy herself. Enjoy the night. Like she was supposed to.

Sin boldly, she thought to herself. Sin boldly, but believe more boldly still.

* * *

Dorothy had recently become attracted to the Off Track Betting location in Ventura. Take the 101. To the 1. Get off at Figueroa. Then park beside the park. She liked it there because she didn't get recognized. She didn't get recognized anyway anymore, but here she never would've. She liked betting on ponies because she felt she had an honest chance to win. As much as anybody else, anyway. And she liked all the numbers. Again with all the numbers. She took the money she made on various acting opportunities and usually tried to double it. Would drive straight from set. But it was mostly just halved. But she didn't think she deserved the money she made, anyway. She never gave it her all. In fact, she got in her own way on purpose—"subconsciously"—scared that if she really tried, then failed trying, then that'd feel worse. Like if she didn't study for a math test and she did poorly, it didn't mean she was stupid, because she left herself no chance. So she punished herself, but had fun doing so. That way it might not feel so bad.

At the OTB nobody judged Dorothy. Or maybe she just didn't feel it because of the Vicodin she'd been prescribed. Her coming root canal got pushed to next week, and when she called and booked the appointment they asked her to describe her pain on a scale from one to ten—one like a pinch, ten like you're dreaming. Ten like delirium. Ten like buried alive. Maybe nine, nine and a half, Dorothy replied. She'd done this before. She'd learned how to get pain drugs. Just describe her pain in its totality, not just what's in your teeth. *How much pain are you in, Dorothy. You know what, Doc? I'm really, really hurting.* Really, she hardly even felt it anymore. She just knew when it hurt she had to call the dentist.

At the OTB people drank beer, even though it was Wednesday morning. Dorothy usually went Wednesdays. But she didn't drink Wednesdays, but that was because of the empty calories. But being high Wednesdays was fine. Fat-free. In fact, it seemed to be encouraged. She appreciated that no one lied to her at the OTB. There were three tellers Wednesdays. Alan Boston wore a Carhartt jean jacket, Rich Marinara slouched and had earrings—silver hoops—and Teddy Covers had white hair that he slicked back and curled up behind his ears behind his sideburns.

It was hot at the OTB—the building's manager controlled the furnace, and he lived in Poughkeepsie—so everyone was sweating. A couple in the corner shared a veal Parmesan from a take-out tray. Today, Dorothy would watch harness racing. Because nobody else did and she could be by herself. Not even sharps know how to handicap harness racing. Only one of the thirty-seven televisions secured to the wall played harness racing. Today's race was at Hanover. Dorothy sat in a corner. She got her betting ticket stamped. She'd conferred with Teddy Covers. She'd bet on Mourning Marvin.

Mourning Marvin had a good record. Two hundred seventeen top-three finishes to one hundred eighty-nine bottom-three legs. His jockey looked good, too. Big ears, small head. Big hands, small body. The jockey threw his paws on the reins. He planked his feet. He looked like a winner. He brushed his hair out of his eyes. Dorothy liked harness racing. When Dorothy felt lonely, she sometimes gravitated toward the addicts and the gamblers. The riffraff. The mole people. The poor—the poorer—because they made her feel better about herself. They made her feel like she wasn't so bad off. Like rubbernecking a car accident. Like stopping your car and watching too long. Dorothy liked harness racing. She may've been the only one.

And we're off.

The jockey gripped his two-wheeled cart—his sulky, that's what it's called—tighter. And Dorothy grabbed her stool's seat tighter than that. Her skin was red and splotchy, warm from the heat and the meds. She was thirsty, but she didn't mind. The horse's carriage strayed back and forth. And Dorothy rocked back and forth on her stepstool.

A betting magazine fell off Dorothy's lap as she shook. *Western Horseman*, September 1973. Mourning Marvin was in third. Dorothy tapped her toes. She moved her hands from her lap to the peg legs of her stool. She put her hands under her ass and pulled on her seat. Her ass was sweating. She was excited. And, again, the painkillers. The side effects of the painkillers. Sweating and dry mouth. Mourning Marvin was catching up. And Dorothy rocked her chair. Dorothy'd exacta'd her bet. Her horse's odds were six to one. She rocked her chair more. And she sweat through her shirt. It was hot and she was high. But who cares? Don't judge her. Nobody there bothered to notice. Why should you?

She smiled and she rocked—big teeth, fangs clack-clacking—even as the porcelain ground beneath her began to crack. The rank smell of Newports and breadcrumbs and sauce didn't bother her anymore. In fact it was comforting. The door to the bathroom was always open. There was only a men's bathroom. People held themselves and wrinkled their eyebrows while they looked up at the one black-and-white TV propped insecurely above the six urinals. The cover article of today's *Horseman* read:

The founding sire of today's Standardbred horse was Messenger, a gray Thoroughbred brought to America in 1788 and purchased by Henry Astor, brother of John Jacob Astor. From Messenger came a great-grandson, Hambletonian 10 (1849–1876), who gained a wide following for his racing prowess. However, it is his breed line for which he is most remembered. The lineage of virtually all American

Standardbred racehorses can be traced from Hambletonian's sons. Lineage, and bloodline, is everything in horseracing. And Hambletonian's bloodline simply can't be beat.

Mourning Marvin came in second place. Dorothy pushed. She didn't win, and she didn't lose. She was the same. She looked over to the bathroom, again. A man held his brown leather jacket over his shoulder. Another in a tracksuit shook himself off and then ashed in the urinal. From behind them, a disabled person pushed open the door to the handicapped stall. Band-Aids covered his bare, shaved-down scalp. He put his cowboy hat back on, adjusted his bolo, and then rolled by the urinals in his wheelchair and left the men's room. Dorothy watched him leave and then walked to the bathroom door. She pushed it softly. It dawdled closed.

* * *

When Dylan was twelve he was home alone without his mother. She'd been gone for hours, and Dylan had school in the morning. He was going through a going-to-school phase. He liked the girls. They'd all gotten much older. They'd grown and *they'd* grown. It was half past one in the morning. Dylan lay in bed, his mother's bed, where he slept until his fifteenth birthday, or when she brought someone home with her, when he slept just outside her door. Until his fifteenth birthday, only because he got taken away. When she was there, and they were sleeping, he'd always make sure he had his foot touching her foot, so that he'd know if she'd gotten up and left. He waited and waited. He didn't sleep. From then on, really. She was out and he was worried. His feet were cold and twitched under the down quilt, which fell on him, heavy as a carcass. He sat up and pulled on the red velvet canopy that hung down over his head, and it felt good in his hands. His hands were cold because he had bad circulation, but he could still feel the rough grain of the velvet in his fingers. He waited and he sweated. Mama had turned up the heat—all the way up—before she left because Dylan said he was chilly. But then it got too hot. But Dylan didn't turn it down. He knew how but he didn't, anyway. She must have left it like that for a reason. It must've been important for something. He pulled on the velvet again. He rubbed it between his pointer finger and his thumb.

Then he heard the front door open and he got up and rushed to it. But Mama pushed past him and through to the bedroom and then to the bedroom's bathroom. Before he could stop her, she closed and locked the door. And he banged, and he banged, and he banged until his right hand hurt. And his hand hurt so he started kicking. And he kicked the door until his big toe began to swell, and then he went back to his hand. He didn't cry though. He didn't like to cry.

She let him in, finally, and he sat on the edge of the bathtub. She stepped back from him and lowered herself, slowly, onto the closed lid of the toilet bowl. He gripped the cool, cream porcelain with four fingers and a thumb. And he watched, as she smacked her arm, and pulled the belt around her bicep, tighter with her teeth, and then sunk a long syringe deep into a dark, round bruise between her wrist and her elbow. She looked at him defeated as she pulled it out and dropped it into a basket beside her with Q-tips and hand towels. She stared at him, defeated, and then empty, but he was okay. He only wanted to be included. He slipped off the tub and sat on her on the toilet and she rested her face against his.

THE THEOLOGY OF PRESENCE

Dorothy got in her car. It was near Christmas, 1977. Dale had the kids for the holidays. The holidays were supposed to be fun. Dale still lived in Malibu, so Dorothy drove from Venice to Malibu. She took the Pacific Coast Highway, all the way. Dale lived on the ocean side of the PCH. He'd bought the house when he was young, after his first hit movie, when he'd first made money. It ended up being quite the investment. Savvy. Brains. Today, Dorothy had made it most of the way down to the house and had only—maybe—fifteen minutes to go before she got there. Dale was having a Christmas party. He didn't want to invite his ex-wife, but the kids wanted their mother there on Christmas. They knew she might be lonely. They pitied her. They knew she didn't have anybody else. They knew it was the right thing to do. Uncomfortable, but probably the right thing to do. But she was nervous. She hadn't seen Dale in a year, and the last time wasn't pleasant. Deep, deep, deep in her heart, though, she still did have a soft spot for him. He was still as handsome as ever. And he was still once a hero, in her eyes. That's what she thought, anyway. First love's a bitch. So she got dolled up. Pink lipstick. Purple under-eyes. Her blonde wig. The blondest. But she was nervous. She saw a bar in the distance on the left side of the highway. A beachfront bar—Moonshadows. She clicked on her left-hand turn signal.

The maître d' met her at the doorway. He was a tall, thin blond. Tan and wiry. He told her to sit anywhere. She found a table by the window that looked out on the water. A waitress came over. She took Dorothy's order. Then she left and came back with a carafe of white wine. Dorothy drank and watched the waves crash. Then Dorothy finished and the waitress cleared it and left and came back with another. Then she cleared that and came back with one more. When that carafe was done, Dorothy asked for some water—if she stayed hydrated then she'd be fine!—and then she asked for the check. She'd been there an hour. Now she was late. Oh no, she was late. She'd lost track of the time. Not really, though. She knew. She knew but she just couldn't. But she got in her car, and she got on the highway, and she drove fast. She drove fast to get to her kids. She drove fast and she'd come to their rescue. That monster is pulling them down! But then there were sirens, and she pulled onto the shoulder. And when the officer stepped up beside her, he smelled the liquor on her breath. And he saw the skew in her eyes. And he listened to her gargled words.

"I've gotta go, sir. You've gotta let me go. I promise it's important. Please, just give me a warning. I wouldn't ask if it wasn't important. Please?"

He stared at her longer. He lifted his sunglasses and rested them above his fading hairline.

"Please," she pleaded. "I'm begging here. Jesus, Joseph, and Mary I'm begging."

When she reached for her purse and removed her pack of cigarettes, he decided to take her back to the precinct. And her car was towed and then impounded. And she was stuck in the drunk tank for hours. And she never made it to the holiday party. And she loved eggnog, too.

Soon after this, Dale requested custody of both of his children, and his request was granted. Dorothy was embarrassed, so she didn't put up much of a fight.

* * *

Dale held his cue stick in his right hand and pointed the green chalked tip at his opponent. Clover, sixteen, put her iced tea down on a bamboo coaster on the small table beside her. Pieces of sea glass and beer bottle caps glassed together atop three uneven, steely legs. She listened to the ocean. She felt the breeze on her cheeks. She sat beneath a large fish tank that hung down over an empty hearth. A fireplace without fire. Once it housed an electric chimney. But that only lasted two days. In the tank were six fish—large and colorful—and, as she stood up, they all seemed to be looking at her, staring into her face. Past the fish stares Clover noticed her own turquoise reflection. She smiled and saw her snaggletooth. And noticed that her face had begun to gain shape. Rounder. Like a heart. But she didn't think it was cute, like a heart. She just thought it was a round heart. It bled out her insecurity. Fat, ugly heart. She turned around. Dale was playing pool with his friends with his shirt off. He was going through a Mexican-cowboy phase—"ranchero"—so he wore his blue jeans tucked into white cowboy boots. The sun was setting, it was getting cold. He wrapped himself in a bandito blanket. His amigo cut one long line—maybe a foot and a half—across a vanity mirror and they all took turns taking it. An inch in the right nostril, another in the left. When they were done, he told them to sit, now, because he wanted to teach his daughter billiards. Drinking beers—Coronitas—and doing cocaine with a hundred-dollar bill after Clover got home from school on a Wednesday—Dylan'd signed up for judo, he'd skip school then just do that—Dale wanted to teach his daughter something. He wanted her to be beautiful, like her mom. But not weak like her. Not pathetic. He wanted her to be wry, and self-aware. Clever, and sure of herself. He wanted her to be brave. A girl that could play pool with men could do anything. Like the heroine in a screwball comedy, whom all the men pine after but no one has the courage to court.

"You're up, baby," Dale said, and he sipped his mini-beer and hit the big end of his pool cue on the Navajo carpet beneath the table on the floor.

"One sec, Daddy" Clover replied. "Let me get some food in me."

"Yeah, all right," Dale answered, but only because he wanted to get back to the drugs. "Make it fast though. And try to not eat too much."

Clover didn't answer. She walked to the kitchen. The house was bright, with high windows, and it hung out over the sand. The front room featured a shag carpet and had two plump, brown leather couches—cracked from years in the sun—that sat parallel to each other in the middle of the living area. The kitchen looked over the living room from one step up. And above the wooden center table hung pots, pans, and skillets. Clover sometimes played Frisbee fetch on the beach with Rex, in the old days. But we all know what happened to Rex. But Clo was still good at Frisbee. She just needed another Rex. The stairs led up to the bedroom, and the bedroom connected to the sauna. She didn't take the stairs. She walked up toward the kitchen and took a serrated knife from the knife block. She halved an avocado near the fridge. She removed some grain crackers from the pantry and cut a lemon into quarters. She plucked out the seeds, and squeezed the rinds onto the avocadoed toasts. Then she salted and peppered the squares before she walked back toward the game. Dale, still waiting—eyes wide and black, owled—knocked his pool cue again against the ground, this time harder.

"Let's do it, baby," he said, and he handed her a stick. She ate a toast then placed the plate on the table next to her tea. She licked her fingers, then wiped them on her jeans. Dale winced. Disgusting.

"All right, so what do I do?" Clover asked as she brushed her fingers against the table's blood-orange felt. Dale's nose flared. He waited 'til she was done to talk.

"Hold the stick like this, and aim it. Put it in the bridge of your fingers, so it feels real solid. The firmer, the straighter. Remember that."

Clover leaned over the table and tried. She tried to bridge her fingers like Daddy's, but she didn't feel strong enough. They began to crumble as she pushed the stick and she missed the ball entirely.

"No, no. Keep your fingers taut, goddamn it." Dale came up behind Clover and smushed her fingers down. "Like that," he said. "Tightly. This is how you keep your hand, okay? You hear me?"

Clover nodded. He let go and stepped back and picked back up his cue. She tried again. She leaned back down, with her hand exactly as he'd forged it, and shot, and missed, and Dale poked her in her ribs with his cue. So she chalked up and tried again, and missed again. She missed again, and again he poked her in the ribs. And, again, and again, until her white mohair sweater began to polka dot. Finally she sunk one. Not because she understood how. More just law of averages. He shooed her to the side and directed with his stick for her to sit down at the table with the gang.

"Jesus, finally."

"I'm sorry," she said quietly putting her head down. "Maybe I'm just not strong enough," and Clover reached for her plate of food. But Dale turned away from the table and stared at Clo, and she knew to stop eating and talking. Then Dale went. And Dale didn't miss. He made one. Then two in a row—a double. Three in a row. A turkey. Four in a row. Hambone. And five a row. All five in a row. Game over. Yahtzee.

"Yahtzee," he exclaimed. "Maybe next time, honey," and he smiled and sniffed, as his *compañeros* cheered him on, and then he walked back toward the mirror. "You wanna try this, by the way, baby? I think it'll help you focus. You seem tired. Plus I know it'll help your appetite if you're hungry too often." And he lifted off his blanket and held it up with his teeth and drummed his flat stomach along to the salsa music that played from the hi-fi in the back. "You look like you're getting a little fat in the face, honey. A little top-heavy."

* * *

Once, after another of Dorothy's arrests, Clover had to bail Mama out of jail because no one else would. No one else cared enough, then. Everyone else was too busy. Or too bored. Just the same story. Just always the same story. Clover was in high school. Her freshman year—her first year—and when Mama first called Clo hung up on her. She refused. She didn't wanna talk. She didn't like the phone. She knew Mama was drinking, again—not like she ever stopped, really—and she couldn't talk to her that way. She couldn't listen to her. She didn't like when she talked through her teeth. Grinding through her molars. She could just see her hanging slack jaw. And her eyes flitter flitter. Clover could always tell from the first word when she spoke to her mother. And that was just too hard. She was in school—she had to try—and it wasn't worth it. It just wasn't worth it. But finally—thirteen calls later—she finally answered.

"What?"

"Clo, baby. It's me. It's Mom. I'm in fucking jail, but it's bullshit. Call Lindsey. You have her number, right? I'm sure I put her card in your purse. Anyway, if she doesn't answer, find another lawyer."

So Clover found Lindsey's number—deep in her wallet, folded in half—and called her and she answered and then she called the precinct and they found out the bail was two hundred dollars and Lindsey paid and Clo promised she'd repay her even though she wasn't sure how and Clo and Lindsey waited in a cab outside, and when Mama came out they gave her purse back and she opened the taxi's yellow door and reached into her purse and found a clear orange bottle and took whatever she had left. Everything she had left. She was anxious, obviously. Jail's sorta hard. They dropped Lindsey off and Clo said thank you and then they took the cab back home. Well, back to her mother's.

When they got there, though, they had to climb over a chain-link, rusted-over fence behind their apartment—thankfully no barbed wire. Thank God, right? They couldn't go in through the lobby. Photographers flanked the front. *White Out: Dorothy, Cooked.* By this time, Dorothy had become less known for her work—her "fame"—which had, obviously, long since dissipated—than for her infamy, in that her exploits as the ex-wife of silver-screen star Dale Kelly, and for her mothering, or lack thereof, of their children. Her arrests—which ones? It's hard to remember—provided her more fame than her acting ever could. Her indiscretions as Dale Kelly's once-other allowed her, in her own way, the recognition she'd always hoped for. Being in the glossies afforded her rediscovery. And, no matter the reason, she could never be embarrassed about that. Press is press. The paper's the paper. She learned that early on. Clover let Mama go first, because she was worried

Mama might fall. And, also, because Mama'd a long night, and she was nervous, and she was scared—about her future—and that's why she had to take all her drugs. She pushed her right leg off Clo's clasped fingers and then shoved her left leg over the top. She fell, a little, as she landed. But she was okay. And then Clover climbed over, and the hole in the knee of her jeans stuck to the rusted rigid wiring of the pointed fence weave. But she was okay, too. She'd be okay. Clover grabbed her hand and she walked her through the courtyard. They reached their first-floor neighbor's window. Clover knocked on the pane glass. It rattled. Clover knocked again. Soon someone troddled over.

"I'm so sorry, Linda," Clover said, as a woman with curlers in her hair took a break from cooking herself a vegetarian meal—probably something "progressive." Probably lentils. Maybe tempeh. Yuck—and pulled open the muntin frame. "But is there any way we could run through your apartment real quick to get to the elevator? I'm so sorry to bother you, but I didn't know what else to do."

Linda stared at Clover then at Dorothy. Longer at Dorothy.

"I'm so sorry to bother you again, Linda. Especially this late." Clover paused. "But my mom's had a really tough night. And we can't go through the front. Please?" She let go of her mother's hand—just for a moment—and placed it flat, palm to palm, to her other hand like she was praying. "Please?"

The woman waited a while longer before she ushered them forward with a limp wrist. Unpainted nails. Curlers. Dirty feet, no slippers. They crawled in through the window. And they were inside. Linda stared, again, but Do stared back. She sloppily smiled. She asked Linda, with her eyes, *I'm okay, right? You don't know anything, right? I look okay, right? I'll be okay, right? Right?* But then she looked down at the floor.

"I'm so sorry, again, Linda," Clover said and grabbed her mother's arm and pulled her home.

When they got there Clover drew Mama a bath. Mama was really tired. And Clover went to her room—Dorothy still kept her a room, even though it had gotten rather dusty—and got in bed. Clover had school the next day. But Clover had trouble sleeping.

* * *

It was a week later and Dorothy was tired. She was tired so she went and sat at a bar to read a book she'd bought from a street vendor. The book was a collection of conversations between film directors. Dorothy liked the look of Peter's ascot on the cover, so she carried it hardcover out.

The bar was dark and empty. Wood floors, white colonnade, which split the room in two—again—and a polished-copper bar top. On their house cocktail menu, they had a specialty Old Fashioned. So she sat alone—just her and her book—and drank an Old Fashioned. Because she was old-fashioned. Wasn't keen on change.

A piano man named Reverend Vince was playing that night, and he played well—like a low, blue flame—and that felt nice, and warming. Reverend Vince wore horn-rimmed glasses and a paisley shirt. The shirt was too tight, but that was okay. It didn't affect his playing.

SCRUPLES

At some point, some summer—I'd say, but there were too many times like this, a microcosmic example of a far greater issue—Clover was sent off to sleepaway camp. Art camp, because that's where Paul Newman's kids went, and Dale was competitive. I think I've already said that. That's where Paul Newman sent them. Expensive art camp, too. Dale thought this was genius. He'd send Clo to camp and Dylan back to Dorothy. Give Dorothy a break. She'd been doing okay—"okay"—a minute, now. Dylan would come back in time for school, and he'd be fine out there. And for Dale—oh, for Dale—finally some time to himself. Jesus Christ, finally, you know? Finally! And Clover didn't hate the idea either. She liked to be alone, too.

So Clover got excited. The night before, she perused the camp's list of things she needed to bring. It read:

CLOTHING

FOR YOUNG WOMEN:
- Bras.

FOR YOUNG MEN:
- Athletic Supporters.

FOOTWEAR

- Sandals / Flip-flops.
- Sneakers.
- Cleats.
- Socks.

- Sleeping Bag.

Now let's go have some fun!

So she packed all that. And she would have fun. But no need for cleats. She wasn't interested in jocks or anything. Tough guys. She didn't like tough guys. She pushed her black duffle bag out by the door and went to bed and waited for the morning when Daddy would drop her off.

However, in the morning, Dale wasn't home. He hadn't come home. When Clover went up to his bedroom—that was a rarity—his bed was made and empty. She had an hour until the bus left from the gas station at the Malibu Country Mart. Near Pepperdine. Off of Webb Way. She walked and sat in the living room unsure of what to do. She could call a cab, she supposed, but she hoped to at least hear from her father before she left. Soon, though, she heard the phone ring from the table beside. She slid over and picked it up.

"Hello?"

"Hi, baby, sorry I couldn't make it back. I called a few people, but they didn't answer, so I called your mother and she's gonna come take you. Okay, baby? You there?"

Clover didn't respond a while.

"Hello? Are you there?"

And nothing.

"What the fuck, *hello*?"

"Yeah, I'm here. It's fine."

"Okay, baby. Terrific. That works, right?"

"I guess so."

"Cool, baby. I've gotta run but I'll see you in a month, okay? I love ya."

Clover waited until she heard the dial tone and then she put the phone down. She went and sat on her duffle and waited for the doorbell to ring.

But Dorothy walked in without ringing and knocked Clover—surprised her father had left the door unlocked—from her bag to the floor.

"Oh, I'm so sorry, baby," she said and reached down to lift her. "I didn't see you there. I just didn't see you there at all."

Clover got up to her knees. And then Mama pulled her up straight.

"What the hell, Mom?" Clover said, sucking on her finger. She'd scraped it on the grout between the tiles. She looked toward the ocean. The waves made her less nervous. She smelled Mama. Mama smelled strong.

"Are you wearing something new, Mom? It's strong smelling."

"Yeah, baby. Freetrapper, it's called. Cedar, bergamot, snakeroot, and black pine. I just bought it yesterday so I remember what they told me at the store. Freetrappers predated cowboys, you know. They conquered the West and were truly independent spirits. That's what they told me, anyway, baby." She pulled her up. "I just thought that sounded nice. Anyway, can I have a hug? Hug your mama, would ya?"

"It's really strong," Clover said as she turned around. She sighed then hugged her then looked up. Mama wore a lot of makeup. More so than usual. It stained the collar of her jacket. And beneath her makeup she seemed to be pocked and scabbing. She wore a scarf over her neck and chin and royal purple Elizabeth Taylor sunglasses, covering much of her face. And an overlarge platinum blonde wig—a cherry on top— but Clover saw through it. She saw right through it.

"Is your face okay?"

"Yeah, baby. What do you mean?" she said nervously. Dorothy put her naily hands in her mouth to cover it. "Just a little rash is all. I'm so embarrassed. I think it's from the cat. I was hoping you wouldn't notice. I was hoping nobody could tell."

Dorothy stared at her for seconds before she could speak. She stared at her daughter both surprised and excited. She stared at her daughter a long while and she couldn't break her stare. Her eyes looked the way they did when she first saw Dale on set. She stared at her daughter with love—in love, true love—piercing through the malaise that usually clouded the glasses of her existence.

IT WAS ONLY five minutes away but the drive felt longer. Probably the new smell. And her disgusting face. What's a freetrapper, anyway? I've never heard of that. Mama's so dumb. Always getting sold on stories.

Suddenly, Clover grew very nervous about what the other kids would say about her mother. They haven't even met me before. This can't be their first impression. I mean, oh my God, what are they going to think? Dorothy seemed to have scratched right through her face, like a bear covered in sticky honey, and then attacked by bees. Heroin addicts often describe this condition as itchy blood. It results, often, in compulsive scratching or picking, which usually results in deep sores, cuts, and bruises. Dorothy's face was frightening. So soon would be much of her arms and even ankles. Once Clover walked in on her mother cutting deep into her skin with an X-Acto knife, the blood on her bed puddling squarely beneath her, quadranting her sheets and boxing her in. Dorothy oft complained of bugs in her room, on the walls, in her sheets, and even hair. Eventually, she became sure that these microorganisms had burrowed into her skin—deep into her pores—and so she just had to get it out. It was for her and her loved ones' safety—and so it was no less than imperative. She was only trying to protect her kin. This condition faded in and out in spells throughout much of this time—masking, clearly, the extent of her usage. A mask amount of makeup, paired with a healthy agoraphobia, allowed her to not notice much of the time. Or, more honestly, too much of the time to not care. Others did, but were afraid to speak up. By this point, the elephant had grown and fattened so much that it filled the room—always the life of the party—and the people, who once inhabited it, were pushed flat to the wall and held there, frozen, fighting for their right to breathe. In other words, she took her sugar with coffee and cream. As they stopped at a red light, a woman turned casually toward their car and saw Dorothy and then looked back again and then quickly forward. She was scared of Dorothy, it seemed. And Clover's fears were corroborated.

As they arrived at the gas station, Clover formulated a plan. They stopped beside a gas pump, the bus parked before them in plain sight, and Clover said, "I'll take it from here, Mama. I love you." And she reached down and grabbed her mother's hand and kissed her on her knuckles. She didn't like the smell, or that her knuckles were clammy, but she kissed it again, anyway, this time harder than the first. "I miss you a lot, Mama. I do. Everything that's good about me comes from you. I love you. I really do."

"I love you more, baby," Dorothy said and Dorothy leaned her head back against her headrest. "Jesus, I do. More than anything. More than the earth, the moon, the sun, and the stars."

"Okay, Mom."

"No, I'm saying I mean it though."

"I know, Mom."

"Well, let me help you now, baby. I'm here already. Lean on me. Let me get out and get your bag and get you on that—"

"No!" Clover interrupted. "I mean, no, Mama. You don't have to do that. I can handle it, Mama. I swear."

"You sure, baby? I wouldn't mind."

"No, Mama. I know you've got a bad back and everything. I've got this, Mama. I swear."

"Okay, baby. Okay," Dorothy said. Clover leaned into her mother and kissed her and got out and opened the trunk and lugged her duffle out onto the pavement.

DOROTHY WATCHED HER daughter line up behind other children—weighed down on her right side as her duffle dug into her neck—until she made it up onto the bus. To make sure she was safe. She hoped her daughter would turn back and look at her before she stepped on. Maybe wave. Like in an Elvis movie. But she didn't, so Dorothy just drove back home.

* * *

Dale pounded his sneakers into the first flight of stairs. Then the second, then the third. He knocked on his son's door. Dylan had locked it. At this time, Dylan's fifteen. Dale twisted the doorknob a few times, and then knocked, again. And then knocked, again. He'd just been called by Dylan's court-ordered therapist. Dylan, it seemed, had been acting out. They told him that Dylan had missed a session. And that this wasn't the first time. This upset Dale. His son's sessions were expensive—two hundred dollars each. For a special therapist. The best at handling problem children—making them feel safe—through their parents' divorces. That's what the judge told them, anyway. And Dale had to pay for these sessions, even though they were required, by law, if a judge deemed them necessary. But he also felt they were important. He felt he was losing his son—even though he didn't quite know him—but nonetheless he'd begun to lose patience. But this more selfish reason paled in comparison to the financial repercussions. Self-lessness comes with humility. Humility comes with an understanding of self. An understanding of self comes with clearheadedness. Clear-headedness comes with sobriety. Sobriety was more than a ways off. Dale's still knocking. Dale didn't want to yell at his son. He'd yelled enough, already. But his girlfriend told him he had to. "He can't keep doing this," she said. "He can't keep doing this to us. He's gonna hurt you if we don't stop him." And his girlfriend was right. But Dale didn't like to get angry, anymore. That's how he lost his ex-wife. Well that's what he told people. And himself, when he was feeling gullible. A few hours in. But he didn't know what else to do. So he had a drink and forced it.

"Dylan," he shouted. "Open the door. Open the fucking door." He heard Dylan get out of bed. Dylan couldn't sleep at night. Nervous energy. So he'd nap after school. If he went to school. Dale heard the door unlock. He heard the doorknob turn. It squealed. And again. Dylan pulled open the door a crack. "What?" he said. Dylan looked tired. Dale pushed the door open and went past his son. Dylan fell back. He looked scared. "What happened?" Dale stepped into Dylan's face. Dylan was still quite short. He'd matured late. But nonetheless he always would be. Dale resented him for that. "Did you miss your appointment with Dr. Seltzer?" And again. "Did you miss your appointment with Dr. Seltzer?" And again. "Did you miss your fucking appointment with Dr. Seltzer?"

Dylan looked down at his toes. "I don't like it there, Dad. I don't need it anymore." Untrue.

"That's not fucking up to you! How many have you missed?" Dale shaped his right fist like a gun and pushed the barrel into the center of his son's chest.

"Like three, I think. Maybe four." Dale pressed harder into his ribcage. He forced him onto the bed. He pressed him down and held him there. He stopped talking. He grabbed his son and flipped him over. He pulled down his pants. Dylan screamed into his pillows. And Dale smacked Dylan's ass. Dale smacked his ass until he was sure he'd bruise. And he continued to do so until he was sure he'd done so. Still down, Dale saw his son's cry slopping out on his pillow. And Dale stopped. He never saw his son cry again. And later that night he'd cry himself. But nobody believed those tears. *Poor me, poor me, pour me a drink.* He put on a show for Kim. The new one. But even she didn't buy it. He was never much of an actor.

A + !

Their court-ordered companion followed the children close behind his nose as he walked in through Dorothy's apartment door. He held them in place and surveyed the apartment, and then he ushered them through. It had been a while since they'd seen their mama. So they walked in sheepishly. Head down. But Dorothy sprang up. She pushed past the stranger and held her children tight. She held them awhile. Dylan tried to shove her off. He didn't like hugging. But she wouldn't let him go.

"My babies," she said in a whisper.

"Hi, Mama," they both replied.

She finally let loose. She walked them toward the couch. This apartment was cheaper than the last. The couch was pleathery. Everything was pleathery. The divorce money hadn't lasted as long as she'd liked. And you don't get the child support when you don't have the children. Clover sat on the left side of the sofa. Dylan sat on the right. Dorothy sat across from them—across a coffee table—in a wooden rocking chair.

Clover looked at her mother. She was a junior, now, and her brother was seventeen in ninth grade. He sat against the armrest of the couch and then reached for a coffee-table book. He picked up the photography of Man Ray. He looked at all the nudity. But Clover looked at her mama. And Mama looked back at her. She'd gotten dressed up. Both of them. Dorothy wore red heels and new glasses—jewel-speckled green plastic. She wore a beige headband around her crimped wig and too much makeup—blue eye shadow, red lips, and clown blush too white. Clover wore a sundress over her freckled legs. She wore makeup, too. For Mama. Like Mama. But hers was more understated. They stared at each other. And then they spoke.

"How've you been, baby?" Dorothy asked her daughter.

"I've been okay. School and everything, you know."

"Well, not really," Dorothy replied. They froze. "But never mind. How's that going? School?" Dorothy leaned back into the love seat.

"I don't know, Mom. School's school, isn't it?"

"Yeah, I guess so. Actually, I wouldn't know. I wasn't much of a student. Anyway, how are you, Dyl, baby?"

He looked up from the book and cocked his head. He picked up his hands and gave her two thumbs up and smiled. Then he looked back down.

Throughout, the court-ordered companion stood in the corner with his back to both walls. He checked his watch periodically. This visit was only allowed to be thirty-five minutes. Talking like this—of little substance—went on awhile. They are twenty-six minutes in.

"Well it's great to see you guys." It was great to see them. And it was great for them to see her. They just didn't have much else to say.

"We love you too, Mama," they both replied in unison.

"And you, whatever your name is," Dorothy swung her arm up at the corner, but kept her eyes pointed at her kids, "can pretty much go fuck yourself."

THE MYSTERIOUS TWO

I n 1980, when her lease was up on her apartment in Venice, Dorothy moved to Santa Monica, where she met her second ex-husband-to-be, Gary. She was at Price Club buying hand towels, toiletries, peanuts, and pretzels. They were introduced when their hands brushed as they both reached for the family-sized jar of Vaseline. She was new in town, and he seemed pleasant enough. He seemed stand-up, and moral. And nothing like Calbert, who stole her Rottweilers and sold them one night she was too tired for sex. Gary was a local preacher. Sold his smile for a living. Could charm the hat right off your head. Dorothy was alone, now, and she thought she needed guidance. She thought it might help her cope with her children getting older. Why they'd stopped calling. Why they seemed not to care. Just why everything went the way it did. Just why, is all. Just why. And it worked for a while. It made her feel clean. Even though he threw out her typewriter. But eventually she got restless and bought another. Kept it hidden. He felt as if they were bonded and fused. Welded or limed. But she never got her wings clipped. She couldn't just stay on the ground.

* * *

Just before she moved in with Gary, though—they moved in together after a fast six weeks—she planned to spend two weeks in New York shopping. Thought she'd have another "me" trip. Had a feeling it might be her last. One last trip might make her happy. Might make it easier to eventually just say yes. Except that she didn't have much money to spend. She could afford three days, two nights at a Howard Johnson. So she booked that, and went. She bought a shark-skin purse, a silk scarf, and a snow globe. By this point, she'd already attempted to quit smoking and drinking and writing—*You know whom creativity's for? The devil!*—because she found religion. And Gary told her to stop. He couldn't be around someone who acted that way. Her actions reflected his image poorly. So she tried. But—but—she smoked those last two nights, because those nights were for her, and she enjoyed those ciga-rettes. And she enjoyed a martini, and she enjoyed a man. She enjoyed every decision she made that trip—her choices—very, very much. But she had to head back home, because back home there was Gary, and she'd become worried she might have to be saved. And he told her she had to stop. Stop everything. He told her religion would make her better. And all that chicanery was considered untoward. But she still held on to her drugs—*These here, baby? These are prescriptions!* But she tried to keep it secret. More and more secret.

CATCH ME IF YOU CAN WHEN
I'M DIPPIN' FROM THE COPS

I t was a long flight, so everyone was tired. But as they waited to deplane with sleepless anticipation—the heads of the tallest passengers tilted down as though they were looking on the floor for change—they noticed that the once slow-moving, single-file line had now crawled to a complete stop, and they began to grow restless. The people in the front third were the only ones who could see why their progress had been stunted, and they were also the only ones who didn't mind not moving. It was as though traffic had forced them to stop and stare at an accident alongside the road, so they felt it their right—almost their duty—to rubberneck. They couldn't continue on before they realized why. The taller ones straightened up and looked over the other passengers. The shorter ones were lucky to be at the front. They—they all—watched a woman at the head of the line hold her tray table in her right hand with all her fight and might, as the three still-working flight attendants— two female, one not, but barely—pulled at her legs to remove her from her seat. Finally, her arm gave way. She might have lasted longer, but, earlier that day, her wig had fallen off, and she'd lost a few of her pins, and she held that—her Farrah—in her left hand while her right hand held on to the plane. She didn't like knowing that if she'd let go of her wig and grabbed on with both arms she could've fought harder—like a good daughter of the revolution—but that was a good wig. One of her favorites. It was important to her—very much so—so she had to let go of the tray table. As she was dragged off the plane, she reflected on her ability to prioritize even through her most trying moments. Her effort made her proud. So she smiled and pushed her wig up toward the sky—with both hands—so as not to get it dirty—as her back scraped the greased-down, chartreuse carpet of the plane.

DOROTHY WAS RECALCITRANT, denying that she hadn't left her overnight bag in New York. That it was on that plane. That she was sure of it. They told her so—"It wasn't on that plane," they said. "We promise." But she wouldn't have it. She sat in an empty room. Blank white walls. White linoleum floor. The sort you could hear when you stepped on it. The three flight attendants entered, and they had called their home-base supervisor so he now joined them, too. There weren't any windows. And the lights were on, high and hot.

"It was in my hand," Dorothy said, "when I got on. I put it in the bin over my head but when I get up it's missin'. I've paid the same amount of money as everyone else. All I want is to be treated like they all are. Be treated just the same." She was sweating, now. Her back stuck to the pleather chair. "Why can't you just give me my bag and let me go?"

They viewed her with curiosity and caution. She figured, perhaps, they recognized her. She'd once even portrayed a stewardess in a spot for TWA! But the staff was just fearful of the oddity. An animal in a zoo. A boa constrictor. Or rare bird. Make sure you don't move too quickly. And don't ever touch the glass. Don't wake her.

"We don't have your bag, Ms. White. We've searched the plane more than once. It's just about been ransacked."

The airport official turned his back to her and whispered to the three flight attendants. He seemed to be talking to only the man. The girls looked over their boss's shoulder. They looked at Dorothy with furrowed eyes. Owl's eyes. Like she couldn't see them back. She couldn't hear what the boss was saying. She just heard his lispy whisper. However, she could see the steward's Errol Flynn moustache—thin and waxy—curl up at something the boss man said. And she figured she might get out today. She fished around in her purse. In the past, she'd been told that her perfume brought out the claustrophobia in people. She dug into her pocketbook and pulled out her atomizer and sprayed herself eight times—twice on each side of her neck, twice on each wrist. She waited a second for the acrid air to settle and then lit a cigarette. She'd just begun smoking Virginia Slims. Finally Virginia Slims. And she loved them. Suddenly, all their faces were smushed and soured. And their wispy conversation came to an abrupt halt. Her sense of smell had never been keen, and had gotten worse recently with her deviated septum—so she sprayed her perfume on heavy. And she didn't care what anyone thought. But that was just an excuse. Once the attendants pulled themselves together and shook themselves off, the boss turned toward Dorothy and walked a few steps and pulled a chair up and sat down. He rested his hands on each of his knees. He wore a blue suit with wide lapels and plastic TransPacific wings pinned above his pocket square. His white socks showed between his suede boots and his pants hem. And his breath stank like cat's breath.

"Is there, by any chance, anyone we could call for you? Anyone who could, perhaps, come pick you up?"

"Sure. Sure, there's someone you could call for me. Call in the person who stole my luggage and have him bring it back." She blew an O in his face and it dissipated around his nose.

He shook his head and put his hands to his eyes. "No one has your bag, ma'am."

Now she shook her head and ashed her cigarette. It fell near his untied red shoelace.

"Who has it then? I certainly don't," she said and puffed another O. Then another. They circled around his eyeballs. He wore them like reading glasses.

"Exactly, ma'am. You don't have your bag and didn't. Now, if you wouldn't mind, I . . ."

"Now I don't mind talking so let me do it," she leaned forward. "Just get me my bag, and don't get smart with me. Get me my bag. I bought it in the city. It's new and it's mine. It has my things in it. It has *my* things in it. It was on that plane, and then I went to sleep, and then I woke up, and then it's gone. Now, if you don't tell me what happened to it, or who stole it, or where you've hidden it, I don't know what I'm going to do. I'll tell you what I do know, though. Talk smart to me again and see what happens. Seriously. Honestly, I'd love to see you try. Do it. Do it just to see. I'll put you across my knee is what I'll do, but you'd probably like that too much. Fucking sissy. Now, go find my bag. Go find me my fucking bag, and go find it now."

He stared into her eyes. And she stared back at him through her oversized, black-framed glasses. With her ire, they'd grown askew.

"No one knows what you're talking about, ma'am," he said and stared into her.

"Go get my bag, now."

He wouldn't look away.

"Go get my bag. Go get my bag. Go get my bag. Go get my bag . . ."

She continued until she ran out of breath. Then he watched, and in the silence there was calm. But then.

"Ma'am, now listen," he said, loud now. Angry. "I promise you we don't have your bag. Please, and this is the last time I'm asking, if there's anyone we could call, or anything else we can . . ."

While he spoke, she removed her perfume atomizer, again, from deep within her shark-skin purse. Before he was finished, she sprayed him twice in the eyes. He doubled over, and the flight staff rushed to help. Then she dropped her cigarette on the floor, sprayed in front of her, stepped into it, walked out of the room—surprised as it was left unlocked—and through the office of the flight superior, who looked up from his papers and over his gold-framed aviator eyeglasses and furrowed his brow and moustache, most certainly surprised to see her, and through the terminals and gates, where people—idiots—sat anxiously, preparing themselves for what was on the other side, and past the food court—and the baggage claim, where those same idiots hugged and kissed their loved ones and watched for their luggage and thought they'd finally made it. And then past the smokers and the taxi stand and the gypsy cabs—poachers—by the taxi stand and then to the other side of the road from the airport—the far side of West Way—where she was dwarfed by one-story-high gray block letters. *LAX* was surrounded by well-trimmed green shrubbery, and she stood underneath in a red phone booth, on a pay phone, awaiting an answer on the other line. She'd already dialed. Ring ring ring.

"Yello?"

"Ah, finally. Thank heavens! Gary, can you come get me? I'm near the airport."

"Dorothy-ody?"

"Yessir."

"Why are you talking like that?"

"Talking like what, Gary?"

"Like that, Dorothy-ody. Exactly like that. You know I don't like it when you speak in your native accent. It's plebeian, and pedestrian. When you address me, you speak formally. Understood?"

She waited and shook her head.

"Understood?"

"Oh my God, Gary, can't you just cut a girl some slack. I mean I was just—"

"Dorothy-ody, you know you don't use the Lord's name in vain in front of me, either. If you expect me to help you with everything—with getting you back on track—you have to at least be aware of my tenets and know that when you speak like that it really hurts me. And it's bad for you. It's really bad form, and it's truly unacceptable. But really, Dorothy-ody, it hurts you more than me—you more than anyone— because, as you well know, I'm not the only one listening."

"I know, Gary, I know. I'm just in a bad way right now. These plane attendants stole my bag and I forgot where I parked my car before I left and I need some help. I'm sorry I used the Lord's name in vain. You know I don't mean nothin' by it."

"Don't apologize to me, Dorothy-ody. You know who you have to apologize to."

"Gary."

"Dorothy-ody."

"Oh, Gary, I'm hot and sticky and tired and really don't want to do this right now."

"Dorothy-ody, recite it for me, right now, full through, or you're staying at the airport."

"I don't want to, Gary."

"Do it, or I'm hanging up the phone."

"Okay, Gary, okay. Love endures long and is patient and kind; love never is envious nor boils over with jealousy; is not boastful or vainglorious; does not display itself haughtily. It is not conceited, arrogant, and inflated with pride; it is not rude, unmannerly, and does not act unbecomingly. Love—God's love—does not insist on its own rights or its own way, for it is not self-seeking; it is not touchy or fretful or resentful; it takes no account of the evil done to it; it pays no attention to a suffered wrong. It does not rejoice at injustice and unrighteousness, but rejoices when right and truth prevail. Love bears up under anything and everything that comes; is ever ready to believe the best of every person. Its hopes are fadeless under all circumstances, and it endures everything without weakening. Love never fades out or becomes obsolete or comes to an end. Love never fails. Love never fails," she paused, and took a few deep breaths. "So maybe now you could pick me up?"

* * *

Dale arrived home to find Clover at the sink doing dishes. Clover took her time with the dishes. She enjoyed it. Sometimes it took her almost an hour, but that was okay. It helped her think less. Or at least more positively. To her thinking was hard. Sometimes she'd do anything not to. Her brain made her afraid. The existential dilemma that sat—relaxed—behind her eyes suddenly got transferred to her fingers—to something utilitarian—and because her fingers were farther from her brain than her eyes it hurt her less. Or it just took longer to feel it. Or something like that.

It was the morning and Dale was arriving home. He was coming home from a girl's house. Somebody from the roster. Just any. One of the many. He probably doesn't even remember her name—this behavior was rather typical—and he was coming home with a hangover. He was also rather annoyed because said nameless girl—let's call her Brenda—hadn't responded to his sexual advances earlier that morning. Brenda said, as he rolled onto her, that she had, during the course of the night, realized that her friend, whom she had known since puberty, had come around, again, and so she couldn't. He said he didn't know what that meant. So she said her "friend"—finger quotes, which she'd indicated with her fingers—who comes around monthly—like literally every month—was back, again, and that's why she couldn't fuck him. He said he didn't know what that meant either. Just speak English, he said. No more riddles. So she said she was on her period.

"Oh," Dale replied. "Well, so what?"

"Well, so," she paused. "Well, so then I don't want to."

"What does that matter?"

"It matters because I don't want to," she said and put her head so far under the covers that only her eyes were showing, like a little girl might. A little girl who thought she was in trouble. "I don't want you to see me that way."

"Well I don't care about your period, baby." And he kissed her ear. "I think you're beautiful always. Always." And he licked her neck. "You know that."

"Well, I don't, okay? So get off, already," and she pushed him off of her and went to the bathroom and closed the door.

"Well fuck this, then. Fuck you, then." He shook his head and thrust off the covers. "Dumb twat." And Dale put his clothes on and went back home.

So then Dale—hung over and frustrated—that cunt—walked into his house and then into his kitchen and found his daughter doing dishes. She turned around when she heard the door open and saw him walk in.

"Oh, hey," she said, and then turned back around. "I didn't know you were home today."

"Why aren't you in school?" he asked her as he walked to the fridge. "Jewish holiday or something."

"Great," shaking his head. "Just burning money over there. And for them." He opened the fridge and looked inside. Yogurt, a half a rotisserie chicken, orange juice, a glass bottle of chocolate milk—still sealed, still thinking about his children—and a quarter-full bottle of Prosecco. "And why is the fucking fridge always empty?"

No reply.

"What is it that you two actually do?"

He waited.

"Yes?"

"I don't know, Daddy," she paused and thought. "I guess dishes?" she smiled.

He didn't.

"Fucking ingrates," Dale breathed as he pulled out the bottle of Prosecco.

He shook his head and stepped his steps hard as he walked behind Clover to the drying rack beside the sink and grabbed a newly clean highball and filled his glass to the top, perfectly finishing what was left of the bottle, as though that last third was meant just for him. But before that, as he reached over her shoulder when he was first grabbing the glass, he noticed that the tag on her shirt was facing outward as it hung off her waifish frame. And as he read the tag it read *Missoni*, which he knew to be expensive from buying it for girls he'd fucked in the past. Not because he knew they'd like it—he hardly knew them at all—but instead because he'd sometimes take them shopping—some mornings—if he thought it might make the next time they saw each other more fun.

"Who bought you that shirt?" Dale asked his daughter.

"What?" Clover responded. She was polishing a colander, remembering her last night's penne à la vodka for one, and how perfectly satisfying it was.

"I said, who bought you that fucking shirt?"

"What are you talking about?" Clover said and turned around, breaking her ritualistic cleaning tendencies—one of the only things that made her happy—drying her hands on a rag.

"I said, *who* bought *you* that fucking shirt." And he stepped toward her and he stopped blinking. "I'm not gonna ask again."

"You did, I guess. I mean, you paid for it," she crossed her arms and put her head down.

"Of course I did. You two are un-fucking-believable." He shook his head and then drank his Prosecco. It was flat, but whatever. "You know what? I paid for that, right? So then give it to me, then. It's mine."

"What?" she answered, dumbfounded. No, not dumbfounded. Awestruck, maybe. Very, very surprised. "What do you mean?"

"Take it off," he said. "I'll give it to somebody who deserves it. Somebody better than you."

"You want me to take my shirt off?" she asked him. "Here?"

"Yes. You heard me. Now."

"Okay," she said and she pulled her shirt over her head. It hung, reluctantly, in her fingers. Dale reached out and grabbed it away. She pulled her arms back and crossed them over her lace bra. She was cold. She put her head down but still looked up at him. Her eyes were sharp.

"And who bought you those fucking jeans?"

She didn't answer, and her stare got even more tight.

"Do I have to ask again?"

"I guess you did."

"So then give me them. Give me them, now," and she waited a moment, and stared into his eyes. But then she pulled them off, one leg at a time, and tossed them to him. This time more confident. This time more true. She stood before him in her mismatched underwear— her panties simple white but thin so slightly see-through—and felt the air on her skin. She uncrossed her arms and put them to her side. She pulled her head from her chest and stood tall, her upper back even arching slightly upward. She'd been relatively full-figured for the past few years, but it seemed, given Dale's face, that this was the first time he noticed. She was a woman. She was nineteen. She'd been with a man, and she knew how much power that gave her. He had, perhaps, not yet seen that side of her, but he would now. This is what he asked for. This is what they wanted. This is what they'll get.

"Good. That's good." He looked down at the clothes and then moved them back and forth in his hands. His voice was softer now, but still strong enough. "I'm gonna give this stuff to someone who deserves them. Somebody better."

"Okay," Clover added.

"Okay is right."

"Well," she stepped forward. "Who bought me this bra?"

"Excuse me," he said with her clothes in his arms.

"Who bought me this bra?" Clover stared into her father's eyes. "Who bought me this bra?"

"What?"

And Clover stepped closer to her father. So close that when she breathed her father felt her warmth. She never broke her stare.

"Didn't you pay for this?"

"I don't know what you're saying."

"Do you need me to repeat myself?"

Dale exhaled and it bounced off his daughter's forehead.

"Clover, I don't know what you're—"

"Who bought me this bra, Dad?"

And Dale breathed heavier. More laborious. With more purpose. With more pulled from his chest.

"I guess I did, yeah. I guess I must've had to."

"Yup," and she stopped blinking. "So, Daddy," and she blew her breath on his chest and he got goose bumps. "What do ya say?"

They stared in each other's eyes awhile but then Dale drank the rest of his flat Prosecco and gave her his glass for her to clean, which he pressed into her ribs and pressed her back so as not to touch her. When she didn't grab it he pushed past her and left it on the sink and left the kitchen. Eventually she turned around and cleaned it. She polished it as best she could. She held it up before her. It sparkled bright and true.

NOW THERE'S A SPECIAL WAY I FOLD MY FLAG

When she got back to her place after two days and nights at Gary's, Dorothy was still in the clothes she'd worn when he'd picked her up from the airport. For the past few nights she'd listened, with her mouth closed, as Gary spoke of charlatanism and harlotry. Ancient astronauts and people of the book. It was the beginning of their budding relationship. He made the short hairs on her neck stand up straight. Not because she was attracted to him, but because of what he stood for. She wanted to change her life. And he wanted to change her life. She wanted to be better. And Gary kept her busy. She thought he must know something. Other people seemed to think so. She thought he might be the answer. She thought he might know the way. And if she was better, the kids would come back. They'd call more, and they'd visit. And then she'd have her life back. Maybe even a career. But without her children—without their love—she was empty. She was alone.

Today, though, she'd go home to bathe and change and eat peanuts in the quiet, all alone. All alone. By herself. She wanted to be in the city today. Spend one night in her little apartment. A one bedroom, with a pull-out couch—well, a futon—and a color TV. She even sprang for cable. She needed a night to herself. They'd recently become rather fleeting.

* * *

The next morning Dorothy awoke to a loud noise outside her bedroom window. She couldn't, at first, place what it was. And she was curious. Before going to see it, though, she hurried to the kitchen and put on a pot of coffee. Loud or not, she wouldn't let it ruin her day. She added cinnamon and chopped vanilla bean in her grounds, and she kept her grounds in the freezer. The noise continued to blare and blare as she waited six and a half minutes for the coffee to brew. She carried the steamy mug and two packets of Sweet'N Low with her to her bathroom. She had a big box of Sweet'N Low. She loved—loved!—Sweet'N Low. It was just so sweet, and it didn't affect her anemia. And no calories, too!

Dorothy got to the bathroom and stared at herself in the mirror, and then into her vanity lights. This was her favorite mirror. Her "mirror, mirror" mirror. She pulled her eyelids open—thumbs and forefingers—and counted each fluorescent bulb. From bottom left to bottom right. And then all the way back again. Eighteen filaments smacked her bright. Thirty-six, as she counted again. She overcame the urge to shut her eyes. To soothe them. They hurt her, but she didn't quit. She held them open longer—like a lemur—and then she finally looked down. She surveyed the countertop with the sort of vision that she imagined an angel might have. She couldn't see much. Nothing was clear. Instead, the world was glowing.

She regained her vision and reached out to one of the three foam heads that stared back at her from a wooden shelf above the countertop. Today, she'd don champagne. One of her favorites. One, only, for the most special of occasion. Because she believed the sacrament didn't represent the blood and body of Christ, the sacrament was, in her eyes, just He. That's something Gary taught her. Something new. He insisted. In a similar vein, her wig didn't represent her. Her false hair was as real as that which sprouted sandy-blonde—still, a little— from her roots. Her false hair was as true as her real hair. Her wig was—truly—part of her. If one day she felt curly, then her wig would be curled. Seeing slightly better still, she dropped it on her head. It sat sideways—she hadn't yet put on her glasses—and she excused herself—I'm sorry, aloud—and used the toilet. Something else Gary insisted. Be proper. Be polite. Hold it as long as you can. Women shan't need to urinate, or defecate, as often as men do. This I promise you. This is a scientific fact.

She flushed and her eyes felt better. She put on her glasses and could see again. She looked in the mirror and fixed her wig—a little to the left, then down on her forehead—and then proceeded with her usual morning routine. In the left-hand bathroom cabinet drawer, festooned between two atomizers, were multivitamins, sleeping medication, pain medication, and those to control weight. She kept her new pharmacological plan—blue for night, yellow for days, and green for hunger, for the most part—a secret from Gary. He wouldn't like it. He just wouldn't understand. Her doctor told her, more than fifteen years ago, about Los Angeles living, and how diet and exercise and a healthy lifestyle must be maintained. "To lose the baby weight," he'd said, "I'm gonna write you a script to kick-start your dietary regimen." She kept that doctor's number. She was with him ever since. She believed in his theories about body chemistry disposition. How some people are just born with disproportional toxin intake. How some people are just imbalanced. How some people need medicine to just survive. She thought of her prescriptions like she thought of her glasses. They were corrective. They made her the way the rest were. They made her capable. They made her whole. They were necessary to properly function. To be responsible, the way she needed to be. She reached down and picked up a yellow square and a green circle. She swallowed both without water. She heard the phone in the bedroom ring. So she hurried without slippers to pick it up.

"Yessum."

"Dorothy-ody? It's Gary."

"Oh. Hi, Gary. I was just freshening up."

"I didn't wake you?"

"No. There was something loud this morning outside my window, so I've been up a little while, now."

"You've been up for a *little* while, Dorothy-ody? Well, I was hoping I'd wake you. But I guess I didn't call early enough. In any event, what was it?"

"Why would you hope something like that?"

"I think it would be good for you if I woke you from now on."

"Well, I don't know what to say about that, really. I'm sorry that it was loud outside."

"That's okay, but as I've already asked, what was it?"

"I don't know. I didn't check."

"Something loud woke you and you didn't check to see what it was?"

"No."

"Why not?"

"Because I didn't care enough. I wanted to put my face on."

"Well then, now that makes sense. Very sensible, actually. Holding yourself responsible for your physical appearance is a true sign of character. Vanity is a quality I truly respect. What did it sound like, then? Let's try and figure this thing out, you and I."

"I don't know, Gary. I was sleepin'."

"What did it sound like, Dorothy-ody?"

"Oh, Gary. I don't . . ."

"Don't say I don't know to me again. You know how I feel about that."

"Okay, Gary. I know, Gary."

"Okay, Dorothy. So tell me what it sounded like, then. And Dorothy-ody, don't worry. I'll wait."

"Okay. Fine. I think it sounded like a train, but in the distance. Yeah, steady like that. But sharp. Like a freight train, I guess, maybe carryin' somethin' heavy."

"Well, it clearly wasn't a train. There aren't any trains in Santa Monica. But I'll ask someone. Talk to someone. I know people out there. Someone sensible. Try to get some real answers."

"Okay, Gary."

"What have you been doing, then?"

"Since when, Gary?"

"Since you've been up, Dorothy-ody."

"Oh, like I told you. I've just been freshening up. I made some coffee, washed my face."

"You didn't tell me that."

"I thought I did."

"No, you didn't. But, anyway, that's good."

"What?"

"It's good to be fresh. I like that. I like it when you're fresh, and energized, as He designed you."

"I know that, Gary. I like it when I'm fresh, too. I just sometimes don't like to shower at your house."

"Well, Dorothy-ody, you and I both know that one day you're going to have to learn how to. If we're going to take this any further, that's certainly true."

"I know, Gary."

"Do you, Dorothy-ody?"

"I do, Gary. I promise."

"We don't promise around here, Dorothy-ody. You know that. What do we do? In the desert? What do we do in the desert? What do we do in the West?"

"We swear on the Foursquare."

"Yes, we do. We swear on the Foursquare. Now, let's hear it."

"I do."

"You do what?"

"I swear on the Foursquare."

"And . . ."

"And I sport the fruit of the Spirit."

"Which is?"

"Oh, come on, Gary."

"Which is?"

"The fruit of the Spirit is love, joy, peace, patience, kindness, goodness, faithfulness, gentleness, and self-control. Against such things there is no law."

"There you go. There you go, Dorothy-ody. I imagine you're feeling good right now. I know I do. I feel great right now. So if I do—if I feel great right now—then you must, too, as well. We are partners."

"Yeah. I'm okay, I guess. Do I have to do this every time we talk?"

"Yes, because it will make you feel better. And if you smile, I smile. And if you don't feel great now, and clean, you certainly will after the congregation tomorrow. I promise you that."

"I can't wait, Gary. I'll be there."

"My house tomorrow, at nine, Dorothy-ody. And we have to be militant. We can't invite just anyone."

"I wouldn't dare bring anyone, Gary. You know that."

"I know you wouldn't, Dorothy-ody. It's just part of my job to remind."

"Okay, Gary."

"I'm just saying we have to militate, and I need your help to do so. You're important around here. Important to me."

"Okay, Gary. I'll be there. Promise."

"Okay, Dorothy-ody. Eight-thirty, then. And remember, you're still in the first cycle of donations, so don't come empty-handed. The house we're renting isn't cheap this time, so remember to bring your purse. Donations are more than welcome."

THE NEXT DAY, on the drive over, Dorothy wasn't sure she was in control of her car. Something made her nervous. Pushed her to the edge. The only way she could stay safely on the road was to drive in line with the vehicle in front of her until he reared off course. So her firebrick-colored Crown Victoria—she'd had to trade in the truck—tailgated a wood-paneled Jeep Wagoneer as long as he stayed en route. The Jeep pulled left into a Mexican restaurant, La Rosa Maria. Surprised—he didn't signal!—Dorothy nervously pulled into a freeway rest area to the right. She made it without incident. She made it safely, thank God. But she took up two parking spaces. Almost three. She put her hands together on the steering wheel and pulled herself off her seat and put her head up through the open sunroof because she was sweating—broken AC—and she didn't want too much to pool up and gather up beneath her. She held herself that way about ten seconds before she sat back down. She breathed. She was uncomfortably wet, feeling it now up her back and down her chest. But she breathed again, and she was a little cooler.

SHE DROVE UP canyons and through valleys. Somewhere in the Valley, in fact. Gary called the West Coast the desert. She never bothered to ask why. She was lost, but she'd find her way. She took highways and freeways. Streets and alleyways. Boulevards, too. She only stopped once more—Gary hated when people were late. She bought an orange from a Mexican for a quarter at a rest stop. He had a full sack at a stoplight and she felt sorry.

"*Uno?*" he asked her.

"*Gracias,*" she replied.

Gary rented a condominium in the hills in a gated community called Cathedral Villas—upper-middle-class housing for families concerned with appearances, but not aware of the distinction—the importance—between old money and new. Not realizing the distinction between living in the Valley and not. The homes were varying degrees of pink—from salmon to the morning sun—and platitudinous. Three-tiered usually, with ceramic verandas and pink hydrangeas. Ornamental palm trees lined the streets, two per block. Fences, gables, cornices, and skylights bordered backyard toolsheds. Chimneys and hedges. Downspouts and dormer windows. Dorothy noticed. Dorothy drove on.

She knew the passcode that let her into the community gate, but Gary wouldn't give her the one for his house no matter how much she begged and bugged him about it. He told her no one knew it. He said it was for his own safety. That he was an important man. That it was "need to know." But she didn't believe that nonsense. She pulled up. A boulder-shaped intercom was silent for a few moments before abruptly shouting at the car.

"Speak into the rock." Analog fuzzy.

"Gary?"

"No. Not Gary. It's Didier-ody."

"Who?"

"Didier-ody."

"Who's that?"

"A friend. A friend of Gary's. I'm here for the presentation."

"Okay. Will you please buzz me in? If he's there will you tell him it's Jo?"

But nothing. But then the buzzer sounded. Dorothy waited patiently for the two gates in front of her to swing slowly forward, as they'd always done so in the past. They were large and wooden, the sort that might protect a moat. But nothing. She waited and waited and looked at her small, silver wristwatch. Red-faced Rolex. A present from the past. She looked back up and then looked back at it again. Finally, a small Asian woman—whose head peeked barely above the five-foot-high fence—undid the stone lock in front of her. She pulled the heavy gates open one at a time as Dorothy waited. Dorothy drove by. "It's broken," the Asian woman yelled, and Dorothy understood, though her English was broken. The woman closed both gates the same way she opened them. Dorothy watched in her rearview mirror as she then closed the latch. Dorothy wanted to thank her, maybe tip her. But when she was finished the Asian woman hurried toward the back door. Dorothy pulled down her mirror and checked her teeth and checked her hair and looked up her nose and then into her wrinkles. She pulled her lips open by their corners. Then she let go and they snapped back into place. She got out and stepped through the gravel driveway. She was still sweating. She thought she might smudge her eyeliner and that made her nervous and so she sweated more. She counted fourteen other cars parked in the driveway. A white taxi on its way out passed her on the left. Thirteen.

She stepped up the two steps off the gravel way and onto the marble-topped stairs. She looked down at her hands. They weren't yellow anymore from smoking. Once mustard, or the yolk of an egg that had faded to fresh butter. Her tinted lotion helped. They often shook, but it wasn't too bad today. And she didn't mind when they shook. It was like her fingers were dancing. It came from the cold or the humidity. Or not enough of this. Sometimes too much of that. She held out her ring finger and pressed the doorbell. As she waited, she looked up at the sun. Stared up at the sun. And she'd do so until someone got the door. She baked her eyes like a sheet of sugar cookies. Maybe with green frosting. And sprinkles. Christmas cookies. *Yum!* Just as she put her hands up and gave up on herself, the door swung open. A silhouette in the frame—larger than expected. The harder she looked, the less she saw. Only visible were his lacey-gold house shoes.

"Yes?" answered Didier.

"Hi, I'm sorry. I'm here for Gary. Gary. He knows I'm coming," she said as she furiously rubbed at her burnt-soaked eyes.

"Are you okay, ma'am?" asked Didier.

"Yes, I'm fine. I'm fine. I'm here for Gary. He knows I'm coming. He knows who I am. Dorothy. I'm Dorothy. He knows. Gary knows."

"Oh, Dorothy-ody. Hi. Come with me. He's waiting for you in here. Inside. We're starting soon. You're just in time."

She stepped up from the stoop and felt the air-conditioning. It was dark and smelled like pennies and eucalyptus.

"Did you have any trouble getting in?" Didier asked. "The gate's broken so we sent Yurik-ody out to get you," Didier said.

"No, it was fine. Thank you. I actually wanted to thank her for her help but she ran inside before I could."

"I wouldn't worry about that. She's somewhere—I think maybe she's folding towels?—but I really wouldn't worry. Wouldn't worry about her at all."

"She went in through the back, I think."

"Yes. She would've."

Didier walked ahead of Dorothy. Dorothy followed close suit. She knew the house, and knew that Gary was most likely waiting for her in the kitchen, by the stove, eating cheese and crackers with a tall glass of whole milk. But she still stayed close, just in case. She was scared today. She didn't know why. Didier stood almost seven feet tall, it seemed. She noticed his head, atop a white-linen three piece. Large at the bottom, it ran inward and formed a point at the apex of his skull. In the suit, and the slippers, he looked like an oversized pencil—the kind she used to win at the fair, when she knocked down bowling pins with a softball. She had a real good arm. As Didier rounded the corner ahead, she caught up quickly behind him. But then she stopped on a dime, startled by the number of people—the congregation—sitting before her. She looked up and noticed Gary beneath a photograph of a dwarf in a black suit with a red tie leaning against an apple. She'd interrupted. They all looked up.

"Ah," Gary said and waved. "Hello, Dorothy-ody."

Gary spoke quietly. Never raised his voice. Dorothy wanted to believe in Gary, and his charisma almost allowed that. He believed in himself, and she was so desperate. She was so trapped. And he moved like a leader—how she imagined a leader might move. With large steps, never shaky—and she wanted to believe in him. She needed to believe in something. He gave her direction, which she greeted with kind hands. Not kind like his, though, as he held a stumpy finger at her straight, like he was conducting an orchestra, his philharmonic responding with beautiful song. Dorothy pushed through the swaths and arrived before him. His hair, curlier and fuller at the back than on top, bounced when he knelt to kiss Dorothy's forehead, but his seersucker suit didn't ruffle.

"Come. Sit at the front with me, Dorothy-ody. At the front is where I want you. I was just about to begin the first."

There was a small wooden rocking chair to the left of the fireplace that Gary had saved special for her. So she sat, and rocked, as Gary began to sermon.

"I would like, before we begin to discuss what you all have read for today, I'd like to express my incredible appreciation for how far you all have traveled to get here. It took a lot of dedication to gather yourselves from such a ways—to take time out of your busy lives—but I promise you it will be worthwhile. Let me ask, first, did anyone here come alone tonight. Are anyone's others in absentia?"

"I did. My spouse and I are separated."

"Me, too. Went out for a pack of cigarettes."

"Okay. That's all okay. Is that everyone?"

"Yes," they responded in unison. Already in unison.

"Okay. No 'plaints. That's perfect. That will be just fine. Will the two of you do me a favor, then? Will you do us a favor? Will you two each pair up with two other couples? Two different couples, respectively? Preferably at opposite ends of the room? Yes. Yes, there we go. Perfect. It looks to me, then, as though everyone is settled. If that's the case, and no one has any objections, I think I'm ready to begin."

Gary's head was wider than it was long. Oblong. The entire congregation, actually, looked like the cast of a turn-of-the-century freak show: tall men and little people. Strongmen. Fat boys and hairy girls. Something even with two heads, maybe. Gary, the P. T. Barnum, was at the helm, indulging in his vulgar eloquence. He'd soon make her feel special. Perhaps she'd join the show.

"I'd like to start by asking you all who can tell me what principles make up the four squares? Who studied?"

"The savior. The baptizer. The healer—" A pause.

"Those are correct, whoever answered, but those are only three. Who's got the fourth for me? Come on."

No one spoke still. But then.

"The coming king," Dorothy interceded, meek and thoughtful from her chair.

Dorothy knew, and she knew she'd studied. And she knew that would make Gary smile. And then Gary did smile. And she beamed. He turned to her and held out his large, white, hairless hand. She was reluctant. Furry arms but hairless hands, like he had gloves on. He squeezed her fingers and then continued holding as he spoke.

"Ladies and gentlemen, I have traveled far, and I have traveled wide, but I have never, in all my years, found a woman with a stronger morality than this one. Dorothy-ody begs and pleads me not to bring her up here when I sermon, but I find her, by my side, to be a calming influence, and therefore I can't but help myself to leave an empty chair no more than two feet from the podium. She's the Bo to my Peep. The apple of my eye. As I said, I have traveled. I have seen much of this great world. I know it. I know it well. I know what it means. I have the sort of understanding that only comes with being worldly. From that learning I've begun to quill something, based on some things I've learned en route. Listen, now, and listen carefully. And if you have a piece of paper, write this down. Is everyone ready? Is everyone ready to hear?"

He let go of Dorothy and stood tall and pointed skyward.

"'*Das ewig-weibliche zieht uns hinan.*' Did everyone get that? Again. '*Das ewig-weibliche zieht uns hinan.*' Did anyone get that? Does anyone speak another language? Does anyone know what it is that means?"

"No," in unison.

Most of them were first-timers. They'd seen fliers—*BEFORE IT'S TOO LATE, GET BETTER NOW! THE WORLD IS UP FOR GRABS. LET'S SNATCH IT!*—hung from bus-stop benches along the road.

"I'm going to say it again, because I hadn't heard it before either, but I still found the sound powerful, and so I researched so as to find out what that man was saying, and when I found out I was awestruck. Would you like to know what that man told me? Do you think you're ready to hear?"

"Yes."

"Are you sure?"

"Yes!" Louder.

"'*Das ewig-weibliche zieht uns hinan.*' '*Das ewig-weibliche zieht uns hinan.*' '*Das ewig-weibliche zieht uns hinan.*' Now, I'll tell you. Now you're ready to *know*. It translates, roughly, as follows: The eternal feminine draws us—pulls us!—upward. It does, members, new and old. It does. It's real. The eternal feminine draws us upward. The eternal feminine carries us up toward the sky. Without a woman, men would never bathe, and our houses might up and crumble. Without a woman, we'd never shave, for fear that a clean face might seem to brutes unmasculine. Without a woman, we'd starve, sick of flapjacks, all we know to cook. Without a woman, our bowties would remain in our closets, exposing our navels a substitute for a test to see who could urinate the furthest. Without a woman, simply sirs, men couldn't be. Our others allow us to be whole on this earthly terrain, and that unity, and the certainty that comes with it, can serve only as a stepping-stone on our path toward heaven's gate. This I promise you. And if, on that note, everyone would embrace their other, temple to temple, cheek to jowl, and if those with three don't mind sharing, then I'd like to speak the first."

Gary stepped on Dorothy's toe as he reached to touch his face to hers. Then he left back for the podium, with a large, round blush spot on his face. She soon forgot that he'd hurt her tootsies.

"Quell matter, ladies, and especially gentlemen. Quell matter, and nurture the spirit. Before the recycling, whence this earthly plain will be wiped clean, renewed. Rejuvenated, refurbished. Spaded under, and new, we must nurture our each and everyone's spirit. We, though, becomes you, for I cannot guide you beyond this earthly realm, and thus must prepare you for your inevitable independence. You must nurture the spirit when you are alone, for when you are alone is truly when you are closest to Him. Nurture the spirit when you are out with your other, though, as well, for He appreciates camaraderie. Nurture the spirit whenever you get the opportunity. Even if that moment is fleeting. Even if you feel it is brief, and you can hardly touch it, attempt to nurture it still, for it will still pay dividends. So go out, dear friends, and find someone that will look with you upward. Look with you toward the sky. That person, for me, was hard to find. It took a long time, ladies and gentlemen. It was more than just a challenge. I met her at Costco, of all places. I met her buying groceries. If you're lucky enough to find your other, while you're in your earthly realm, then you must cherish her or him. A swim pal at summer camp, you watch out for each other. You must be brave for each other. You, and only you, make sure they never drown. I, all, am lucky enough to have found mine. I found my Dorothy-ody. My everything. My number one. And I shall cherish her. I was lucky, for He works in mysterious ways. So now that person sits here beside me. This girl, this Dorothy-ody—the Mysterious Two, as in my own mind to us I've begun to refer—has meant more to me than I can verbally qualify. And members. Members of the community. We fit together. We fit right, like corner pieces in a jigsaw puzzle. And that, my friends, is all a man can ask for."

* * *

When Dorothy got up another morning, Gary was gone. She hadn't been woken up today. She'd had a long night, so she was allowed to get some rest. She rubbed her eyes, then noticed her wig head had been removed from her bag and now sat next to a picture of Gary and his mother on the bedside table. Mama Gary was half his size. Just last night Dorothy had finished moving in, but she hadn't unpacked yet. Suddenly Gary entered wearing a rust-colored vest, with a matching flap hat that covered his ears, and wax-cotton knee-high boots.

"I'm going birding."

"Oh. Okay. Am I supposed to come?" She was hoarse from hardly sleeping.

"No. No. Just be here when I get back. Be ready when I get back. Get in the shower, maybe. And do something about your face."

He reached down to grab and kiss her left hand. With his lips on her wrist, though, he slapped her lower back.

"It's time to rise, now. You see?"

He looked at her, and winked, and then turned around and left her. She put her wig on and then her glasses.

* * *

She only wanted her driver at her bachelorette party. She liked her driver. He was fat, but he listened. She didn't invite Gary and she didn't want him to come. But he showed up, anyway. He had picked the invitees, so that figured. Sometimes, some mornings, she thought about the loud noise that woke her the last time she slept at her apartment in Santa Monica. It was the last thing she remembered from when she lived alone. She never figured out what caused it. She wished she'd checked. Maybe then things could have changed. Maybe then things would be different.

STABAT MATER DOLOROSA, JUXTA
CRUCEM LACRIMOSA

G ary had booked their honeymoon stay at the Mountain Home
Christian Retreat in Acton, California.

*Mountain Home is nestled in the foothills of the Sierra Pelona Moun-
tains, near the southern upslope of 5,517-foot Houser Mountain. Mountain Home is at 3,500 feet elevation, about 55 miles north of Los Angeles,
and some 15 miles south of Palmdale and the Antelope Valley.*

*Mountain Home is open year-round to provide a peaceful place for indi-
viduals and groups. This is the right place to be "Alone" with God.*

They got married in August 1981. Gary liked the heat—he said
it was cleansing—and he wanted to wear a powder-blue linen suit, a
fairytale he'd always imagined. They held the ceremony at a church in
the hills. Gary said only the congregation—only just believers!—could
be invited. Dorothy, then, was forced to keep it a secret from her children. Clover was considering college now. Dylan was in and out of
a few different high schools. She rationalized this by telling herself
that they might not be able to understand Gary. That they couldn't,

yet. They might find him off-putting, and then they might try to talk her out of it. Talk her out of everything. There's no way they'd get it. They couldn't possibly understand. She needed help. She needed to fix everything. Fix herself. And then down the road she'd explain. Down the road she'd say why. She'd tell them once she got better. Dorothy had spent too many years living in blackness. And Gary, hairy toes and all, just might live closer to the light.

"It's a four-hour drive," Gary said the night before they were to leave. "I've already called and written out the directions. I figure we'll wake up at the crack tomorrow and get there by early afternoon. If you need to rest you can sleep in the car. I don't mind drivin'."

"Okay, Gary," Dorothy replied. "That sounds good, I guess."

She sat in his Barcalounger and watched one of her stories. She didn't care for the show but she liked the break. She liked not talking. Or listening. But now Gary stood before the TV discussing their itinerary. He wore red Christmas pajamas—footie pajamas—with a white snowflake print. It was a quarter past six. Three quarters before seven. They'd already eaten dinner. Gary liked supper ready by four. Eating in this light is better for the soul. Plus then we can get to bed early. That hour—four to five—was his favorite hour. He referred to it as "the magic hour."

"Well, *I've* already packed," Gary said emphatically, implicating.

"Okay, Gary, whatever. That's fine." She motioned with her right hand for Gary to pick a side to stand at.

"Have you packed?"

"No," Dorothy replied, still trying to get him to move. Now flailing, "You make a better door than a window!" And then she finally stared him in the face. "Of course I haven't packed. I have hours. Now would you get out of the way, already? I'm watching television."

"No. No, you don't have hours. We're leaving early so we've got to go to bed early."

And then she got angry.

"You don't have to worry about when I go to bed, okay? I'll be ready by tomorrow. I'll be ready before we leave. Now move. Jesus, just fucking move!"

"Oh, please, Dorothy-ody. Would you just listen—"

"No, I won't listen. I'll do it after this, okay? I promise. Now move, already, or else it'll take twice as long!"

Gary left with his hands in his pajama pockets shaking his head. Dorothy heard him enter the bathroom and then close and lock the door. Gary had irritable bowel syndrome, and Dorothy cooked her chicken with a lot of butter. She refused to change that. In fact, she liked the clout. The amount she used gave her the break she deserved. A stick gave her about a half hour. Often she used two.

THEY PULLED UP to the security checkpoint before the parking lot the next day around 2:30 P.M. A wooden gate stood before them and a guard booth was to their left. A brown-leather-skinned guard poked his head through the window. He wore a white, short-sleeved button-up—tight on his biceps—tucked into his khakis with a red tie and black suspenders. He had a thick sandy moustache, crusted with what appeared to be dried minestrone soup, and an oiled, bald, freckled head. Too much sun. Too too much sun.

"Good afternoon, all. What can I do for ya?"

"Well, how are you?" Gary replied, rolling down his window. He stuck out his hand and shook the guard's, his face even redder than usual from the heat. This car had air-conditioning, but he didn't believe in air-conditioning. Embrace the heat. Bake a little. Bask. "My name is Gary Gascoigne. I have a three-night reservation in one of the cottage suites."

"Okay, then. Let me check to see if we have your name here." He picked up a wood clipboard and stared over his gold-framed readers at a sheet of sun-baked, once-white paper. "Ah, there you are," he said and reached toward his desk. "Mr. and Mrs. Gary Gascoigne. And there she is. The Mrs."

As the security officer repeated their names, Gary looked at his new wife and smiled. Dorothy, instead, pursed her lips and leaned her face against the glass window. The glass felt good against her freckled face. It was slightly cooler than the air temperature.

The guard leaned over the driver-side window and handed them a stack of papers, as he pushed a button to open the gate. Gary handed the papers to Dorothy and then drove on. Dorothy read the one atop the stack.

1. All guests must make reservations. No "Drop-ins" are allowed!
2. Remember, people come to Mountain Home for rest, for prayer, for meditation, and for quiet spiritual refreshment.
3. Let us all help to maintain this retreat for that purpose. Water is very precious! We are on a very limited water well supply. Please conserve in every way possible. Like He'd want us to!
4. Please report any leaky faucet or toilet to the manager.
5. NO smoking or alcohol is allowed anywhere on Mountain Home property.
6. Solicitation of funds or distribution of literature is not permitted anywhere on Mountain Home property, unless approved by the manager.
7. For your convenience, there is a pop machine, public telephone, and drinking fountain located on the patio next to the main dining room.
8. ALL GUESTS MUST BE QUIET and in your room or chapel between 10:00 P.M. & 7:00 A.M.
9. When night meetings extend past this time, curfew starts when the meeting is over. Preachers and/or Leaders MUST RESPECT THE QUIET HOURS. NO EXCEPTIONS!

They arrived at their room, and Gary removed his sweat-soaked clothes. Rather than see his wilted, naked skin—yuck—Dorothy went to the bathroom and closed the door behind her. She grabbed the sink and leaned forward and breathed. She dropped her head against her chest but then picked it up and saw herself in the mirror. She watched the clouds of perspiration grow and then disappear and then grow again. She turned on the faucet and splashed some water on her face. She took a washcloth off a rack and wet it under the cool water—let it run—then patted the damp cloth against her forehead. Then under her armpits, and then in between her thighs. She reached into her purse and took out her reddest lipstick—a primrose. She applied it to her lips, from left to right, then smacked and pressed them against a piece of toilet paper. She crumpled the kiss-stained sheet and threw it in a corner. As she was about to put the cap back on, then, instead, she twisted the silver swivel-up tube all the way out, exposing two rose-colored inches. She took it and, in the center of the mirror, penned *you cunty bitch* in her most precise cursive. She looked at her work and smiled, but when Gary knocked she grabbed the tissues and rubbed it out. Then she opened the door and entered the bedroom.

"Well, you were in there a while," Gary said, zipping his pants.

"Sorry. I had to wash my face."

Gary walked over to his bag and grabbed his wristwatch and strapped it on. He wore a tan safari shirt, with matching safari shorts and a white hat and white tennis shoes. Around his waist was buckled a brown leather fanny pack—gum, ten dollars in quarters, and a pocket New Testament—and his red cheeks hadn't gotten any less rosy.

"It's fine, Dorothy-ody. But let's get going. This place is very important for us."

"I know that, Gary," she sighed, and put on a cardigan.

"It is our honeymoon, you know."

"I know, Gary," she sighed. "I can't wait."

They walked along a stone desert path and made their way from building to building. They started at the chapel. The chapel was flanked by four square columns at the front. A stone bell tower, with a thin-stone steeple, sat atop four columns. Inside was hotter than outside, and the smell implied the death of at least one wild animal, yet unfound. A jackal, Dorothy guessed. But she didn't really know much about jackals.

After the chapel they went to the tabernacle, but this time Dorothy didn't go in. Gary took his time. Dorothy sat on a bench and waited. Then they visited the two prayer towers sitting at the two opposite ends of the property. Gary seemed at peace in the prayer towers. Dorothy could've used AC.

They had dinner in the main dining room with the rest of the guests. Dorothy's lipstick had been used up earlier, so she didn't bother with much makeup. It didn't seem appropriate, anyway. This occasion's importance didn't quite stack up. They sat at a communal table with a church group visiting from Arizona. Gary ate mutton and green beans and cauliflower mash. He told the group—a table of seven, including the man and wife—about the Message, attempting to expand his brand. Although the tourists seemed interested, Dorothy considered telling Gary that we could get kicked out for that—that the rules are strict here, and solicitation breaks more than one. But she held her tongue. She hoped, in fact, that someone—someone in charge—might hear him preach, and then they could go. But her wishes again went ungranted.

Dorothy looked up at the blood-orange sunset as they walked back to their cottage. The sun set later here, and the pinks and reds and greens were bigger and brighter and true. It was the pollution, she'd heard, that allowed for such beautiful sunsets. It's the smog that shines the filter. She looked up and smiled for the first time since she'd arrived. Or, wait, the second. The night sky, too. But, as they got to their room, Gary stepped in front of Dorothy before they reached the door.

"Dorothy-ody, if you don't mind, I was hoping I could take a few minutes to myself in order to get the room ready. I have a few surprises in store for us tonight. It won't take long at all, I promise. Forty-five minutes, I'd say. Maybe an hour. An hour at the most. Maybe you could take a walk? Or actually, if you'd prefer," Gary reached into his pocket and handed her the keys to his leased Lincoln Continental. "Why don't you go for a drive? Just be back in an hour." Dorothy nodded. "Make sure you're back in an hour." And he kissed her. "Pretty please?"

TWO HOURS LATER, Dorothy arrived back at the gated security checkpoint. She was smoking, and she pulled into the wrong side—the exit side—of the booth. The guard walked over to her driver's-side window. He noticed an empty bottle of wine. And then he noticed another.

"Are you okay, ma'am?"

She pulled on her cigarette, took a moment, and then exhaled into his face.

"I'm fine, thanks. Would you mind opening the gate for me?"

"You're on the wrong side, ma'am. You're gonna have to turn around and go back the other way," he said, and he stared at her. "You're also not allowed to smoke."

"Oh, really?" she answered. "I had no idea," and she blew in his face, again, before dropping the butt in the remains of the Riesling. "Now, again, and seriously this time. Would ya just open up the fuckin' gate?"

"Sure, ma'am. Sure. Give me just one sec, would ya? I'll get right on it."

The security guard walked back to his booth and made a phone call. He informed his supervisors that a guest was drunk and smoking and driving a car. And so, while Dorothy was taken into the security officer's custody—they didn't believe in police—the hotel manager walked to their room and found Gary wearing only a white robe and white socks and white tennis shoes. The hotel manager told Gary that his wife had been detained, and that he'd have to remove her from the premises. Gary had placed, on a chair beside the bed, a matching white robe—in her size—and matching white socks and white tennis shoes. And he had fashioned a crucifix atop their bed sheets in rose petals— Jesus and all, his work in fact quite impressive. But Dorothy-ody—but Dorothy-ody—she never got to see. They left the premises later that night, and their marriage was left unconsummated.

* * *

Once they returned from their honeymoon, Dorothy's emptiness only doubled. Then tripled. And quadrupled after that. She began to drink Shiraz or Pinot with dinner—sometimes even Merlot—even though Gary forbade drinking. Even though she wasn't supposed to. She'd hide it at first. She'd siphon it into quarter-full Diet Cokes. Then sometimes she'd call her old boyfriend, Seth—old meaning not recent, because he was still then not even thirty. But sex in parking lots didn't quell her nervous energy. Or her fluttery hands and feet. Birdlike forever but never able to fly. Neither did a slipped disk in her spine that required—required?—she take OxyContin. They didn't specify how, and they worked faster if she crushed and snorted it, and she liked the way they tasted, so that's what she did. On top of everything else. She began to feel disabled. What she was getting just wasn't enough.

So, one day, Gary slapped Dorothy. He was angry. She'd begun to disobey. She'd begun to outwardly question his authority, from the way she was supposed to dress to the penance she was told to inflict upon herself to the tithing. This, the percentage of her paycheck, he felt he was due. Her money, now, was accrued as such; from her grandfather, once he'd passed—he, worried, allowed for a trust wherein once a month she got some of his leftover retirement—enough to spend but hardly anything to save—that was an easy rationale, though, especially when you were born a junkie. Oh, and something still came in from the divorce. Palimony, or alimony, or whatever. Whatever the difference is. It didn't matter. No matter what she always spent it all. Always believed she deserved to feel better. No one should feel this bad. And never much on anything important. Unless, that is, you're into alligator-skin belts. Or monogrammed emu loafers. Or drugs. When all this was through she'd eventually be supported by her daughter. But that's not 'til later. Now, though—but now—she began to cough on Gary's message. She refused to swallow. Any of it. Any of it at all. Gary was old—let's say sixty—and his slap just didn't hurt her. She was tougher than he was. She'd been through more. It's like, fuck him, you know? So Dorothy, high as a kite, slapped him back. Once in the ear, once on his cheek. And his fat, red face was throbbing. She packed her things in black garbage bags, wished herself a traveling mercy, and got in her car and drove east, to Palm Springs, to a rented condominium her daughter had helped her find. And she started smoking again—sigh—and drinking whenever she wanted. But at least she could say she was her.

She'll live here for the rest of this, until this whole thing is finally over.

ACT 3

1982-1990

AND I ARE ALL

Slowly, over the next few years, Clover gave up on Mama—even though Clo still paid for everything—because she just wouldn't quit the drinking. Or the wrong men. Or the strong men. Or the everything else. Or the always and obvious everything else. Back when Clover turned eighteen, it wasn't up to the courts anymore whether or not she was allowed to see Mama. It was no longer her father's say where she went and what she did, although to be honest he'd given up those duties quite a long time ago. She was now, technically, allowed to visit her mother. She was an adult. If she wanted to go she could. But she didn't want to. It hurt too much. At a certain point, to survive, Clover decided she couldn't leash her happiness to her mother's well-being. After a party she'd thrown in high school, one of the many weekends when Clover ran away to her mother's, Clover was downstairs drinking boxed wine and telling her friends not to tell her mother. Dorothy was upstairs drinking boxed wine and asking Clover's friends not to tell her daughter, please. Eventually they both ended up asleep with boys in beds they didn't belong in, and when she woke up, to her mother still sleeping, she realized that Mama might never get better. That there might be no such thing as better. That this might be, and perhaps always was, just her. And then suddenly Clover was free. And Clover was happy. And she just lived. She just was. But that didn't last long. It didn't suit her. She found it unbecoming. But throughout this—Clover referred to the times when she felt forced to cut her mother off as being "without her"—Clover never stopped thinking about Mama. She never stopped wondering why she was the way she was. She never stopped guessing what she was doing and wondering how she lived. Even day-to-day things, like whether or not she went to Starbucks or the Coffee Bean. But, in a bigger way, she wondered why she made the decisions she made. She wondered why those decisions always seemed misthought, or skewed. Without any perspective. Without much interest in the truth. In the end, Clover finally just realized that her mother was unreliable. Well, beyond unreliable. Out of step. Without footing and afraid. Toothless and hairless. Untethered, in every sense of the word. But Clo also decided that that wasn't Mama's fault. That it wasn't anyone's fault. That it just was. That she just was. Hope and hope swallowed.

Clover eventually got married. At twenty-one, she married young, just like Do. She was beautiful, like Mama, too. And thin, once she discovered cocaine. And a model. Eventually an actress. And good. So she had her pick of the litter. After an audition in New York, she went to a party at a club with the city's movers and shakers. A real who's-who. The word "bougie" comes to mind. She went with some friends. Or some other models. Not really friends. Competition breeds resentment. In the corner of the room, in the section roped off for those considered VIP, she saw a tall, strapping, oh-so-handsome man hunched over a table. He was chopping glassy cocaine shards into a powder across a mirrored coffee table and pulled that powder into lines, approximately the length of a snow pea. Long, thin lines, like canes, or poles. Lowercase *l*s. She walked over to him and asked if she could have some. He, of course, said yes. Coke-talk for hours— what else is there to do? She found out that he was the starting quarterback for the New York Jets. He saw her and knew that she was beautiful, and once he spoke to her he found that this was true of every part of her. He particularly loved her voice. One month later they married. His name was Jack. They'd move to New York, and then divorce in eight years. They'd also have a son. His name's Jack too. Well, technically, his name's Jack Jr. Sometimes they called him J.R. I hated that.

* * *

Clover lives in Manhattan. This is while they're still married. They also have a country house in Long Island. That's where she and Dorothy would stay. But not yet. That's a little later. When Clover got pregnant, she got sober. The coke got her skinny enough to get the guy, but now that she got him, what did she care? She romanticized the idea of being a mother, and also, if she didn't quit, Jack swore he'd leave. This is how he got her off drugs. How romantic. She wasn't a fun cokehead. Sort of a pain-in-the-ass cokehead, eventually deciding upon it in lieu of morning coffee. But when she got pregnant, she got sober. And she was happy to be sober. As an athlete, Jack wasn't always home. So she spent her days at the gym in the morning—endorphin addicted, which is I guess as good as you can do—and Alcoholics Anonymous meetings at night. Sometimes Narcotics Anonymous. Sometimes the other way around. When she was feeling indulgent. In fact, she's at a meeting now. Drew Barrymore was there, and she used to take thirty Vicodin a day. Five in the morning, ten with lunch, and fifteen at bedtime. Or something like that. Maybe it wasn't her. Maybe it was someone else. Obviously. Dorothy was coming to visit Clover soon, and she'd never visited her home before, and she was nervous. Both of them. It's been years. But Clover, sober and happy enough, had just had her baby boy, and she decided it was time for Mama to meet her baby.

* * *

Tinkerbell was Dorothy's new toy terrier. She thought he looked gay, so she made his name Tinkerbell, even though he was a boy. And she needed something, you know? The two pals sat uncomfortably on a plane from Los Angeles to New York in the fall of 1983. She was on her way to see her daughter, and she couldn't find anyone to dog-sit Tink.

Dorothy's knees ground against the polyester of the seat in front of her and she pulled down the plastic window cover to her left. She didn't like that she had the window seat because she liked to have room to cross her legs. And the fat person next to her walked onto the plane with a white sack of McDonald's. The whale had already asked Dorothy if she wanted a bite of her McRib, and Do looked past her pores and into her eyes and declined, as politely as she could. She opened the window cover again as the plane sat on the tarmac. The pilot had said that they were sixth in line to take off. Outside was bright and the sun shone into her face, but she looked into it, and then back down at her seat, but then back into it, and smiled, because she liked the way the sun hurt her eyes.

* * *

This is the Christ Church meeting on First Avenue and First Street. It's on Thursdays. It's in the morning—seven, sharp!—because it's a meeting for the types of people who need two meetings a day. Today, too, Clover was the meeting's moderator. She made the coffee, bought the Styrofoam cups, and chose which chips and pretzels and crackers to bring. She also brought cookies and Hostess cakes and candy for those who liked candy—she'd found that sobers, when recently sober, broke down into sugars and salts, and so she offered everyone a chance to get what they wanted. Everyone needs something. She aligned, and realigned, the hollow tin chairs, and she gathered the literature and stacked it, neatly and with reason, next to the wooden stirrers beside the Mr. Coffee machine.

* * *

The sky was bus-station bright outside the plane. Above the white clouds. Cozy. So cozy. The fat ass beside Dorothy took a portable tube of lotion from her purse and squirted some into her hands before she dug into the rest of her French fries. She stank like lemonade, lard, Lysol, and petroleum. Maybe that was partly the plane. Maybe not, though. When she cracked open the white bag that housed the rest of her lunch— she'd saved some—Tinkerbell started barking from the traveler's bag she was housed in under her seat. As the people around her began to stare, Dorothy got nervous and grabbed up the carrying case with Tinky and put it on her lap. She unzipped the front and Tink's head popped out. Dazed—Dorothy had fed her baby Benadryl to keep her calm on the plane—she opened her mouth and rolled out her tongue and stared at the fries. Her ears went back like a rabbit and her blonde bangs hung down into her eyes and she began to fidget her way out into the world. "Oh, well isn't she cute," Do's seatmate said, spilling over into their seat. She finished her fries and licked her greased and salted fingers clean and then pet the hairs out of Tinky's eyes. The grease and spit from her fingers slicked back and clumped together Tink's bangs. Dorothy's mouth furrowed. It was disgusting. Dorothy got out the baby Benadryl and gave her another teaspoon. Tinky coughed, then stared a beat, before dropping back into the bag. Tired. Again tired. Do zipped the carrier and pushed it, again, beneath the chair in front of her. The doctor said up to two tablespoons of baby Benadryl was acceptable. But Tink was acting disorderly, so Dorothy gave her a third.

* * *

Clover already knew all the literature. Backward and forward and frontward and back. Red Ricky got his nickname from the way his cheeks looked, mornings, before he'd given up drugs. Extreme dehydration due to Riesling, over-exercise, and amphetamines. He always called it Tina. He learned that from a masseur. When he went out— the good old days—he didn't even iron his jeans until midnight—his own special routine. He loved his little routines. The real parties don't start until after, but you already knew that. Ricky walked up and stood behind the podium. He'd been assigned to speak first.

"This week, I just wanted to thank everyone for sticking with me and being here. Thank you guys for showing up. I know people can get tired of me. I know I don't have the cleanest résumé in the group. But I'm trying. I'm trying as hard as I can. This past week, I went out to eat—a Japanese place that I hadn't been to in a while. The last time I remember going—with friends I don't even see anymore—I remember doing sake bombs, cheap sake and cans of Sapporo. And more sake bombs. And more sake bombs. And then I'm drunk and tired, so then I call for blow. Oh and sheesh, I don't remember much after that. I think we drank more. Definitely more drugs. I remember that. I remember trying not to be tired. But, anyway, they let me back in to eat. And I made it all the way through dinner. All I drank was ginger ale. So I just wanted to thank you all for supporting me and believing in me, 'cause I think, maybe—just maybe—I'm finally starting to believe in myself."

And he sat back down. And applause.

He took out a red bandana from his bag and wiped at his eyes. Clover found this routine off-putting and decided, for the time being, not to share. Red Ricky put on this performance if he noticed new men at the meeting. He liked sympathy to spin-cycle around him. The podium, at the front of the room, stood square and vacant. She didn't like the silences. It'd been too long since she'd seen her mother. They'd have dinner later, she thought. And she'd look at her mother, and reluctantly she'd see herself. And then she'd look back down at her plate of food.

* * *

Turbulence made Dorothy nervous. Not intellectually, in that she didn't think this meant that the plane was actually malfunctioning, but in terms of her equilibrium—unsound footing made her uneasy. Turbulence, like seasickness, made her miss where she was from. Turbulence, like seasickness, made her miss the pavement. She didn't like the warning from the loudspeaker, and she didn't like when the stewards rushed by her to get to their seats. She didn't like that her seat was next to the emergency door. And she didn't like that the doors had instructions on how to open them. Twist the middle lever, then pull. Dorothy gripped her armrests as tight as she could as the plane began to wobble and dip. She closed her eyes. She tried to think of being somewhere else. Somewhere that made her happy. She was at a beach, and there was a boy there. And she was young, and he was young, and muscly. Beefy. And they were together. Just them two. She'd just begun to forget when her seatmate dropped her slippery hand on top of a few of her fingers. She'd fallen asleep even through the turbulence, of course. Dorothy didn't want to share the armrest. She pulled her hand out and watched her seatmate's fall like a dead flounder between her fat thighs.

* * *

About a week before, Clover's husband Jack did a celebrity autograph signing appearance at a car show at Lincoln Center. To avoid state taxes, he requested that he be paid in cash. In fact, he said that if it wasn't cash, then he wouldn't be attending. So five thousand dollars was arranged. This money still sat in a canvas overnight bag in the kitchen. Also, about a year ago, Jack did a commercial for a local car dealership. In exchange for his talent they offered him two small sedans—a Chrysler and a Plymouth. Instead, he requested a limousine. As a lark. Half-serious. But his request was granted. And so a boxy stretch Lincoln sat untouched in the far-off dank garage. Keep this in mind. This'll come up later.

* * *

"Because somebody like me—somebody as fucked as me—well I could do anything, and I did. Because, for what they call normal people, there's a line—an equilibrium—that they're at all the time. But for people like us, or people like me, anyway—they tell me to talk in the I—I'm either too high above—way too high above—or too low below, because'a what I been through or whatever, and I spent years trying to get there. Just trying to even out. Trying way too hard to feel normal. Because I quit drinkin', and quit cocaine, and meth. I quit smokin' weed and takin' pills. I quit everythang. And I are all. Now I just gotta quit smokin' smokes, but I guess nobody's perfect. Anyway, thanks for lettin' me share," and he got down from the podium, to fervent but scattered applause, and cowboy'd his way back to his folding chair.

Clover raised her hand. She would share next, she finally decided. She'd talk about her mom. And then about her dad. And then about the Mamas and the Papas.

* * *

Unable to relax—pharmaceutically or otherwise—Do pulled open the Lego-gray window cover halfway to see the shade of the sky. It was clear, now. The shaking had finally quit. The light broke through the plastic, wedged between cramped necks and knees. It smacked Dorothy's face and stung her eyes. She squinted, and then closed the shade halfway so it split her seatmate in two so just her dimpled legs were glowing. Like a black-and-white cookie—top-heavy, but still in the shade—her head fell forward against her bosom. Dorothy opened the window cover all the way in hopes of waking her to subside her snoring. But it didn't—she hammered and hammered away—and Dorothy sighed. At least she wasn't scared anymore. She looked back out the window. An American flag was printed on the white wing. It had faded, a little. Sun-dyed—pale and peeling. It stung more, this time, to look out at the incandescent sky. But it was a good hurt, so, again, she opened her eyelids wider. And the red sting made her forget that she was nervous, like when she'd pinch her belly when she used to take shots at the doctor's. And Tinky would finally stop yipping from her carrier. For the first time the entire flight, she was quiet. The drugs were working. She'd cried herself to sleep.

* * *

Clover waited and waited, perched on the brown wood steps of the porch. Mama said don't pick me up. Mama said. Everything will be fine. *I'll find a cab, baby. I've flown a million times. It's easy as pie, baby. I promise.* But Clover was nervous. She should've gotten her, she thought. She should've driven to the airport and picked her up. But Mama was insistent that she'd be fine. That you don't have to worry about Mama. *That I've always been fine, and I always will be.* But now she's late. Oh no, now she's late.

Finally, a green taxi—an airport taxi, Newark Cab and Town Car—pulled onto the seashelled driveway. And, after a moment, the door swung open from its green rusted hinge.

"Baby. Baby, baby. Do you have twenty bucks? I spent all my cash on magazines."

Clover reached into the back pocket of her corduroys. She had sixty dollars folded up. She walked to the car and gave it to her and Mama snatched it quick.

"See if he needs a tip," Clover said.

"K. Thanks, baby."

Clover watched Dorothy pay the driver. She looked at her mother and her mouth smiled. Her eyes looked sad, though. Dorothy gave him two twenties and put the other in her shirt. She hopped out of the car. Her head fell toward her shoulder.

"Hi, Clover. My girl. My little baby," Dorothy said, and dropped her purse by her feet.

"Hi, Mama," Clover replied and ran into her. She took her hands from her pockets and ran as fast as she could.

They eventually made it inside. Dorothy wore too much perfume. And Clover squeezed her tight tight tight. Until she smelled like Dorothy. Until she made sure she smelled like Mom. Clover dropped Mama's bag by the screen door and it fell down heavy. She'd over-packed. She was just staying the weekend. Dorothy unleashed Tinkerbell and Tinkerbell ran free. They walked through the kitchen. Then sat in the den. In the middle of a gray leather couch. They sat close. Together. Their knees just barely touched. Tink ran in, eventually, and jumped in Clover's lap. Clover pet Tink awhile with an immense focus and intensity—she surprised herself—until she realized she was just forcing her mother to speak first.

"Where's the baby?" Dorothy finally shouted. She was excited. She was there.

"He's napping, Mom. I'll bring you up real soon."

Really, though, Clover had to make sure her mother was right before she let her meet the baby. Jack Jr. was still sacred. Jack Jr. was still pure. He didn't have any LA in him. Well he did, but only in his blood. They'd refused to have him baptized. They didn't know any better. But they thought, understandably, that good parents might be enough to keep him straight. Idealism is just another way of saying naiveté.

"Come on, honey. Can't we go wake him?"

"Soon, Mama. Real soon."

Dorothy huffed. Clo continued petting Tink. Dorothy sat with her legs crossed. She wore a tweed pantsuit. A white purse. Big hair. Big, blonde hair. And a pearl necklace tight around her neck. Her lips were dyed Bloody Mary red and were crusty at the corners. Clover leaned in. Mama stunk like horseradish, Tabasco, and tomato juice. Celery salt, Worcestershire, and lemon. Oh, and vodka, of course. Everyone knows plane Bloody Marys are the best Bloody Marys. It has to do with the air pressure. The air pressure makes you crave salt.

"Fine. Jesus. Where's Jack, anyway?"

Dorothy had only met Jack once. At the wedding. That didn't go so smooth.

"He's at practice, Mama. He won't be home for a few hours."

Really, though, Jack had gone away for a time. He and Clover had fought, and he was sick of it. Sick of everything. Sick of playing second fiddle. It's like every day can't be a bad day, you know? This doesn't bode well for this couple's future.

"Well I'd love to see the little one, for cryin' out loud. Isn't that the point?"

Dorothy leaned back and sank into the couch.

"You will. I promise." Clover waited. "How are you, anyway?"

And then again Dorothy fell forward. Nervous. Tough time sittin' still.

"I'm good, baby. You know I'm good. Why do you ask, baby? You know I'm good. I'm always good. I've been good forever. Forever always just the same."

"Oh, I do, huh?" Clover pruned, putting her hands behind her head. "I know you're always good?"

"Well, what the hell is that supposed to mean?" with her hands dancing.

"Nothin', Mama." She leaned on her knees with her elbows. She didn't want to push her. She spent too long too far away. "Just that I love you is all. I'm just really happy to see you. Happy to see you doin' well."

By this point Clover was well aware how Mama was doin'—not all that great, given that she controlled and supported her finances entirely—but she didn't care. Right now, she didn't care. She was just really happy to see her. Well, in any case, is subjective. Mama seemed well enough to love her. So she should just leave it, then, right? Leave well enough alone.

Clover walked Mama up the creaking steps to the second floor. Clover noticed the sound more than she normally did. Perhaps she was uncomfortable. They walked up the dark, wood stairwell. Clover in front of Dorothy. Clover led the way. They gripped the handrail tightly up to the landing. The first door on the left led to Jack Jr. Clover held the doorknob, then shushed Dorothy—her humming could wake the baby. Then Clover turned the doorknob, and then they walked in. It was dark, but they stepped forward. Little Jack Jr. lay sleeping in his crib. Little snores came from little Jack Jr. His head shook—swung back and forth—but he didn't open his eyes. He stopped squirming and turned on his side. One leg over his blue blanket, one leg under. A Teenage Mutant Ninja Turtle onesie. And a Nerf football, just like Daddy, under his arm.

"He's really a stunner," Dorothy said too loud.

Jack Jr. turned over on his stomach and opened his eyelids wide but then closed them and started to snore.

"Yeah," Clover whispered, shaking her head. "Be quiet though, Mom," and Clover pet her son's hair, and she smiled. "Let's come back in a little, though," Clover whispered. "I don't wanna wake him, yet."

"You sure, baby?"

"Yeah, Mom. I'm sure."

"Okay," she said and put her hands to her neck and squeezed it. "He really is an angel," said Dorothy. "I haven't seen anything so pretty since you were born."

"Oh, please."

"I mean it."

"Yeah, okay."

As they left, Dorothy's clunky bracelets and anklets rattled and chirped. But Jack Jr., then, was quite the sound sleeper.

They walked a few doors over. Clover showed Mama her room.

"You can put your stuff in that thing, Mom. K?" pointing to a round armoire. "I'm gonna get some rest. I was up all night with him. I just gotta lay down for a little, okay?"

CLOVER GOT UP from her nap after about an hour. She outstretched her arms. She felt better. She'd slept over the covers in all her clothes. She was tired. Stressed. She shook off, patted down the bed, and walked to the guest room. But Mama wasn't in there. She walked to the baby's room, but he was asleep in his crib in overalls, his football torn in half now, one in each heavy hand. Tink slept in there, too. Tink liked the baby's breathing. So Clover walked downstairs. Mama wasn't in the kitchen either. She wasn't in the bathroom. Or the parlor room. Not in the den or the foyer. She wasn't in the game room or the guesthouse or the pool house. Oh no, Mama wasn't anywhere. Mama isn't anywhere.

Clover went back to the kitchen and poured herself a glass of water. She looked around. The canvas bag was gone. Jack's overnight bag was missing. And when Clover walked to the garage—the last place she checked for Mom—so, too, was the limo.

THE NEXT MORNING, after Clover searched everywhere all night—everywhere she could possibly think of—she found Mama at the Sunoco mini-mart, leaning against the outdoor bathroom and holding the bathroom key. She was standing outside, her eyes were open. Her hands were shaking and she looked older than her years. She held her wig in her right hand and a brown paper bag in her left, crumpled in her fingers. She wore bare feet, and they were dirty black. Chipped nails and clackling teeth. Chipped nails and click-clackling teeth. A patchy bald head and holes in her leggings. And, again, wide eyes, like a marmoset.

"Oh my God, Mom. What the fuck is going on? What are you doing here?"

The bag was gone, and, again, the Lincoln.

"What do you mean, baby?"

"What the fuck are you doing here and where have you been?" Clover screamed.

"Don't yell at me. Your house is stuffy and I wanted to get out for a little. So I got a motel room. What's your problem?"

Clover shook her head and closed her eyes.

"This is so fucking nuts."

"Oh, please. I'm a grown woman and I can do what I want."

The bottle in her paper bag was capless.

"Well, where's the car?"

"What car?"

"The limousine!"

"I don't know anything about a limousine."

"Oh Jesus Christ." Clover stopped. She collected herself. "Let's just go home, okay?"

"In a little, baby. Let me finish."

"Whatever." She sighed and dropped her head and winced. But then she sprang up, curious. "But if you don't know where the car is what are you doing at a gas station?"

"Two-for-one cigarettes," Dorothy winked. "Sunoco's the only place for that."

* * *

When Clover revisited her mother in rehab—this wasn't the first time—she was shocked how far it was away. All the way in Malibu. She was paying for rehab all the way in Malibu? Malibu rehabs don't even count. Clover didn't much like to drive. She'd flown to LA, and she'd got a hotel room, and the hour drive to Malibu was, at the very least, quite taxing. Driving didn't come natural, so the focus it took tired her out. When she called Dorothy, before she got on the road, Dorothy insisted they meet at the green grocers—instead of the hospital—so that way they'd get to eat well before she came up. Dorothy was sick of the food on the hill. Everything was fried, or buttered, or both, and Dorothy was suddenly vegetarian. They met at PC Greens—a local healthfoodery—and had carrot-apple juices before they sat down to their vegetarian Chinese chicken salad. Chicken tofu. Looked the part. They split it. They were both worried about being judged. Also about the calories.

"How you doing, Mom?" Clover asked between round bites of fried garlic and sliced mandarin.

"I'm good, baby," she said, still slightly slurring. The antipsychotics, for her nerves. Those didn't count. Those were prescription.

"You swear?" Clover asked.

"I do, honey. I really do. They took me off mood stabilizers today, so I'm feelin' a little wonky. A little tired. Wish I felt better but I know I will be soon. But other than that I'm good, you know? I'm gettin' better."

Some time passed. They both ate their half-salads slow. But then Dorothy succinctly said, as though she were prompted, "Hey, you wanna see something funny?"

And Clover nodded sure.

Dorothy pulled up her sleeve and revealed a white taped-down bandage on the outward-facing side of her wrist. She peeled it off and revealed a deep cut, sutured and healing but still with the black stitching sewed through.

"See," she said and she pointed. "See, I broke a needle off here. And they went in and tried to find it but they couldn't find it."

Clover stopped eating and waited.

"What's funny about that?"

"Well, what they told me is, believe it or not, is that now it's in me. Forever, I guess. And there's nothin' they can really do about that. So, now, they said, at the airport I'm gonna beep when I go through the metal detectors. And they said there's nothin' I can do about it. I just gotta explain everything every time."

"That's it?"

"Yeah, I mean, I thought it was pretty funny when I thought about it earlier."

"I don't know, Mom," Clover replied, but started eating again. "I'm not sure that's very funny at all. In fact it's pretty disgusting."

"Well, I guess we're gonna have to agree to disagree on that one. Do I have any arugula in my teeth?" And Dorothy smiled wide open with some greens stuck between her fangs.

"A little."

"Excuse me, honey?" Dorothy called for the waitress. "Do you think you could get me a toothpick? Thank you, honey. You're the sweetest girl alive. Did anyone ever tell you you look like Kristy McNichol? Well, if they haven't, they should've, 'cause boy is it ever true."

DOROTHY EVENTUALLY ORDERED an avocado and sprout sandwich on flax-wheat toast—wasn't satisfied by the near meat—but couldn't eat the whole thing and wrapped up the second half. They went shopping afterward—PC Greens was also a healthy grocers—and Dorothy bought a bag of vegan popcorn and some instant vegetable soup. When they got back to the facility, Clover parked and then carried Dorothy's bag and purse up the hill to the main entranceway. They walked inside and were greeted by three orderlies.

"Say hello," Dorothy told Clover.

"Hi," she said, and they all commented on how tall she was. She was two inches taller than Mom.

"You mind leaving your bags here and we'll bring them out to you in a minute?" one asked. "Thanks."

"Sure," Dorothy replied. But she preferred to wait while they inspected.

And they dug into the grocery bag, which was okay, but then her purse, and pulled out a sleeve of Tylenol.

"More Tylenol?"

"I had a headache."

"You have enough Tylenol."

"Yeah, but I had a headache when I was out."

"And what are these?" She pulled out three loose orange and white capsules.

"How should I know?"

"Because they were in your purse?" Calfskin, by the way.

Dorothy squinted and looked up, remembering.

"Oh, I know what those are!"

The orderly waited. And waited. "And?"

"They're antidepressants."

"I know that. I recognize them. Why do you have them, is what I'm asking? They're not from us, nor are they on your charts."

"Oh?" and Dorothy snapped the elastic scrunchie on her wrist. And then did so again. "Well, that's 'cause I got 'em from another patient."

"Excuse me?" the orderly stood straight.

"Yeah, well," she put her head down and looked at her pink sandals. Real cute sandals. She'd shopped for the trip. Rehab fashion. "And you know I've been a little down in the mouth. So I just figured, I guess . . ."

The orderly looked at another orderly and he held Dorothy's elbow and escorted her to her room while Clover stood in there in silence. Then Clo walked back solemn to her car while the orderly shook her head and went back to digging.

THIS IS A DOG RUN, NOT A PLAYGROUND

This is later.

* * *

With a Dodgers hat turned halfway backward and dready blond hair, a boy with blood in his eyes mashed open the first gate into the North Fork Hills Community Park Dog Run and then closed the silver latch behind him. He then propped open the second. Before he walked in, he stopped to read the rules, which were written beneath a plastic sheath.

> *Monitor your dog at all times. If your reading material keeps you from doing this, please do not use them here.*

He undid the knotting and then pulled the list from the fence.

He dropped it to the ground. It fell when he walked and he stepped on it. It stuck for a moment to the gum sole of his tan, used Timberland boots. He kicked it away. He saw his friends around an American elm tree in the back, near the street. Near a dirty, red Kia Sorento, and shouted, blindly, "Pup-a-doodle-doo," before he laughed sideways. He knocked the ash from his cigarette, pulled at it again, and then flicked it into a pile of dead leaves and acorns. The acorns came from an oak tree, of which there were four. The elm, though, was the only elm. Near them was a larger, albino-looking gentleman with a goatee that hung long and colorless from his chin and a clerical hat bent up at the front. His denim vest was covered with patches—*USA!*, *Romeo Void*—and his chain wallet sometimes got stuck between the slats of the seat built in around the tree's base. Around him, two girls—maritime-tattooed, one's a consistently tropical theme—palm trees, mermaids—and the other's mostly, entirely etched on skulls—seemed just along for the ride. One of the two ate cinnamon Life cereal from a family-sized box and dropped a few pieces behind her. And so behind her three dogs followed her in step—a pug, a Pekingese, and a Pomeranian. They ate what she didn't. Later they threw it up. She didn't have a dog of her own, though. None of them did. The other girl looked up at the sky and noticed there were no clouds. She fiddled with her nose ring. All four walked around awhile. Soiled wood chips crunched beneath their feet. The girls wiped the sweat from their foreheads with the ends of their unwashed hair. Then they sat around the elm tree with crossed legs and opened cans of malt liquor beer that they'd kept hidden in a rucksack made by L.L. Bean. It was nice out and they passed the Becks and tipped their heads back with each foamy sip. They didn't seem like they slept, really. Maybe here or there in the park. Maybe locked in the bathroom of a coffee shop. Maybe that's why they liked the dog run. Vagrants, maybe, or wanderers. Drifters, or grifters. Mole people, but who didn't sleep in the subway. They weren't allowed, anymore, to sleep in the subway.

Do whistled for Tink and they left the run. She followed and Do leashed him. She tied him outside a café and went inside for a hot tea. When she got back out Tinky's tongue dripped out from his mouth. She kneeled down and pulled on it—not too hard, though. She didn't want to hurt him—before she walked him home.

* * *

Dylan is twenty-one now. He doesn't much speak to his mother. He lived there, but he didn't see her too much. Or his father. Just reiterating. Both points. His parents were celebrities. *Were* celebrities. Well Dale was still known, but not all that well regarded. Dale had turned back toward television when his career began to parch. A weekly crime serial. Mediocre, at best, reviews. But good ratings. And Dorothy. We all know about Dorothy. Dylan thought he'd like to go out tonight. He wanted to get drunk. Maybe meet a girl. Maybe a few. I mean, why not, right? Everyone in the family has, at least, charisma. It was the eighties and he wore holed jeans and a white T-shirt, with a pack of cigarettes rolled into his shirt sleeves—he loved old movies—and his green flannel tied around his waist and a shaved head and still freckles. Still covered in freckles. Worn-out combat boots and white socks. That's what he wore out, even though he wanted to go to a nightclub. Fuck them if they don't like it. Fuck you. But girls were at the nightclubs. And he liked girls. But not girlfriends. That wouldn't make him feel better at all. So he had a friend who also had a shaved head and they got an eight ball and then went out to dinner. They had Israeli food—they thought it'd be fun to scare the management. Chicken liver giblets to start and then steak with hummus then salted chocolate cake and beers and whiskeys and then, eventually, coke in the bathroom after. He ran the faucet and then dipped his house keys in the matchbook-sized plastic bag then breathed in and licked them when he was finished. Metally. Yuck. But the best kind of yuck. He licked his keys again and then licked his fingers and then looked at himself in the mirror. He ran his hands under the water and then turned off the water and then rubbed his nostrils clean.

They went to a few bars and drank more and often had to go to the bathroom, but now they're at the front of the club line. They are third in line, behind two muscly gentlemen in mesh. Their tank tops gave clear view to the contours of their shaved backs, and their slicked hair was shiny, too. Full body buttered. At this point Dylan had done a lot of drugs. Wide-eyed. Owled. Ready for fun. So he could fuck all night. He was excited, but he wasn't nervous. He knew the owner of this club. The proprietor was one of Dorothy's old boyfriends, and while he hadn't spoken to his mother in a while—unsure, even, of how and when they'd split—he didn't think he'd have a problem. Perhaps it was his altered state. He knew the relationship was back when Dorothy was young. Back when she was still pretty. Back when she trusted herself more. When she'd only just started wearing wigs. When they weren't too big. When they didn't, yet, get in the way. When the attempt wasn't to be unrelentingly gregarious. Anyway Dylan was now at the front of the line and the gentlemen before him were ushered to the side. Weren't cool enough. They didn't look the part because this club was happening. This club was cool. A real LA who's who. A real social register. "Hardest door in town," he'd heard. But not for Dylan, Dylan thought. He knew someone, and that someone was impressive. Because that's where the girls were. And Dylan liked the girls. The prettiest girls. So they'd tell him he was handsome. And thin. And he'd take them to the bathroom. And impress them. He had the good drugs. And then everything would be okay. So we're at the front, now. Velvet ropes drooping.

"What's up, my man?" Dylan said with his hand out.

An Asian—or half-Asian—stood before Dylan with a list. He wore tortoiseshell Wayfarer eyeglasses. He held the list with both hands and didn't let go. So Dylan pulled his hand back.

"Who you here to see?" the half-Asian asked, eyes scanning Dylan from above. Dylan was little. He never quite grew.

"What do you mean?"

"We do private parties," he said, his round eyes now down at his clipboard. But not for long. He never quite looked at it. Just stared down blank. It was probably empty. He probably just held it so he didn't have to touch people. Maybe he didn't like germs. People are disgusting. Dylan got that.

"No. I mean, I know Ron. Is he here?"

"No, he's not here. He doesn't come 'til later."

"No, no, I mean I really know him. He used to go out with my mom."

"Yeah, okay, kid," he chuckled. "I'm sure. I think it might be time for you to move to the side." And a large black man opened the rope to the right of him and pointed toward the sidewalk with his hand out flat. He ushered them away. But Dylan wasn't ready to give up yet.

"No, I mean. I know Ron. The owner. He used to go out with my fucking mom, okay?"

"What does that have to do with me?"

"He told me to tell you that. He told me to come and tell you that."

"Well, he didn't tell me anything. I don't know you. That's all that matters. I've never seen you. So move."

"Let's go, fellas." And the large black man pulled on Dylan's shirt.

"No, no, get your goddamn hands off me. I know Ron. He told me to tell you that. So you're supposed to let me fucking in." Dylan shook himself. "What's your name?"

A beat, then, "William." Sniff.

"I'm gonna tell Ron about this, you fucking loser. You fucking joke. I'm gonna tell Ron and get you fired. See if you remember me then. See if you know me then. You tell me then if it was fucking worth it!"

And then the black bouncer grabbed Dylan by his shoulders and tossed him toward the street. Like a garbage man would toss garbage onto a garbage truck. Dylan crumpled heavily to the ground. As he tried to right himself, Dylan tripped over a few black trash bags that were waiting for the next morning's removal.

"You fucking loser," Dylan said as he stood up. And as he wiped his face he noticed his nose was bleeding. "Good job. You're doing real well for yourself." The half-Asian smiled. "Real fuckin' well. You should really be proud of all this," he said, and he wiped his nose with his shirtsleeve. "I'm sure your mother's somewhere smiling."

And Dylan wiped his face with a napkin he found on the street and then pushed it up his nostril to tamp it. He lit a cigarette as he walked away but then turned back and watched the fucking half-Asian loser let in the cute couple that had been standing behind him in line before.

SO HE'D FINISH his drugs elsewhere. His friend was embarrassed so he didn't come with. Dylan would find a dive. Somewhere without a door guy. Somewhere definitely without a door guy. The next morning he felt bad—felt awful—about what he'd done, and where his life was. How this stacked up against his prior rock bottoms. His hatred for himself was relentless. "Oh, Dylan," said Dylan. He'd hit a low. But that was just a chemical imbalance. Cocaine hangovers aren't any fun, you know. Or maybe you don't know. I guess that's possible. So I guess then trust me. You're just gonna have to trust me.

OUR TOWN

After what she considered a long and full repose, Dorothy decided it was time to go back to work. She didn't have much left after all the divorces and the moving and the surgeries. The booze, the pills, and the needles. And the everything else. The nameless everything else. The always and forever everything else. And so, on Wednesday, July 12, 1989, the fifty-year-old left her house and walked four blocks east to Flageolet, the local performance theater. Sponsored in part by the YWCA and run six days a week by a Frenchman and his age-less child—a sexually ambiguous, overlarge woman who dressed like a man—they were holding open auditions for a production of *Our Town*, which, as a film, was once Dorothy's favorite. She had a crush on William Holden. That dark skin and dark hair. The continental part. And those dimples. Stop. So she decided she'd do a play. She'd act, again. And this time might turn out different.

* * *

It was summer in Palm Springs—wind turbines, golf carts, visors, and pink flamingoes—and Do had just received a phone call from a man with a lady-voice who told her that she'd earned the role of the

Stage Manager. The Stage Manager? Fancy that. Given that the rest of the cast were locals, she'd gotten the part on résumé and reputation alone. They'd never had a real actress—former or not—so she'd earned the lead. The role she'd always wanted. She sat on her couch and watched TV, but that was making her dizzy. She wore Gary's tortoiseshell reading glasses, the only thing of his she'd kept. They bore Gary's strong prescription—8 by 7.5—but she didn't mind. They made the news anchors look fuzzy, but they really framed her face.

THE NEXT DAY, Dorothy arrived at the theater in overalls and freshly capped teeth. Rehearsal wasn't 'til three, so she had booked her dentist for the morning. The teeth were big and bright and whole. Big, juicy smile. She was her, again. She was happy. The rest of the cast stood fidgety outside the theater. The man playing George Gibbs dyed his hair too dark to look natural and had a lazy eye, but that was okay. At least he had hair. He turned, and they made eye contact, and then he walked toward her. She sat back and waited in reproach.

"I understand you're taking over the role of Stage Manager," he said as he arrived. "Brenda's done it for years, but between you and me that act's been getting pretty tired. I've never seen you around before. I mean, most of us are pretty regular. All of us, I guess. But, by the look of you, it seems that they've made an interesting choice."

Dorothy was five foot six inches. But five nine, wig included. He was an inch taller than she. Wrinkles crawled out from his eyes. Dorothy knew hard living—she, too, knew how hard it was—and he, too, was weathered—leathered—like a sea captain. His skin salt-crusted from years of sun and waves.

"Yeah. Yeah, I guess they did," she responded. Hopeful but unsure.

"Oh, I meant that as entirely complimentary. I did. I just meant that, with this one, they made a choice, for a change. They always just take whoever first auditions. But now this one might not be the same old story. This one might be different. And that's a good thing. I'm just happy there's new blood around here. I'm excited. I swear."

Dorothy was bashful, momentarily, but then fell back into being her.

"There's always a new girl," Dorothy winked. "Haven't you ever been to the movies?"

But then, suddenly, she was aware of her charm, and thus nervous to expose it. She looked down. She couldn't find her compact in her purse; she felt for her cigarettes. But they weren't there either. What the hell?

"I'm just happy they're making a change. I didn't know they made 'em like you anymore," he said and he put his thin hand out. His knuckles sprouted salt-and-pepper hairs. The drapes didn't seem to match the curtains. "I'm Marcus, by the way."

With this gesture she considered walking away—her instincts becoming more acute—but she liked his chin and his jawline and she was trying to be different, so she went against her gut. He was old-strong. Man-strong. Like her daddy was. Charlton Heston. She stared at his hand until she put hers out sideways, parallel to the sky. Dorothy found him endearing. She didn't care how hard he tried. Since she'd moved to Palm Springs she'd mostly stayed in. She got used to TV, and white wine, and filling her ashtray shaped like a ten-gallon hat. And Tinkerbell. She loved little Tinkerbell. Between her and Marcus, with whom she held hands, walked Bernard—the director, the Frenchman, and so they unclasped. People gathered around the three, but Bernard simply didn't want, yet, any extracurricular relationships to form—taskmaster that he was—and so he broke them up and walked toward the theater's entrance and waited for others to follow suit.

"Should we head in?" Dorothy asked

"Sure. Yeah, don't ya think?"

"Do you want to know my name?"

"Yes. Yes, definitely." He looked up from his feet. He wanted to stay in good standing with the director, but then suddenly didn't care. "I think I'd like that."

"It's Joanna-Rae."

She'd use Joanna here. Her birth name. She'd use Joanna-Rae here. She'd try something different. Here things would be different.

"Joanna-Rae. Well, that's wonderful. I'm Marcus. Marcus Scythe. It's very nice to meet you."

"I already knew that."

"Already knew what?"

"Your name. Your name, remember? You already told me."

"Oh, I actually think you're right. I apologize."

"But not your last name. You never told me that."

"That's true. It's Scythe."

"Scythe, huh? Like a knife?"

"Scythe like a knife. You got it. Spelled that way, too."

"Okay. I think I can remember that. I'm Joanna-Rae Cook. My name's Joanna-Rae Cook."

"Joanna-Rae Cook. You got it. I can remember that. That's pretty."

"You wanna go in?" she asked as she looked around and noticed others filing in. "I'm done jackpotting."

"Let's."

They walked and queued up behind at the door. She thought Dorothy was prettier than Joanna, in general, but Dorothy needed a rest. Dorothy was burnt out. The last time she was Joanna-Rae she was having sleepovers and drinking Nehis with her Coney Islands. She was learning geography in grade school with the rest of her class. She was wearing velvet and eating licorice and rice pudding and talking about boys. She was going to pre-proms and proms and post-proms. Back then it was all so easy.

THE DIRECTOR'S NAME was Bernard Boudreau. He had a round head and wore glasses. His beret covered one of his eyes. A red face from over-shaving. His shirt was green and his tie was beige and polka-dotted. His double-breasted, linen summer suit was beige, his fashion, clearly, an extension of his art. The cast was inside, sitting in the audience. Bernard was onstage. He took off his jacket and hung it on the back of his folding chair. *Very* dramatically. Really stretched it out. Real thespian stuff. Actors, you know? Enough already. He sat down and put his elbows on his knees. He rested his forehead in his palms. His tie hung between his quadriceps.

"It's good to have everyone here, today. It's good to see everybody." He pulled his beret down closer to his nose at a diagonal so one eye was entirely covered and his hat's bottom tip was close to his chin. Two-faced. "Where to begin, where to begin. Dorothy, you're new. Why don't you start? Let's start with your opening monologue?"

French Canadian accent. Again, high drama. The thespian way.

Dorothy immediately didn't like taking her orders from this director. It seems she had a problem with authority.

"Joanna-Rae."

"Hmm?"

"It's Joanna-Rae."

"It is? Well, it says right here that we have a Dorothy playing the role of Stage Manager. Is that not you? If they screwed up this damned call sheet again I—"

"No. No, it's Dorothy but it's also Joanna. Joanna is me, too. I just want you to call me Joanna, if that's okay. I'm trying something."

"Okay, Dorothy. Okay. Well, can we begin then? And can someone please fix this damn sheet then? I don't have a pen."

She walked up the aisle and onto the two steps to the stage. She walked to the middle of the floorboards and looked out onto the audience. She stood there, about to begin her monologue, but instead looked up at the set lights that hung down above her. They were opera lights, pleasantly blinding. Dorothy was spotlit like she hadn't been in years. And that light reminded her of a time she guest-starred for a three-episode arc on M*A*S*H. The lights on that set were different—more archaic, like her—but they were the same sort of blinding. They provided the same sort of attention. They allowed the same sort of attention. The same sort of an inability to see. It was that lack of vision that allowed her to stop thinking. Stop thinking, and worrying, about what she was supposed to do. It was that lack of vision that allowed her what she remembered as perhaps the best performance of her career. As good as she could do. As good as she could possibly do. Without her eyes, and thus her memory, she could just react to those around her. And then, suddenly, she was just herself. She wouldn't pretend anymore. She trusted her instincts, truly, for the first time in remembered history, and then those that acted with her followed suit. And she listened, instead of waiting for her turn to speak. Maybe if she'd trusted people, from the beginning, then she wouldn't have turned out this way. But she'd been fucked too much to think that anyone was really—really, actually—good. Deep-down good. She thought back on her time with Alan Alda. She was so pretty then. And then she thought of herself, now—diasporated, an upside-down version of what she used to be. Since she'd stopped working, for reasons that the tabloids were unable to ascertain, she'd been empty. Especially since they took her littles away. That cored her. But today, as she stood under floodlights that made her vision blurry and her body sweat—she didn't sweat anymore from pharmaceuticals—she felt full again. Tired maybe—a little hung over—but certainly not empty. Not alone. And she'd pull, from deep within herself, a real voice. She'd be herself. Born in Georgia. Miss Americus. A model and an actress. A wife and a mama. A woman. A woman, for the first time on her own.

She'd been onstage for upward of six minutes, staring straight up, and she hadn't said a word. But her castmates and director watched intently. Her unusual intensity made them think that the pause was a part of her method.

* * *

Dylan works in a bar. Twenty-seven now, he still shaves his head. There's a girl he likes there. A pretty girl, named Clementine. He's a barback, she's a hostess. Greets people as they come in. One Friday night, Dylan's shift ended at 3:30 A.M. They didn't need him anymore, they said. You can go. But he hadn't eaten dinner, so he sat at a table alone and ate a salad and bread and olive oil and drank two large beers and a whiskey with his pain medicine. He'd fallen, once, carrying boxes moving, and he'd been prescribed pain medication, to manage his pain. A large bottle of Vicodin. With refills. And it was easy, too.

LA doctors. By this point he'd begun to take two before he arrived at work—two during—and then two more when he got off. Symmetry was very important to him, you know. He was always counting. And he drank when he got off because he needed to swallow his job. And he needed to forget—he didn't care for being talked down to—and he didn't know how else to do so. He always had one too many. Maybe a few. On top of everything else, especially. The combinations were what usually did him in.

When he was done, he left. He opened the door to the bar's staff exit. But before he punched his clock-out card.

Time In: 3:58 PM
Time Out: 4:33 AM

He stepped out into the dark, and the September rain stuck in his nostrils as he sucked in, and he snapped awake, but then took another step, and he noticed the coming light. Anxious, exhausted, with whiskey still in his mouth, he tingled with opiated joy. He took four tonight, because two times two is four, and that made sense, and this was that sort of night, and so this was what he needed. The sun loomed just below the horizon, but the early Sunday streets were still muddled with leftovers from the night before—mostly the ones who were still high and were, therefore, out of cigarettes. Dylan stepped on an empty, licked-clean-dry plastic bag—square, a half-inch wide and thick—and it stuck to his wet, black boot as he made his way toward home. He didn't have a car. He'd totaled his last one. Before that, DUIs. He tried to zip his green bomber tighter, but it was already full closed. These days he walked home. He lived close enough. But he didn't have an umbrella. His jacket began to soak through, and his pants and his feet were getting swampy. He needed a cab tonight. He just needed to get home. He needed something warm. His bed, maybe. Maybe more. He pulled his hood over his head.

He walked down the dark street. Only one streetlight—an oddity in LA, but Dyl did this on purpose. He knew those streets well. He knew where reality cracked through the shiny, sunny, snow-globe sheen that facelifts, and hiking, and auditions provide. That tummy tucks, and chardonnay, and perfect weather do. That Thai massages, and Catalina, and Jacuzzis let you have. And sunblock, and rhinoplasty, and surfing let you be. He knew how to look past that—past those people. Through them, he saw the fringes of the world, and he found comfort there. Drugs helped with this. Often made people ugly. Just last year he'd lost his first tooth to meth. The fringe—the heroin addicts splitting their sandwich with their dogs, the waiters that gave up on acting—the moment when they realize that they'll be refilling water glasses forever, and how that often pairs well with them losing their hair—and the misery that's the rest of it. A misery you could eat off their cracking chins. And the musicians that became roadies, and the car guys that worked at the Valero. The father with nine kids, seven moms, and a factory job. The after-college kids waiting for the bars to wake up at seven, up all night doing cocaine—the blues in their eyes too blue, the whites in their eyes too long. These people made him comfortable. These people didn't just live. These people felt, and made him feel. The fringe was his family. And he didn't put parameters on his family—he let them be them. He knew they'd fuck up, and so he could count on them for that. They were reliable, and his love for them existed without condition. They were all he ever wanted—scumming was all he ever wanted—and they only wanted him. Everyone else is just too sunny. Too sunny to find anything to do. Everyone else's sandals—how can a man wear sandals?—and tans, and hair—you're supposed to fry out your hair—got in the way of their hustle. They walked too slow, and drove too slow. Freeways. Too slow. They lived. That's it. They didn't even know what hustle meant. They could never survive here. They could never survive with us. Why the fuck are you next to us? He hated them. And they hated him, too—or perhaps, more aptly, didn't notice him—which is why he lived here, with his kin—guala— and does, until this is finally over.

And now he walks there, past the one streetlight, the only one that worked. He walked past two bars—Homer's and Mac the Knife! They were closing up so their lights were lit on high, and their staff was drunk and high and smiling. A few had their shirts off. Past the bars was a green-painted apartment stoop. Curled up to its right was a local homeless, Butch. Butch used to come into the bar and ask for soup. He'd salute the manager and say he was a veteran of two foreign wars. He'd say we owed him. But the manager said they weren't allowed to feed him. For legal reasons, or company policy. At least that's how Dylan understood it. The manager was hard to hear. Or hard to understand, actually. Dylan walked past Butch and noticed a rusty syringe near Butch's feet, which hung out past the stoop. With his wet leather boot, Dylan kicked it out of his way into a drain grate—Butch seemed to have had enough—and then kept walking.

He waited for the crossing light to change from red to green. His pants were now soaked through. And his underwear was making him chafe. And his toes were wet. And he hated it.

He thought maybe he'd call the hostess when he got home. They'd already fucked. Maybe she could come over. She had light hair, too. They could be together and sleep close and then wake up early in the morning. They could wake up face-to-face. Even though he was tired from working. But he had the day off tomorrow, and maybe she was free, too. And they could go to brunch. They'd have Bloody Marys. He knew a place. And hold hands as they walked back home. And then they could have dinner. And more drinks. And maybe she'd stay again. And again and again. And then he'd be happy.

He reached Santa Monica Boulevard, entirely wet through, and the light turned green. He walked halfway across the street—Santa Monica has four lanes, with a tree line down a center island, parting them, and benches for people to sit on—but, really, who wants to sit in the middle of the street? Dylan, tonight, didn't want to be alone. He was hurt, and his hurt made him scared, and his scared made him feel, and he felt lonely. Dylan liked to be alone—or he told himself that—'cause he grew up alone. He wandered about the house, then the school. Then the city, then the world, and he just wanted to feel better. Eventually he just wanted to feel. His dad paid for his lawyers if he got arrested, when he got arrested. And for acting classes—he wouldn't go, but he thought the idea might make Dad happy. The "creative" career path tends to lower expectations. And Mom left, but she did that even when she was around. And then Clover. Fuck Clover. But he didn't have to be alone tonight. He'd be home in ten minutes. He could change and get into something comfortable. And he'd wait for Clementine. He'd be nervous. So he'd drink some more. Maybe take some more. But when she got there he'd be okay. When she got there he'd be okay.

He saw the orange light flash, and he looked left, then right, like Mama always taught him, so then he kept walking.

But, as he stepped off the one-foot cement ledge, just as the light finally turned, he heard tires squealing to his right, trying to grip the wet, grease-soaked pavement. The car attempted to beat the light but failed. The driver obviously wanted to get home quickly, too. He must have been antsy. Something important must be waiting for him. Maybe he had a long night. Maybe he had a pretty girlfriend.

HE LAY ON the ground staring up at the sky, blinking repeatedly to get the rain sting from his pupils. His body shook with fear as he sucked in breath. He was soaked in adrenaline. Oh yeah, and drugs. He was suddenly warm. He could feel the heat in his belly, and it crawled out into his hands and then his fingers. His knees and then his toes. His neck and his shoulders. But it was the hottest in his cracked ribs. He pulled his arm out from under him and held it above his eyes. He could move his thumb and index finger. His *fuck you* finger and his pointer. His pinky, even. But not his wrist. He blinked more. He pulled his hand in closer. Pieces of glass and spit and pavement stuck to his palm. He pulled his other arm out and tried to brush the debris off but it was dug in. He stared and stared. It was hot in his eyes now. And not just from the rain sting. He stared more and kept his arm steady. To see if it was okay and because it blocked the rain. He heard a door open to his right. A black car had stopped in front of him, with its red hazard lights flashing like a lighthouse. Cars and trucks still flew by in the other lanes around him, but his lane was blocked. He heard honking and confusion. He turned toward the car and his face fell in a puddle. His neck cracked and his head was heavy. At the bottom of the puddle he saw one of his teeth. A molar.

Then a waifish man stepped out from his black sedan and walked toward the front of his car.

"Oh my God," he yelled. "Baby, get out here."

A bleached-bobbed blonde in a mini and red shoes joined him and they both put their hands to their mouths. The car's hood was dented, flat through, and the brittle windshield was splintered. Spider-webbed, but still connected to its frame.

The driver leaned in on his girlfriend. He looked at Dylan and then at his car and then at her. "What should we do?" he whispered. But Dylan heard.

"I don't know," she said. They both stood still as the rain continued drip drip dropping.

"Should we just go?" he responded nervously.

"No. Go see if he's okay." She shook her head. Then stopped. "I mean, he's awake, right? I saw him moving. I think he's okay. I bet he's okay."

"Fine," he sighed. "Get back in the car."

"You know I didn't . . ."

"Just get back in the fucking car, okay? Jesus."

She wandered back to the passenger seat and slammed the door behind her.

The driver stood and stared awhile longer, staring at his windshield. Then at Dylan. Then the hood. It began to rain harder. And then even harder still. Finally, the driver walked toward Dylan. He stepped steady, in reproach. He put his hands on his knees and leaned over. He tried to stand steady. But his equilibrium was certainly—most certainly—compromised, to say the least.

"You all right, man?"

Dylan hadn't tried moving his legs yet. So he tried. He kicked his right foot. Then lifted his left ankle. He leaned up on his spine and pulled his neck out of the puddle. His hair was dirt-water soaked through.

"I think so," Dylan said. He grabbed his knees and pulled himself forward and hugged himself. The driver got behind him and pushed him up. And Dylan stood, but his legs were shaky and he felt unsure, so he stumbled toward the car and leaned against the rattled Saab. And, from the LED light inside the interior, Dylan looked at the driver. For the first time. He saw his skinny suit and his skinny tie. His straightened, jet-blacked hair. The tear penned under his eye, most certainly based on his penchant for new romanticism when he felt down. He saw the steel-silver earrings in his ears and the tattoos across his knuckles. *SELF-MADE.* He saw his gaunt and pockmarked face and his running eyeliner. And his thin chin and thin nose and sideburns. Jewish looking, too. A *band guy*, Dylan thought. A *fucking band guy*. Dylan grabbed his stomach and leaned forward. The driver held him up. With his head down, Dylan saw his pointy shoes.

"You sure you're all right, man?"

He leaned forward and Dylan smelled his breath. He stunk like gin. He stunk like tonic.

"Yeah," Dylan replied, trying to right himself. His ribs and wrist and face still pulsing. But nothing hurt. Everything was glowing. Like he was high. Which he'd forgot he was. Dylan breathed and breathed and then tried walking.

"Are you positive? Can I at least give you a ride home?"

"No, no," Dylan said, and fell forward. "I wanna try and walk."

Dylan tumbled toward a payphone. But he didn't have any quarters. He pulled three dollars from his soiled pocket, and he got twelve coins from a twenty-four-hour deli. The Indian behind the counter handed him the quarters slowly. Before he fell back in the booth, he saw the Saab drive away, the driver's head out his driver's-side window like a thirsty sheepdog. Dylan leaned next to the black plastic phone box and onto the silver poles that held it up. He thought of the numbers he knew by heart. He pushed the stiff, silver wire to the side and then picked up the handset. He inserted a quarter and dialed. A voice monotoned that it cost another. Area code's too far away.

His mom didn't answer. Voice mail. Ten quarters. He called again. She didn't answer. Voice mail. Eight. And again. She didn't answer. Voice mail. Six. Again. Didn't answer. Again voice mail. Four. So he tried his dad. More local. But he didn't answer either. Three. And voice mail. And again. Two. And again, voice mail. Even his sister, and they didn't talk, but he didn't have enough to make it cross-country. But it ate his money anyway. One left. One. It was too late. He didn't blame them. But he didn't know anyone else's number. He leaned back on the silver phone booth. A piece of pink gum stuck to his back. He reached back and pulled it off and then slunk down to his knees. Maybe he could just try to find a cab home. But what if he wasn't okay? It was hard to tell, really. He noticed a soaking-wet, overused advertisement. *Dudes with a Van Movers: We're cheap cuz we're just like you.* He checked the coin return slot for any extra change. There wasn't any.

DON'T MESS WITH THE MAYOR

But Dylan remembered that once—before—Clementine had sat down at the bar when she'd finished her hostess shift. She had a few drinks. Dylan gave them to her for free, even though he wasn't allowed to do so. He'd risk his job for her. Who wouldn't? When she wanted to leave, in place of a check, Dylan left her an empty piece of paper clipped to a postcard—*Greetings From Sunny Los Angeles: Find Yourself Here!*—so she'd be surprised that he bought them for her. And she smiled, and Dylan went to the bathroom. But when he came back she was gone. When Dylan, disheartened, went to throw her check away, he noticed she'd written him a note.

D,
You're cute. Call me. (XXX) XXX-XXXX
C.

Dylan had had her number already from work. And she knew that. But she knew he was old-fashioned. And he loved her for that. So he'd saved it. He kept it in his wallet. He reached into his back pocket and took it out and he used the last of his quarters. And he called her. And she picked up.

"Hello?" she said. Surprised, not tired. Not much able to sleep. Back then she partied.

"Hi," Dylan replied. "Hi."

* * *

When Dorothy got home that afternoon, Tinkerbell ran to the door and started scratching. Dorothy turned the key, and Tinky jumped and jumped. As she swung it open, Tinky stood on his hind legs, and gnawed at Do's pants. She liked the name Tinkerbell, even though he was a boy. He looked like a Tinkerbell. He was cute—blond, and teeny-tiny, like a pixie—and she always wanted a Tinkerbell. What's emasculating to a dog, anyway? What does he know? She thought maybe she was even being progressive. She might even be doing some good. Anyhow, she picked him up and put him under her left arm. She brought him to the couch. Tinky lay down on his back. Dorothy ran her hand across his stomach, and felt his pinky belly with the tips of her fingers. Then she lifted him above her head, and his front arms came together, and his back feet split apart, and he froze. A tripod, too scared to try and move. She shook him and his tongue fell out. She got bored and let him go. He dropped by her on his side, rolled and jumped off the couch—over his initial excitement to see her—and sat on his bed—a blue blanket, folded four times over—in the corner of the kitchen. She brought her fingers to her nose and sniffed—garbage and graham crackers. Dorothy walked to the fridge.

"My little seal," she said. "My beautiful seal needs a bath," she trailed off. Tink was already sleeping. He didn't hear. She put her head in the fridge. Clover had refused to spring for central air. "My beautiful seal needs a bath," she said again. "My beautiful seal needs a bath, and so do I."

She opened a diet soda—maybe a Tab—took a sip and put the can to her head. The phone, which sat by the white couch, then rang. And rang and rang. She rushed and got it before the answering machine.

"Yello?"

"Mom. Mama. It's me. It's Clover."

She coughed before she answered. She hadn't heard from Clover in months. Clover was busy now. She had herself a seven-year-old boy—who she dressed in velvet, like a doll. Dorothy had called Clover last night and left her a message, and Clover heard something different in Mama's voice. She sounded good, which was hard for Clover to admit. She sounded happy, which is almost impossible to say. She sounded like she was telling the truth. And Clover knew when she was telling the truth. Even over the phone she knew if she was telling the truth. It was something in her cadence. Something in her throat. Something in her husk that Clover could pick up on. Something that Clover could always pick up on. An instinct that had never failed to disappoint Clover, even though the truth often disappointed Clover. But today. But today. Dorothy had always tried to be something different than she really was—always trying to reinvent herself. I guess maybe she'd finally given up.

"Clover. Oh my God, it's you! You're calling," she said and picked up her pack of cigarettes and lit one with a white lighter. "I didn't think you had this number. I left it on all your machines, but you know I don't trust those things. Don't trust them for a minute. But I haven't spoken to you in forever. How are you, my most beautifullest daughter? My only daughter. My love. How are you?"

There was a momentary pause on the line. Clover had put the handset by her side. It was difficult for Clover to hear Dorothy, even on the phone. Dorothy spoke loudly. But that wasn't it. Dorothy was Clover's mother. And she worried she'd turn out just the same.

"Oh, I'm good, Mama. I've been good. Busy, you know. Jack's always playing or practicing, so it's just me and little Jr. Me and the little one. But it's okay. You know. Things are okay."

"That's amazing, my sweet. That is just amazing. That little angel. I can't even tell you how good that makes me feel. You know, I really can't even tell you with my voice. I really, really could just cry and cry. Cry and cry and cry."

"Oh, Mom. Relax, will you?"

"Oh, sweetheart, I'm relaxed, sweetheart." She couldn't find an ashtray so she ashed in her Tab. She'd bought a case of them. One could be spared. "You know I'm relaxed. How is he, anyway? How is my gorgeous grandson? I feel like it's been a year since I've seen him."

After she said this, she counted backward in her head. It had, in fact, been fifteen months.

"He's great. He's really great, actually. He's very handsome."

"Oh God, that's just terrific. I can't even tell you how good that makes me feel."

"Yeah. Yeah, I guess it is."

"He's got good genes, baby. Of course he's handsome."

"Yeah."

"You're not still dressing him like a sissy, are you?" Dorothy barked.

"Oh, Mother. Stop."

"I'm just saying. You know how I am. I'm just saying a little boy should dress like a little boy, that's all. He just had all that hair the last time I saw him. I'm not saying anything bad."

"Mom, I'll hang up."

"Oh, don't, honey. I'm sorry. Please, honey. I really am. I'll stop. I promise I'll stop."

Dorothy whimpered. She could hear Clover breathing heavily on the phone. The way she did when she napped as a child. When she thought she was alone.

"Well, how are you, Mom, anyway?"

"I'm good. I feel good for a change."

"Well that's great, Mom."

"Yeah, I mean, I auditioned for a play. That made me happy. Or actually I'm just gonna do it. They just gave me the part. And I think I have a crush on a boy. That's been sort of fun," she said, and she took an accomplished pull of her cigarette. "Yeah, really sort of fun."

"You're trying to work again?" Clover questioned her. "Wow."

"Yeah, baby. I thought I would. Nothing serious, or paying or anything. Just local theater. But yeah. I thought I'd try."

"Well that's real good, Mom. Crazy, kind of. I mean, at this point—"

"What is that supposed to mean? Why would you say that? I mean, what do you want me to be some lonesome—"

"No, no. Nothing, Mama. I didn't mean anything by it. I just meant you just moved up there. I just meant you just moved up there is all."

"Yeah, whatever. I just don't know why you'd—"

"Oh, Jesus. Stop already, would ya? What sort of boy? How old is he?"

"He's old. He's older, like me. I just met him today," she said and pulled at her cigarette and blew out slowly, so as to make her daughter wait. "He dyes his hair too dark. He's not fooling anyone. But he was sweet, and sort of pathetic. I think he's fond of your mother, though. That felt nice."

"That's great, Mom."

"How's Dyl? I haven't spoken to him in forever."

"Who knows? It's hard to get in touch with him. I'm pretty sure he's struggling."

Indeed he was.

"Oh, my boy. I do love my boy. I hope he's okay."

"It's like you have to remind yourself."

"What?"

"Nothing."

"Yeah, well I—"

Clover interrupted. She had to.

"Listen, Mom. Listen. The reason I'm calling you back is I've been thinking recently. I've been thinking a lot. And I think you should see him. I think you should try to be a part of little Jack's life. I mean, I think we should really make an effort—a concerted effort—to get you to be here for him. And me. He asked me about you."

"He did? He asked about me? Why?"

"I don't know why. But he did," she said, and she waited for a moment and put the handset on her thigh. She didn't want to hear her mother breathing. But then she gathered her thoughts and put the phone back on her ear. "Yeah, he did. He asked about you. And I didn't know what to say."

As a tear rolled down Dorothy's face, she reached to wipe it away with her left hand, but as it passed her nose she smelled Tinky, and her sadness quickly dried.

"You really mean that? I mean, sweetheart, you'd really want me to do that? All the way up here?"

"Well, yeah. I know we're far, but I've got a friend who lives up near you and I was thinking I'd come stay for a few days. Maybe a week even. Would that be okay, Mama? In a few weeks? I was thinking in a few weeks."

"Really, Clover? Really? God, I'd love it. You know I'd love it. I'd love it more than anything. I'd love it more than the earth, the moon, the sun, and the stars."

"Oh, Mom, Jesus. Stop being so dramatic."

"I mean it, baby. And don't be mean to me about my words. I'll love that little boy more than anything. I love him more than anything. I promise. I don't mean to soliloquize but—"

"I know, Mama. I know you mean it."

"You do?"

"Yeah, Mama, I do. I mean, you are his Nana, aren't you?"

"Yeah, I guess I am."

"You are. You have to know you are."

"Well then, I'm his Nana. I'm his Nana. I know I'm his Nana."

* * *

When Dylan finally went to jail—DUIs, and then finally when his girlfriend Clementine tried to leave him so he shot out her tires, so she was stuck—he didn't feel safe. It wasn't a long stay—a month, maybe— but when he came back from the detention center he had a swastika tattoo on his torso. He'd been getting beat up and The Aryan Nation were the only ones who would accept him. He thought they looked cool, too. The leader of the group—they called him "The Mayor"—had forced him to get it, and then he promised they'd protect him. He scratched it into his chest with a blue ballpoint pen.

HIGH NOON

Five weeks later, in preparation for her daughter's visit, Dorothy drove to Albertsons to buy a turducken. This was Clover's favorite meal as a child. Dorothy would cook for Clover when she'd come back for supervised visits. Then, she was only allowed to come twice a month. Dorothy tried her best to make these visits special. She made turducken every other time. Switched off between that and taco salad. And Clover always pretended to like it.

But when Dorothy got in the car to go to the supermarket, it was past five, and she'd been drinking, like she did. And she made it along for a while, too. Down sandy Bob Hope Drive—she lived on Varner. Wrong turn on Frank Sinatra. She turned back around. She had to go to Albertsons, in the desert, about twenty minutes away—off Fred Waring—because they had the best produce. She'd also made friends with the cashier, also Sandy, who was young and pretty with braces and shiny hair and skin like the sun. "You can fry an egg out there, huh, gorgeous?" Dorothy didn't respond. "I'm just sayin' it's hot, honey. Anyway, paper or plastic for your thangs?" Dorothy described the heat that way—her heat, her surroundings—for the whole of her life. "You can fry an egg out there," she'd say. "Right there on the sidewalk." She turned onto Portola. She had to go backward in order to get back the right way. Left on Country Club. Dorothy noticed the high-up mountains. Right on Monterrey. She looked past the signs. She looked past the palm trees—transplants, anyway, and the too-green shrubs. Past the telephone polls and condominiums, where the pools were the same temperature as the sky. And past the cacti and the ever-vast sand and the tumbleweeds, which she still couldn't believe were real. Which she still couldn't believe were everywhere. Sorta like in the movies. *High Noon* comes to mind. Then past the "desert modern" homes and chain-link stores and restaurants—all beige, forever beige—and past the churches—"modern" churches— one on every corner, the sort of place where the preacher might wear a shirt and tie tucked into his blue jeans, his belt buckle as shiny as his hair. As shiny as his boots. As shiny as his complexion. As shiny as his truth. And past the vast desert ocean. And then finally past the heat. That she could see in the air. That gave the ocean waves and microwaved her vision, blurring and glowing her view. Like a going grill does to a pool, and its inhabitants, as they enjoy drinks in coconut-shaped glasses and laugh with their heads back and wear sunglasses in the water even though they know they'd get wet. She looked up to where the sky kissed the mountains and the clouds looked like they were happy, too. She saw the hills' dark green apex and the trails hikers hiked on. And the water towers and the trailers where nearby people lived. They didn't wanna be found. She saw the umber of the terrain and she felt it burn beneath her feet. And she saw two rams, with long, round horns, meeting each other just past a crag and staring into each other—thinking of the damage they could both do if they put their heads down—and live up to their God- given names, and feel they were justified—but they decided against it. Deciding not to fight, they moved forward, cautiously, hoof before hoof, and pressed their faces against the others. They trotted over the mountainscape in tow, together, and found shade from the baking, draining, egg-frying sun beneath an overhanging rock. That pro- tected the stream, perpetually, and they both drank it, and drank it, and drank it, until they felt better, too.

CLOVER CAME TO visit her mother in the hospital. She came to hold the mirror. Dorothy wanted to see her face. Clover tried to pick up Dylan on the way, but he wouldn't leave his house. She knocked and knocked, but he wouldn't come out. A pregnant black woman was smoking menthols on his porch. She told Clover that he wouldn't come outside. That he'd been awake a week and that he'd grown paranoid. That he'd been hiding in the bathroom, and when he did come out all he wore was a shower curtain. And that there was a possibility, and it was in fact likely, that he'd have with him a handgun. Perhaps two. But now he was sleeping. Clover knocked once more, but decided it wasn't worth it. She tacked a message to his door, then left.

You're a fucking loser. Come visit Mom at the hospital,
when, or if, you ever wake up.

Clover sat by her mother's side alone for a few days while Dorothy watched soaps and smoked menthols and recovered. She'd lost two fingers in the accident and she'd killed her little dog. The third day Clover was there, they got a call at the hospital from a police officer. He said he'd just arrested a man who was coming to see her. That man claimed to be her son. She put the phone on speaker.

"What's he been arrested for?" they asked in unison.

"He was driving on the highway," the officer replied, "and he ran his truck into an off-ramp. But he wasn't injured."

"Thank God," they replied.

"But when we walked over to his car," he said, "it was crushed. It was totaled. We leaned down and peeked inside, wherein we found your son."

He paused.

"And?"

"He was naked, behind the wheel, which was pretty strange. Completely soused, too. Naked on the road. But at least he was wearing his seatbelt."

"But why was he naked? Did you ask him?"

Again, in unison.

"I did ask him."

"And?"

"He said he was hot."

WHEN CRANES DANCED

Clover cried like a little baby girl when she lost her Mama. She had a relapse—coke, I think. Maybe OxyContin. Maybe both, after overtaking one in an attempt to balance out, but whatever. It's really all the same. It all just keeps going. Hope and hope swallowed. Swallowed, then swallowed again. Before that, though, while Dorothy was in the hospital following the accident, they realized she had lung cancer as they tended to her wounds. Her diagnosis was thenceforth bleak. She refused chemotherapy, so she went fast. She died in October of 1990, at the age of fifty-one, and Clover was the only one there. Dylan never made it—he couldn't make bail. He was still in jail from the wreck. He'd defended himself at the hearing and his statement that, due to his truck's faulty air conditioner and his genetically inherited tendency toward heat-born "spells"—which would explain both his loss of control of the vehicle and thus his indisposition—was unable to be sold to the judge. Nor his father, whose embarrassment in his son made not paying to bail him out—to not allow him to go to his mother's funeral—both scrupulous—Dale's unwavering integrity still very much intact—as well as fiscally responsible.

Dale would eventually weep at Dorothy's funeral. He would walk to the podium, head down, shoulder's lowered, and then eventually raise his hands up to the sky. "*Why*, God? *Why?*" he yelled, and then sobbed, putting his right hand out before him, gesturing that those were the only words he could muster, his tears bleeding into his thin goatee, nearly full enough to cover the incision scar on his chin from his facelift. But his gesture felt like no more than that, so nobody there quite believed him. Like I said, he was never much of an actor.

Just before she died, though, Dorothy asked Clover for another cigarette, and Clover gave it to her. She'd parceled them out like dog treats. For good behavior. "Only one every few hours," she'd told her. "Otherwise you might get sick." And she'd stuck to it—to her plan—but she couldn't stop her all the way. She just wanted Mama to be happy. She couldn't let her go with a long face.

"Mama's on her way," she said to her daughter, as she looked wistfully through the window and down the sunset's blue. "Give me a minute, would ya please? I just want a minute with my maker."

So Clover went to the bathroom. She wanted to freshen up. But when Clover came back, Mama'd put a gram of cocaine—cooked down with a lighter from her purse in the rounded, mirror side of a sunset-blue old compact—into the IV bag that was connected to her arm. That was keeping her alive. Who knows where she got it from. Maybe she paid off a paramedic. That made her have a seizure. Then cardiac arrest. But when Clover came back she wasn't having a seizure anymore.

And that was it.

* * *

Before all that, though—maybe a month before, probably, just after the accident, just before the cancer forced her from her home—Clover brought over Jack Jr. and Dorothy babysat while Clover saw old friends. Clover felt comfortable and confident that her Mama would be okay with her son. She didn't know why, she just felt it. For the first time she just felt it. Clover knew that this would mean a lot to her Mama. Clover knew that Mama might not have much time left after the accident. And Clover knew, even though it made her nervous, that this was the right thing to do.

Then, though, Clover came back from her friend's house. She sat with her Mama at the kitchen table. Jack Jr. played outside in the yard. Clover told Mama how great it was to see her friends. How she hadn't seen them in years. How it felt good to catch up. Dorothy sat across from her. She'd prepared two Arnold Palmers, and they both drank them and enjoyed them, even though the ice in their glasses had melted and they were watered down. Then Clover asked how it was watching Jr. and Dorothy replied it went swell. Then Clover told her Mama that it was great to see her, too. How she didn't like waiting this long between visits. How much she'd missed her, and how happy she was that Mama had gotten to be a nana. And Dorothy smiled and showed her big white teeth and looked down at her feet and then up at her daughter, and she was bashful, and she was shy. And they were both happy. But then Clover had to go. She took little Jack Jr. and they got in her car and drove back to the airport and then back home. The flight home felt shorter than the one she came out on. Maybe she was more at ease. But maybe it was just the air stream.

WHEN CLOVER GOT home she kept it up. At this point it was hard to care. This was a cheap relapse. A real relapse. She wanted to get dirt high. Ugly high. Not like pills, which she could always rationalize. Those were necessary. Her doctor told her so. Those were for her overwhelmingly paralyzing anxiety. Her doctor told her so. Otherwise they wouldn't have been prescribed. She had to treat her pain—physical and emotional—as well as the other various ailments from which she suffered so. But this wasn't that. This time she'd get dark with it. She'd test herself. Push as hard as she could. She'd overdosed before and survived. And, anyway, who gives a shit, right? She has a disease. She doesn't have a choice. This isn't up to her. This is just protocol.

And so she went downtown to buy crack where she used to. To the East Village. Anywhere on Avenue C. She asked a Spanish kid at a bodega if he knew where she could score. He said he could help, but he came back in a police car, as he happened to be an off-duty cop. So she got arrested. And when Jack found out he left her. He thought when they got married she'd left that behind her. Sympathy was never his forte. So he left her and he took Jack Jr., too. And Clover fought for little Jack Jr. And she saw him when she could. And she tried her hardest to be a good mama—she had so much love to give—but something in her never let her quite do so. Something inherent seemed to paralyze her belief that she could do so. She just couldn't get out of her own way.

* * *

Dylan, later, was coming home from his dad's house on the bus. He saw him sometimes when he needed money. He'd gotten fired from his job, and Clementine went back home to live with her parents. And then he got another girlfriend, and he got her pregnant, and he had a kid. But it turned out he wasn't a good daddy either. Once he tried to become a Scientologist, noticing that that's what seemed to be a prerequisite for financial success in Hollywood, but once he couldn't make the payments—sorry, "donations"—he was no longer allowed a seat in the service pew.

DYLAN GOT OFF at his stop. And again he got off at his stop. Different houses, different buses, but Dylan, now, only went to work, and then took to the bus, and then got off at his stop. Perpetually got off at his stop. There were more women, and more kids—three girls, two boys, four mothers—but he didn't much care. He wasn't particularly interested. He wasn't a family type of guy. When he got home, he snorted a roxy—30 mg. rapid-release oxycodone. A blue—slipped disk and another slipped disk, all sorts of different doctors. And enjoyed a Coors, poured deftly into a tall, chilled glass and watched the History Channel.

* * *

Known today as pulmonary tuberculosis, consumption was referred to as such, in antiquity, because it seemed to consume people from within, from bloody cough, fever, pallor, and long, relentless wasting. In the early twentieth century, some believed TB to be caused by masturbation.

Before the Industrial Revolution, consumption—tuberculosis—was sometimes regarded as vampirism. When one member of a family died from it, the other members who were infected would lose their health slowly. People believed that this was caused by the original victim draining the life from the other family members.

TB—consumption—was romanticized in the nineteenth century. It was believed that TB sufferers acquired a final burst of energy, just before they died, that produced feelings of euphoria and a final burst of energy and life. This phenomenon was referred to as spes phthisica, or "the hope of the consumptive."

THE HOPE OF THE CONSUMPTIVE

"Baby, don't ever smoke ever ever," Dorothy spoke to him softly but nervous. "Worst things in the world for ya," she said like she would to a suitor—coquettish—she didn't know any other way. We've at least learned that already—and then paused to kiss the lipstick-stained, barely burning Virginia Slim—here, still, Virginia Slims; she ended with Virginia Slims—she just finished to the still pearly-white one hanging from the end of her mouth. Tobacco spit stained her long, painted, pointed nails, but the rest of her was done up proper. She'd taken time to get ready for the occasion. She liked the opportunity to play dress-up, and she was aware this was potentially her last. And she was right about that. "Smokin's the worst thing ever," she whispered, again, breathing earl-gray colored breath through her nose, like the world's most prettiest dragon.

When Nana—henceforth she'll be Nana, Jack Jr. doesn't know any better, so henceforth she won't be judged—wasn't smoking, her breath was pulled and dry and heavy, and her Georgia-anxious cackle turned quickly to a cough, but with a thin cigarette hanging from her three-inch nails, or at the corner of her blood-stained lips, Nana was lovely again, and capable—capable enough for this, anyway—like cigarettes were invented just for her. Like when she wasn't smoking she couldn't really breathe, a thought she both had as a lark and a reality due to her continually closing, cancer-shorn esophagus. "Like when fishermen drop their fish back in the water after they catch them," the boy thought, still young enough to believe that this was the life of a fisherman. Because out of water, fish cough and fight and squirm, attempting to escape the body bestowed upon them. Out of water, fish hate themselves and struggle, unable to ascertain the meaning of their own existence, or really of anything at all. But in water, fish were lovely—fish were home—like water was invented just for them. At one point in Jack Jr.'s life he will become jaded and distant. He'll smoke, and he'll hate himself for it. He'll become aware that the world around him and the people who populate that landscape—this landscape—tend to disappoint. But not her. She never disappointed him. Even if he had to patch her life together—even as its threads, often, fell apart in his fingers, she never disappointed him. Even if he had to make it up—especially if he had to make it up—she never disappointed him. No matter what, he understood that they had something in common. That they were both alive and they knew what living meant. That they were together. That they were real. That this is real. In the end, he was her. She was him and he was her. And that's all that ever mattered. That's all this was and will be. That's all that this is about. But he's not there yet. Thus far, in his short life, he just likes to be outside—in the day—and he just likes things that are pretty. And he thinks his Nana is the prettiest thing he's ever seen. He thinks his Nana's pretty as a picture.

"Please don't ever smoke," she said to him again, this time blanketing him in her gray, chardonnay-flavored breath, soft and wet and comforting, like the dew that built when she left her wine glasses on her porch overnight. And overnights. "Worst things in the world for ya. That's about the only thing I'm damn sure," and this was, in fact, true. Certainty wasn't in her character. Being certain, in her eyes, disallowed spontaneity. It disallowed what she referred to as "real living." It disallowed allowing yourself to make mistakes. It disallowed no consequence.

Jack Jr., though, had heard all this before—I mean not only just earlier that day, but a few times—but he still stared at her, not because her telling him the risks of smoking, using herself as the example—Exhibit A—had captured him, and not because her large, blonde wig had, as the heat grew upward of 115 degrees, and her scalp began to sweat, become parallel to her ajarred, black-framed glasses—Gary's, but she'd finally had her prescription switched in—that sat lazily upon her reddening nose, but instead because recently she'd been in an accident—an "accident"—severing both the ring and index fingers of her left hand, luckily not her smoking hand, and that nonsmoking hand now stared at him, swishing white wine on ice, its fingers perpetually trapped in a pose that he knew to be, from all his schooling and all his friends, dirty.

"It was in my blind spot, baby, I hope you know that. Baby, it was a dark tunnel, and I don't know. I don't know. I was trying as best as I could."

Waking him from his daze, Nana spoke at him, still nervous, as she put out her cigarette atop an anthill of butts in the ceramic ashtray—shaped like the state of California, and with its motto, *Eureka*, inscripted beneath a mountain of accordioned filters—that sat at the center of the white tin table.

"What? Nana, I wasn't staring at you, Nana. I swear I wasn't."

"The streets here are so bright, baby! I couldn't see at all! I musta just got in some sort of spell, and just sorta lost it, I mean, baby, Tinky didn't even make it," she cried out now, nearing tears, because while she loved Tinky, she was still acting. She couldn't really cry anymore. She couldn't much feel anymore. She'd forgotten how. Her trade allowed her the ability, though, to conjure up faces of embarrassment and guilt when she felt they could be beneficial. Casts she thought might look empathetic. The different masks she wore. Of all different types. Like her wigs, her face had become malleable, and she'd become able to choose the proper expression for the proper occasion beforehand. A bob and a wry smile for a party, say. Bangs and a teary scowl at a funeral. A Farrah and a smirk on a date. That last one, though, stood out as more of a fantasy, or perhaps a memory, than the others. It had sadly been a while since her last date, but maybe she was better off? Earlier that morning she stood before her mirror and chose a sandy-blonde updo—her Dolly, one of her favorites—and the face of somebody empathetic. Today she'd be likeable. Today she'd be somebody about whom we are supposed to care.

"Nana, I wasn't staring at your hand. I wasn't. I swear." He looked around the garden sheepishly, boyishly, playing up his refined youth. Acting. He looked for an excuse in the shrubbery. Nope. Then he scanned the walls of the house. Nothing. Then the roof, and up at the chimney. Still no. Dammit. He looked back down at the ground. "I was just. Well, it's so hot. And I just, well. I'm thirsty," he said, reaching for a way out of the conversation as he reached his arm toward her. "Can I have some of that?"

He understood her answer from her stare and pulled his hand back and clasped it to his other and looked back down. He knew his Nana had seen him leering at her most newly acquired insecurity—she had many he knew, but what she now referred to as her "mongoloid side" had become her most readily available, in that she hadn't yet found a way to cover it up. She'd looked into a glove with false fingers, but she didn't want to always wear a glove. I mean, she would—she could make it elegant—but at this point she hoped she could be brave enough not to bother. Jack Jr. didn't like to see his Nana sad, so he couldn't quite, yet, look at her. He saw a snail was under his chair. A big snail, the kind you only find in the desert. He watched carefully its lasting trail as it crawled away. Tinky used to nest under the lawn chairs, with the snails. A big, happy family. Amigos. But Tinky died in the accident, so now the snails went back to being alone.

"Well, baby, this drink is no drink for little boys. This drink's just for me. But let me run in and make you some lemonade. I think I have some concentrate in the freezer. I'll make some up right now. Won't take me more than a minute. Easy as pie."

She spoke softer now, feeling her drink more, and thus more secure. She got up, whipped her neck back, and snapped her wig into place.

"And remember, it's hot up north for a reason. That's why our lord, Jesus Christ, our savior, lived in the North," she preached as she walked away. But after a moment, she stopped and looked back and cocked her head. She stared at him, paused, and smiled, exposing her newly finished pearl-white veneers.

"You know what I mean?" she whispered, nearly. "Now don't you go anywhere, beautiful. You just look too beautiful in this house. As handsome as anything. Pretty as a picture," she said, before trailing her way back inside. As she stepped her first step her knee buckled between her shoe and the sun-soaked brick. She remembered that about fifteen minutes before she'd enjoyed a Vicodin. From then on she took more care in stepping, though her carriage was still slightly unsure.

She was so convincing, as she stepped through her AstroTurfed garden and toward her wood-paneled condo, that he was compelled to believe her. He didn't quite, in his heart, but he wanted to, and he appreciated how much she tried. She stopped once more, before the glass doors, and looked back at him, and winked somewhat sloppily, but so cute. I mean, no less than precious. Then she turned around and slid inside and pushed the translucent glass door to a rubbery close. This shut him off from the oscillating fan that spun off cool air by the cactus.

Sweating, now—again, Palm Springs is the hottest, third-hottest place in America, they say—through his loosely buttoned, short-sleeved, "hunter's green" shirt—as he'd heard his mother dub it once before—and onto his red velvet vest, he got up from his seat, brushed his sun-dyed blond hair to the side, and followed the path of the slippery snail he'd seen under his chair. His feet followed close behind his eyes. His stare was sharp. He was on a mission. It had only crawled about six feet since he'd last seen it. But, as it reached the end of the oval plywood deck, before dropping out of sight into the imported garden—the greenery was mostly purchased at an artificial plant shop called African Queen, as Dorothy didn't care for watering—it popped its three-pronged head out and snapped its shell back into place.

"Oh, she's just putting her face on," he imagined his Nana saying, while she, in fact, admired her reflection in the steel-shiny tin of the toaster oven while the lemonade thawed. She filled her wine glass to the top and cheersed her smiling likeness—proud that she felt she was doing a good job. Proud to be a nana—but as she pushed her wine glass forward triumphantly it slipped from her hand and fell to the floor, so now she'd spend the next few minutes cleaning. And so back to the snail, who eventually returned her head to her shell and climbed over the edge of the deck and dropped out of sight, into the thickets of bamboo, and then onto the mossy edges of the chlorine-soaked pond water. The snails, too, had become immune to the dangerous chemicals. "She's the hare," he thought to himself. He'd be the turtle. He followed her off the deck, into the garden, and stepped out onto the dirt, praying not to lose her. He strode silently from the tall ledge—he'd removed his sneakers, so as not to make a sound—but she was gone. He couldn't find her. She wasn't anywhere, anymore. She was lost. All is lost. But no, not yet. He was determined. He wasn't ready to give up. The tropical grass tickled his nose and ears, but he walked into the bushes confidently—a predator aware of his prey. This wasn't his first time at the rodeo.

He stepped two steps but then backed up quickly and pressed his palms flat against the wall behind him. He'd crunched something under his toes; he thought it was her—he thought he'd killed her—and he was frightened. He closed his eyes, then lifted up his bare foot, held it in his hands, then opened them. The remains of a stale pretzel—pieces of rock salt and knotted bread—stuck to his heel. Thank goodness. He brushed it off and breathed and breathed and wiped the sweat from his brow with his shirtsleeve. He didn't want to be a predator anymore. He lost it as quick as it came. He retreated again against the wall, but was put at ease by the mossy rocks on the back of his neck. In the shade and the brush—cultivated tall enough to protect them from the ogling neighbors, who weren't particularly fond of Dorothy's brand of fun—the wall seemed the only cool thing in the desert. It certainly was the only cool thing outside. He'd scared himself, but he'd gathered, and now he was ready. Again he was ready. He paced forward, and moved slowly, and wearily, and he watched his steps as he made an inroad on her territory. He saw three plastic birds—cranes—spinning around on their white, plastic axes. He came upon a rock—one of the many rocks of the same color and size mined strategically throughout the artificial greenery, and lifted it, to see if that's where she was hiding. She wasn't there, but *Serenity*—he sounded out—was etched into the bottom of the stone with a small ™ logo beside it, and *MADE IN CHINA* printed beside that. His taste, even at this age, was evolved enough to find this off-putting, so he placed the rock *Serenity*-side down and continued on pretending.

"Baby. Baby boy. Gorgeous. The lemonade's ready. Ready for you to drink. Come and get it! Come on here!"

He sat low in the bushes and listened to her muddled voice address him.

"Come on, baby. Baby. Little one. Where are you? Where you hidin'?"

Then he stood up, the snail—well, don't worry about the snail—and he watched his Nana smile—a big smile, pushing a cigarette past her teeth. She struck a kitchen match on her clog and lit it. And he smiled too.

"There he is," she said as he hurried to her, still wishing he was drinking what she was, but happy all the same. "Were you prayin' in there again, angel?" she asked him, holding out her arms. He ran and jumped into her and only they—together—mattered. She held him tightly and whispered, "Like an angel. Prayin' for Nana's little hand," her voice even grayer than before.